# ON THE TIPS OF
# HER FINGERS

# ON THE TIPS OF HER FINGERS

*Sophia —*

*I hope this book inspires a little more magic in your day...*

## BIBIANA KERPCAR

NEW DEGREE PRESS

COVER DESIGN BY KRISTINA CAIZLEY

*This is a work of fiction. Any resemblance to actual events or persons, living or dead, is entirely coincidental.*

ON THE TIPS OF HER FINGERS

ISBN   978-1-63676-515-0   *Paperback*
         978-1-63676-043-8   *Kindle Ebook*
         978-1-63676-044-5   *Ebook*

*For my mother, who let me stand on her shoulders.*

*For my brother, who shared my passion with all who would listen.*

*For my love, who read the first words and pushed me forward.*

*For my beautiful family in Stará Ľubovňa, especially my grandparents, who conjured up magical stories for me at bedtime.*

*I hope this book makes you proud.*

# CONTENTS

———

"Stories you read when you're the right age never quite leave you. You may forget who wrote them or what the story was called. Sometimes you'll forget precisely what happened, but if a story touches you it will stay with you, haunting the places in your mind that you rarely ever visit."

—NEIL GAIMAN, *M IS FOR MAGIC*

# NOTE

———

You will find out soon enough that people can't transport themselves via tactile touch, nor can animals talk, nor do islands inhabited by witches who conjure practical magic exist.

Or maybe they do.

There is an inherent vulnerability in creating something from nothing, conjuring a world and characters that feel wholly real: reflection opens us up to all moments. It does not discriminate against the good or bad. You are left with a library of feelings to parse through. And you begin to parse through them chronologically.

In 1993, I was living in the Slovak Republic, where I was born. I had recently begun to read and write (in Slovak, of course). My writing consisted of my nickname spelled in varying upper- and lower-case forms, jammed into the plaster walls of my bedroom with crayon. And at night, after a bath, my mother would brush my hair, help me into my pajamas, and sit with me while my grandmother read from a thick book of fairytales propped in between us.

With the mountain air whirling outside, my grandmother regaled me with stories about howling werewolves and insomniac princesses sleeping on a stack of mattresses that were, in turn, balanced on top of a single pea. I listened with bated breath at night and continued to practice writing with crayons on my bedroom walls during the day.

And then life uprooted. We moved to the United States. My mother sacrificed her education and worked hard to put food on the table, teaching me the importance of perseverance and strength along the way. I started a school without knowing English, and spent my formative years—six, seven, and eight years old—hearing calls of "alien" and feeling aware of my otherness.

My small brain buzzed with grown-up worries. Those grew and snowballed for decades, and that's where the vulnerability kicks in. I became fearful, anticipating what would come next, and coping with my emotions how I best saw fit. Developing coping mechanisms, especially when you are young, is powerful. As a child, you don't realize there are many types of soothing behaviors, often unwittingly dangerous. Anxiety can be "fixed" with food. Or emotional compartmentalization.

But at night, with the pages of a book between my fingers, I escaped into different worlds. Despite these changes, books—and reading and writing—were a positive constant. The idea of escapism resonated. I yearned to leave reality behind.

The weight of fear, stress, and the unknown can be crippling for young children and adults alike. Grappling with my emotions, I found myself drawn to the fantastical worlds that my favorite authors conjured up—worlds where the protagonist was like me, dealing with unique struggles, yet simultaneously coming out of their fantastical adventures with a newfound understanding of themselves and the world around them. Stories where the protagonists were awestruck by the idea of magic, hidden in plain sight, exploring its wonders with a childlike lens.

Fairy and folk tales are the natural ways we imbue magic in the everyday, especially when we are children. They feel real. The stories have real-life people and places that seem like they can be touched, just out of reach. But they also have princesses and talking animals, expressive and fantastical worlds. It is precisely this magic we often need more of the older we become.

As a young adult, I found myself dusting off the fantastical books I loved as a child. I pulled them off my bookshelves and returned to them, remembering how much they impacted my life. From *Coraline*, I learned that you can always push through the difficult moments. Hermione in the *Harry Potter* series taught me that it is always worthwhile to be yourself, regardless of the judgment that comes with going against the grain. *Matilda* taught me the value of literary curiosity, and that, out of the bad, you can find a happy ending.

Lives become clouded with harsh emotions and realities: depression, stress, and on and on. And, with time, we realize that even with our feet firmly planted in reality, there is a desire to escape and to experience the unknown.

Fairy and folk tales are often written with children in mind, creatively teaching lessons and instilling a love of magic. But they can also be written with adults in mind, recalling us back to those lessons and allowing us to dig deeper into stories, using them as soothing works to help us make sense of the changing and oft-crippling world around us.

Magic is the perfect route for escapism—for people who are struggling, for children learning to understand their feelings and emotions. Books are a beautiful medium. But there is a twist.

Fairytales always have a lesson. And magic can become dangerous if used for the wrong reasons, even if our initial intentions were positive and sound. There comes a time when we have to use the lessons we learned, gleaned from the weathered pages of a book of fairytales, and continue to go through life with them, hopeful and inspired enough to face our fears head-on and address the monsters—literal and metaphorical—in our lives.

*On the Tips of Her Fingers* is a momentary act of escape—an opportunity to delve into a mystical world of magic and find ourselves in characters that feel real. We are all struggling and stumbling through life, at every stage, and often need to lean on our imaginations to help us cope.

This is for anyone needing to step outside of their reality for a moment in time, anyone who wants to gain that bit of magic they felt as a child.

Just like I did.

If you love fairy and folk tales filled with fantastical worlds, my hope is that you can find yourself in this book.

# PART ONE

# PROLOGUE

———

Moonbeams reflected back in her irises, like silver flecks dotting a deep emerald landscape. She ran her fingertips through the coarse grass, which was dampened by the afternoon pocket of rain. The packed dirt underneath released a sweet, earthy scent, petrichor rising from the ground. Her body tensed as she conjured the energy to take the next step. Cortisol built up as her leg muscles poised themselves to move, to stand. She strained her ears to the hollow air around her: the faint howls of circling wolves interwoven with raised voices from behind her, inching forward, as if catching a ride on the still air. She closed her eyes. Eyelashes trembled on her freckled cheeks. Clutching the grass in her hands, she fell through time.

# ONE

# HOME

———

A puff of cold air escaped Adela's chapped lips. Opening her eyes, she found that she was on top of the world—or, at least, a small hill that overlooked the glowing lights of the pastoral village directly below. A crescent moon loomed above, same as moments before. Or ahead. Her strawberry-hued hair whipped in her face as she looked over her shoulder.

There she was. Her other self.

Her non-traveling body.

She tilted her head down to the other Adela's reclined body, tracing the path of long hair spread alongside her face like rays kissing the sun. The look on her face—the face down in the nook of the hill—made her laugh, and she inhaled a small breath in surprise at the sound. Her upper lip was scrunched atop her lower lip, and her eyebrows had a tendency to furrow with a confused scowl, despite the fact that she was neither confused nor ill-tempered.

The rise and fall of voices interrupted her thoughts. They came from the cottage where she—the "she" currently moon-gazing—had departed only minutes prior. The cottage was on the same plane as she now stood, and the Adela of fifteen minutes ago was carefully out of sight, tucked into a recess of land underneath the house. But still, the traveling

Adela was careful to stay hidden; she crept forward, the damp grass she had ripped out of the earth still clutched in her hand. She passed through the grass effortlessly, the surrounding flora giving way and then gradually settling back into place once she had finished traversing through the area. She inched closer to the voices.

As she approached the yellow glow of the inside world, she inhaled deeply and caught it, keeping the air in her lungs. Her cheeks bulged and shifted upward, almost meeting her eyes. Adela crouched low, clearing the structure's windowsill. Grazing the wood grain with the pads of her fingers, she slowly rose above the ledge, squinting in an attempt to fight the poor visibility from behind the frosted glass.

With bated breath, she eavesdropped.

"...come home to stories about stealing bread and imaginary friends. I shelled out nearly thirty gold on the spot—"

A firm, calm voice cut in. "I already apologized. I won't do it again."

There was silence and then a scoff of incredulity. His voice became louder.

"You're sorry? And what about her? I tell her the stress she's giving me and you know what she does?"

"What's that?"

"Her eyes get empty. She digs her nails into the palms of her hands! She, she—leaves! Ignores me! She's too quiet. I don't even know what she's thinking. I liked it more when she talked back."

Adela caught movement coming from the right side of the pane and strained her eyes as boisterous hand gestures took up the width of the window. As she lowered her head ever so slightly to avoid detection, the burly figure threw his hands in the air, his face blotchy from anger.

In the corner of the room, a small woman hummed softly as she clicked the stove on and topped the orange fire with a ceramic tea kettle. The red linoleum cabinets creaked with age as she searched for a suitable mug, emerging with a pale cream variant that was chipped on one side. Adela smiled. That was her favorite mug. It had a certain character.

"She's young. She has an active imagination."

Adela's face pulled itself into a scowl again, scrunching up. That wasn't true. It wasn't her imagination. Everything happening to her was real. But she could never tell her mother. She would never understand what it was like.

She dug a fingernail into the palm of her hand, and her body became flushed. She hated when they argued over her.

It was why she had run out of the house earlier. Adela could not bear to sit in her room while the voices found their way upstairs. She had places to see, time to traverse, abilities to explore. But at the same time, she couldn't quite pry herself from the sounds. Her curiosity consistently got the best of her. She needed to hear more.

A loud, brash laugh silenced the room. "It's those books you let her read! Every time I ask her to help around the house, she's reading. Off somewhere in her head! I tell her to clean up, and she stares blankly ahead. If she were *my* child, I would—"

"And she's not. So you won't."

But that wasn't true, either.

Silence enveloped the world as both voices fell quiet. Around her, insects and bugs emerged from the trees surrounding the house, landing on Adela's arms as she quickly swatted them away. Her adventure was nearly over; it was time to return to her original body.

Stars filled her head, and she grew lightheaded. Slowly, she exhaled the air she had been holding hostage for the last minute. She had heard enough. She had traveled far enough.

As she followed the curves and angles of the house to the hilltop, the weeds left over from the earlier months scratched at her ankles. She pulled her coat closer to her frigid torso with a single hand, making her way back to her body, currently sprawled in the middle of the rustling field. Any minute now, the raised voices would once again get louder and travel to her as she picked at the grass stalks.

The familiar howl of a wolf broke her train of thought, joined soon after by the pack, raising their night song to the sky. A raindrop escaped the cloud cover above, and she anticipated the patter that would begin to fall, an evening moon shower preceded by an afternoon moon shower.

Adela knelt low, keeping her traveling body hidden so that any passerby would not be able to see two Adelas in the field. Rubbing the last remaining grass stalk between her pointer finger and thumb, she let it fall.

Adela's original body awoke, eyelashes fluttering open, like green curtains that would slowly reveal a surprise hiding behind them. Her eyes fixated on the moon as her mind fought the grogginess that was often an unwanted souvenir of her travels. This time, she had traveled in both space and time, albeit a short distance.

She propped herself up on her elbows, softly cradled in the grassy knoll where she had found herself twenty minutes ago. Or was it twenty minutes from *now?* Or was it now? Leaving her own time always confused Adela, her brain like a melting cauldron stirring together the feelings and experiences of both bodies.

The rain continued to sneak through the air, peppering Adela's clothes with dark, damp dots. She picked up her book and hid it within the confines of her coat, protecting it from the harsh environment. Her hair stuck to the side of her face, her eyelashes catching and releasing small droplets with every blink. She looked back at the quaint house where she—or another version of her—had eavesdropped. Tufts of smoke escaped from the chimney, and she could faintly make out the strengthening whistle of a tea kettle.

She waited. Another minute. Then another.

Nobody came to collect her, to scold her for running away from home or getting drenched in the rain. Nobody peeked outside the frosted window, curious as to where she was when they realized she wasn't in the bath or in her own frigid bed piled with layered blankets and quilts to help keep the warmth in and the cold out. She dug her nails into the palm of her hands.

The howl of wolves edged closer. Once tense, her muscles relaxed.

As she once again snuck back in the direction of the house, Adela put one bare foot in front of the other again, and again, and again until she reached the distressed, wooden front door. She waited for what seemed an eternity, time ticking by; then, she gripped the worn doorknob and introduced the creaking of the wooden door to the night.

Entering the quaint alcove, where worn boots and too-small coats lay strewn around, Adela took off her extra layers, starting with her knit long-bottoms and then her damp coat. She stacked them one atop the other, and tiptoed into the hallway.

"There you are."

Adela jumped in place, her feet lifting off the ground briefly. She gasped.

"You knew I was gone?"

She turned toward the red kitchen, dimly lit. Inside, her mother cradled the cream mug with tea, steam rising off the top as she dipped her head to blow on the boiling water.

Her mother paused and sighed. "Of course, I did." Her brow furrowed, and a sheepish smile pulled at the corners of her mouth. "I heard some stories about you today." She pulled her lips back in an effort to disguise a small laugh.

Adela faced her mother. Her own lips pursed into a mischievous grin, mimicking the characteristics in front of her.

"I know."

Adela fidgeted with her wet clothing, allowing room for the conversation to continue. Out of the corners of her eyes, she took in her mother's figure, which had now stepped out from behind the kitchen table. Adela was only eleven years old, but she was beginning to look more like her mother each day. Where the latter had dark blond hair peppered with coarse, gray strands, Adela's own hair was slowly shifting from its strawberry color to a mature shade of blond. Even Adela's eyes were ever-changing; in the sun, people often told her they skewed translucent. It was difficult to determine their true color.

"You have such pretty blue eyes," an elderly woman in the village once told her unabashedly. As she and Milo, her friend, walked back from the market, he'd spun her around in place and placed his face close to hers, noses touching.

"She's wrong," he'd breathed, his stale breath biting her nose. "Your eyes are gray."

But Adela's eyes were green. At least, that was how they appeared since the Last Sun. Before the event, she would sit in her room by the window with a hand mirror, twisting her face toward the sunlight so her pupils would dilate, her eyes shifting in color.

"Where did you go just now?" Lucia's warm voice pulled her back into the creaking cabin.

"I think I need to clean up." Her damp, fine hair whipped in her face as she shook her head abruptly, snapping herself out of her daze. "I'm going to take a bath." She realized she had been chewing on the inside of her lip for the last minute, her teeth finding a soft spot and filling her mouth with a trickle of the metallic taste of warm blood.

"That's fine. Don't run the water too hot. The other day you came out looking like a ripe tomato. I'll bring you tea when you're ready." Her mother held her eyes on Adela for a millisecond too long and then retreated back into the kitchen to pour boiling water into another mug.

Adela took another step into the house as it creaked around her. She had lived in this cabin as long as she could recall. It groaned with age from before she was born. The alcove gave way to a small hallway that branched into three sections of the home.

The cozy kitchen she had peeked into earlier in the evening was large compared to others in the village, the back wall covered with crimson linoleum cabinets, worn with time and peeling at the edges. The wall that ran alongside the alcove housed the banquette where the family would have dinner in the evenings, often in silence interrupted only by cleared throats and coughs.

A small master bedroom with a frosted-pane window kept watch over the vegetable garden. The door to the room was often shut, but today it was open a hair, giving Adela purview over the snoring, slumbering occupant. Straight across from the alcove, visitors would be met with a decision of sorts. Down below was a pantry and wood-burning fireplace that provided warmth to the home. The descending steps were stone, a cooling sensation in the heat of the summer. But with the never-ending cold, she shuddered at the idea of going down.

Adela lumbered up to the second-floor landing—a lofted area with three secluded rooms. The first was a small bathroom with a porcelain tub for washing and other things. The second was a gathering space for when visitors called on her family, often eating and drinking until the early evening hours around a small fireplace, the darkness outside never transitioning. Adela's bedroom was the third. She stepped into the tiled bathroom, the floor marking patterns of black flowers atop a white backdrop.

She drew a bath, leaning over the tub to open the small window near the ceiling as the room steamed and made her eyes water. As she slipped into the tub, Adela scrubbed at her knees, her feet, and her arms. Light brown freckles peppered her skin—"sun kisses," as her mother once explained. Her skin blushed a deep pink the more she scrubbed, becoming inflamed. Adela hated her freckles. Milo had once told her that his own mother's great-aunt was covered in freckles and that she scrubbed for hours every evening to rid herself of them. It took her seven years but she claimed to now be unblemished, rid of the blasted things, although she refused to show her arms beyond her wrists.

Adela believed that if she just kept at it for a few years more, she'd be able to shed enough skin to make them disappear completely. But tonight, she was tired and cold. Giving up on this activity, she sat in the bath listening to the grandfather clock in the hallway tick on and on and on. Her mind leapt from one topic to another, like a traveler seeking new shores and towns to visit. She never quite understood how people could shut their brains off; it was a foreign concept to her.

If there was nothing for Adela to worry about, her quick-thinking brain could conjure something up with ease. Yesterday, when Adela and Lucia were in the field picking green apples to store in the pantry, she thought a tree could fall and crush the cabin or fall on her mother. When she dipped her feet in the frigid lake with Milo last week, her face flushed with blood as she realized that their toes could freeze and snap off in the chill, or that they could be carried away by a strong undercurrent, or pulled down by sea monsters, even though she had learned how to swim in this lake when she was a baby, spending summers by its edge.

The habit followed her everywhere.

"What did I tell you about the water being hot?"

The sudden voice cut through Adela's thoughts, and her head snapped to her mother standing in the doorway.

"Mama, but it's so cold out," she groaned.

"I don't care. Up, let's dry you off."

Adela emerged from the water, now cold and cloudy with the dirt and grime that had fallen away from her encounter with the outside world. Stepping out on the tile, she dripped in place until her mother rushed over with a thin, worn towel.

"Will you read to me tonight? You haven't read to me in a long time..." Adela's voice tapered off.

Lucia sighed. "I have a lot to do tonight." She paused. "But yes. I'll be up in six minutes. And I have just the story in mind," she whispered mischievously, her eyes gleaming.

Adela grinned, her body instinctively lighter and warmer as she thought about her mother's stories. She followed behind her, with her mother descending to finish her kitchen work and Adela tiptoeing to her room, aware of the noise she was making as the floorboards creaked underneath. She had aspirations of becoming a ballerina as a child, and now tiptoed out of habit. It hurt the balls of her feet, inflamed and painful since the skin had hardened over time. But the sensation made her heart race with pleasure.

Her room was not special. The floral wallpaper peeled at the edges and the windows were drafty, letting in the cool air now associated with the Last Sun. A bed just wide enough to sleep two was pushed against the wall farthest from the window, scrapes on the wooden floor showing its journey to escape the biting cold. A threadbare rug lay central in the room, collecting dust bunnies and all other creatures hiding in the shadows.

But Adela's favorite part of her room was her bookcase. It spanned the wall opposite her bed, made of rosewood her great-great-grandfather cut down himself. He had shaped it into a grand literary home, three times as wide as Adela was tall, and nearly her mother's height. Adela dreamt of one day filling it.

On the top-most shelf lay knickknacks Adela had collected over the last few months. A wildflower lay wilting on its side, petals decomposing by the stem. Next to it was a tooth—an incisor, to be specific—slightly shorter than Adela's pinky. A porcelain doll slouched in the corner, smooth lips pursed into an oval and eyes forever unblinking. In the nook of the doll's dress were three cave pearls, smooth and round, each slightly bigger than the doll's eyes. A modest notebook and pencil finished off the strange assortment.

They did not look like much but were Adela's most prized possessions.

The rest of the bookcase was a marvel, too.

When her mother had been pregnant with Adela, she loved to open all the windows in the room and bring her paints upstairs. From when the roosters crowed "good morning" to when the stars began to twinkle, she created imaginative scenes with the flick of her brush and colors of blue, gold, emerald, and pink.

Adela's spine had tingled in awe when she'd first learned about this, taking in the tapestry in front of her—a humble depiction of the village below the verdant hill. At the top, Lucia had painted a heavenly sky, made lighter with whites and darker with blacks so it was impossible to know what time of day the wood depicted. The sky gave way to yellows, the rays of the sun in the scene poking out behind the grassy field where Adela and her mother lived.

At the base of the bookcase, the greens of the hills coalesced to create the greens of the village. Grays and blacks formed the rocky edge of the main road, and pink and gold wildflowers completed the scene. Behind the main road were the snow-capped peaks of the mountains, a glistening lake humbly sitting in between them. They were joined by the deep greens of the pine forest just behind their home, within which a small plume of smoke rose over the treetops.

It was a simple scene but exhilarating to take in. Her mother was a magician with colors.

On cue, her mother pushed the bedroom door open with her toes, holding two hot mugs of tea. "I let them cool off for a bit. Mint, your favorite." She deftly placed one mug on the floor and lowered the other into Adela's waiting hands. "Careful... and I added bee honey, too."

Adela knew she had to savor the special concoction; the honeybees had disappeared since the Last Sun and nobody knew if they would ever come back.

Her mother's soft voice cut through the silence. "You get into your head a lot. Like me when I was a little girl."

"Mama, do you ever feel like there's something more out there?"

"Of course, there is. There's a vast world of forests and deserts and magical landscapes."

"Have you ever seen it?"

Lucia hesitated, considering the question. "Yes," she finally answered. "I've seen a few places."

"Are they better than here?"

"I don't know if *better* is the right word. Different. Peculiar."

"When can I see these places? Can I see them soon?"

Her mother's posture stiffened slightly. "You're too young, for one."

Adela scowled, her wet hair dripping onto her arm as she moved to dry off the patch of exposed skin.

"And what's so wrong with home? It's quiet here, peaceful too."

"I don't know if I want to be *here*." Adela hesitated for a moment, scared she would give too much away. Her eyes closed, and her mint tea sloshed in the cup with the subtle movement. She loved Sunseree, its subtle beauty. But because of all the stories her mother had told her, she yearned to be in far-off places. And with home no longer the happy place it had once been...

Adela sighed. "I don't want to be here. I want to be..."

"Now, why would you say that?"

Adela opened her eyes. Her mother's face hardened, eyes filled with a sadness Adela could not place.

"Forget I said anything," Adela said.

Her mother bit the side of her lip, a habit Adela never knew she had inherited until today.

The mood in the room dampened.

"I want you to be happy, always."

Adela inhaled, dust filling her nostrils and mingling with the scent of fresh mint and sweet honey.

"I'm sorry," Adela said and sighed.

Her mother waved her hand away, and her face softened. "Don't say 'sorry.'" Hushed excitement crept back into her voice, and her eyes turned up as if there was magic behind them, hoisting them up. "Now then, should we read a story?"

# TWO

# STORY

———

*Once upon a time, there lived a young girl. She lived in her family home, as young girls tend to do, up near the hills and nearby the sprawling wildflower fields that sat damp with dew each morning. Her mother and father were her favorite people in the world. They kept her happy and warm and safe.*

*And everyone loved her.*

*She was kind to those she encountered, family and strangers alike. They all marveled at her ability to make people smile. But perhaps what made them smile the most was the peculiar gleaming gold sun on her forehead.*

*This gold sun appeared when she was a baby, like an unusual birthmark.*

*Each day, as the sun's rays extended toward her bedroom windows, the young girl hopped out of bed to make tea for her mama and papa. One morning, the house was still and quiet as a mouse. She skipped down the stairs, the joyful sounds of her footsteps reverberating through the walls and entryways. Her hair flowed behind her as she ran, the strands like a running brook. She loved the morning, when everything began to groan awake, as if shaking out the sleep from the night prior.*

*But today, something felt different.*

She entered the pantry, where her mama was usually stationed; but she was nowhere to be found.

She turned the corner into the kitchen, expecting the smells and sounds of the morning to meet her; but her mama was not at the stove.

She checked the garden outside, where wildflowers peeked through the dirt and rabbits passed through in the springtime, nibbling on bright orange carrots; but her mama was not there either.

Back inside, she noticed the closed door separating her parents' bedroom from the rest of the home. It was usually open. The young girl would often jump on the bed while her papa was off at work and while her mama tidied up inside. When she pushed the door open, she finally found Mama.

Her mama lay in bed, beads of sweat pooling on her forehead, her eyes closed. Next to Mama was Papa, kneeling with his head low, his gaze trained on the floorboards below. When her papa heard the door open, he turned to check the noise and his eyes found the young girl. His eyes were heavy, tinged with a quiet sadness. With a gentle touch on her mama's forehead, he came outside to talk to the young girl.

"Mama is sick. Her fever came back last night, strong and suddenly. The doctor has been here since dawn."

A doctor with his bag of medicine stood in the dark corner of the room behind Papa.

"What can I do?" asked the girl.

"Nothing," her papa sighed. He hesitated for a moment but then continued, "The doctor says there is only a single flower that can ease her pain. It is found on the Isle of Vila. But it's too far away."

The young girl's golden sun began to tingle, tugging at her skin as if trying to catch her attention.

"I know what you can do!" Papa exclaimed, clapping his hands together. "How about you go make some hot tea for us all? I'm sure Mama would appreciate it very much."

As her father retreated back into the room, the young girl went to the kitchen to brew some water in a pot. She picked tea leaves out of the small container where her mother stored them. There were only five leaves left, and she added them to the water, waiting for it to boil. She spooned the honey, which their neighbor had delivered, into three mugs. Their neighbor brought the honey, like clockwork, each month. It was as gold as gold itself and peppered with honeycomb.

When she entered her parents' room to deliver the tea, giving one to the doctor, one to her papa, and setting one at the bedside for Mama, Papa winked at her and thanked her. But the girl wanted to do more.

Leaving the adults downstairs, the girl ran upstairs and closed the door to her bedroom. Acting quickly, she pushed her heavy dresser drawers as far as they would go, blocking the doorway slightly. She hoped nobody downstairs could hear her.

She dropped to the ground and pulled out her paints and favorite paintbrush. Lifting the brush, she began to paint on the wall directly ahead.

It was hard to picture the Isle of Vila when she had never seen it before, but she remembered people in her village describing it: its dense forest, covered with blue and green leaves, each gleaming with golden sparkles that shone when placed against the blue sky.

She saw the deep indigo sky, featuring a big, white moon.

She heard the flutter of bird wings, whizzing by tropical flowers that strained toward the moonlight, drowned out only by the sound of rain battering the forest.

She smelled bread baking and, just like that, a small house appeared, smoke billowing from the chimney and windows steaming with heat.

A young woman in the distance fixed an apron around her waist, tying her black hair up. Her hair was as dark as a raven, as deep as a smudge of ink on a piece of paper. She was beautiful.

As the young girl's mouth began to salivate with the taste of warm bread she couldn't reach, she opened her eyes.

The young girl surveyed the scene in front of her. It had been replicated almost perfectly on the wall in front of her, like magic. And, with a look behind her shoulder, she knocked on the wall alongside her bed four times. A door appeared, and she painted its doorknob. She got on her knees and crawled through, leaving it slightly ajar.

The Isle of Vila was more beautiful than she could have imagined. A faint buzz enveloped her, little lightning bugs welcoming a new visitor to their environment. The rainforest was so grand. She had never seen trees like those before, rising to meet the sky. She wanted to take this world in, explore all of its treasures, but she knew she was running out of time to help her mother.

So she began to walk, and then run, forward, careful not to slip and fall into the stream running at her side.

After a little while, she came upon the stone house, mirroring the one in her painting precisely. The house was near the magic door's entrance, mainly because the young girl had drawn it that way (for whatever the girl drew, she could conjure it up in reality, just like that).

She was excited and rushed to the house, throwing up mud and dirt on her legs along the route.

Knock. Knock. Knock.

The door creaked open, and the lady she had painted mere minutes ago opened the door.

"Yes? What is it?" The woman's gaze flew to the golden sun on the young girl's forehead, her eyes widening.

"My name is—"

"No need. I know who you are. And why you're here," she said as her eyes glinted like stars. "Come in. Come in."

Inside, it was warm, and the house smelled of sourdough bread and paprika.

"Would you like something to eat?"

"No, I'm sorry to interrupt but—"

"I know," the woman cut her off as she put her hand up. "Wait here." She left the warm alcove and disappeared into a small basement, hidden behind a door near the stove. The young girl sat and waited for what seemed like hours, watching the seconds tick by on the grandfather clock, until the young woman appeared with a jar.

"This is what you need."

The young girl reached out, brushing her fingers against the woman's. "Thank you, I—"

"I sense that you are very special." The woman kept her fingers wrapped around the jar, refusing to let go. "How did you get here?"

"I don't know..."

"But you do."

The air was thick, no longer heavy with the smell of baked bread; if air could taste like something, it tasted like dread and anticipation. The grandfather clock ticked the seconds away until the young girl spoke.

"I stumbled upon your house while wandering by the path."

"That's a lie."

The girl tried again. "I got lost at sea and washed up at the edge of the forest."

"Another lie?"

The young girl gulped, sweat beginning to pool under her arms. She paused and then...

"I painted this world to life."

The woman nodded, finally accepting the young girl's answer and seemingly able to understand her strange ability. She laughed. "But you didn't. This world exists. What you did was you painted your view of the world. And you were able to enter it. You're in the real version of this world, but there's a curtain over it that shows you only what you imagined." She paused. "What do I look like to you?"

The young girl's head hurt trying to process this information, but she obliged. "You—you have dark black hair, down to your waist."

"And what's my name?"

"Well, you don't have one."

"Oh, but I do. And I don't look the way you painted me."

The young girl caught her breath in her throat. Everything, even the clock, seemed to stand still.

The young woman smiled, and time resumed.

"I know what you want. You want this jar. You heard about the flower that can heal your mother. I have its petals here. Simply steep them in hot water and give it to her to drink. Easy. And she'll get better."

"Thank you." The young girl exhaled, reaching for the jar once more.

"But I need something from you. Your abilities, when did they appear?"

"I-I've had them for as long as I could remember."

"And the sun?"

The young girl's hands rose to the golden sun on her forehead, the outline of it slightly raised but imprinted in her skin since infancy. "Always."

"I see..." the woman mused. She tapped her long fingers against the glass of the jar in a strange rhythm. Finally, she spoke again. "Take the jar. But return next week, to show me how you paint. How you can pass through worlds with ease."

Her gold sun tingled, and the young girl sensed something was wrong. "Yes... of course," she lied. She pried the jar from the young woman's grasp and began to back out of the stone house. "I should really get going now," she stammered, as she reached for the doorknob.

"Don't forget what I said," the raven-haired lady called after her as the young girl leapt over rocks and squawking animals to get back to her door. Finally, she found it—still ajar—and crawled through on her stomach, keeping the jar in one hand and pulling herself forward with the other.

When she entered her room again, a small wind-burst from the Isle of Vila followed before she could shut it. Catching her breath, she looked out the window and noticed that night had fallen. She had been gone all day.

Her golden sun throbbed with pain, as if fingernails were trying to peel it off her skin at the edges. Tears rose in her eyes.

She moved the dresser back to its position next to her bed, tracing the path of the existing scratches in the floor.

Throwing the door open, she ran down the stairs and gently knocked on her parents' bedroom. She opened the door and found her papa hunched over, his face in his hands while he sat at the foot of the bed. Her mama lay still, her chest slowly moving up and down. The tea at her bedside table was untouched.

"Papa!" she gently exclaimed.

A sad smile made the corners of his eyes turn up as he answered the young girl's call.

The girl thought quickly. "Mama didn't drink her tea, so it must be cold by now. Let me make her a new cup," she whispered, her fingers turning white as she tightly grasped the jar behind her back.

"Okay, little sunbeam."

The young girl followed the same routine, putting water on to boil but only enough for a single cup. Instead of the tea leaves, she thrust her hand into the jar, scraping her wrist on the edges in the process but escaping with wilting marigold-colored petals. Taking most of the flowers, she tucked a few in her pocket, vowing to hide them somewhere safe in case she ever needed them again. Most of the petals, she steeped in the water until it turned orange, draining them before pouring the water into a mug. The darkness of the night would help hide the color.

Returning back to the bedroom, she swapped out the new mug for the old and placed her hand on her mother's arm. "Mama."

Her mother opened her eyes and smiled, opening her mouth to say something.

"No, Mama, don't waste your energy, please. I brought you tea. Drink it."

"She'll drink it tomorrow," her father interrupted. "She's too weak."

"No, no," the young girl insisted, "she should drink it now."

Papa complied, curiously. He helped prop Mama up so she could sip the tea, slowly so as not to burn her tongue.

The young girl stayed in the room all night, making sure Mama had drunk every last drop. And then she fell asleep, curled up at her mama's feet while her papa rested on the cold, hard floor.

The next morning, the sun's rays extended toward the bedroom windows. The young girl awoke, the grogginess of the previous evening falling off her in the daylight. She lay on the bed, alone. Mama and Papa were nowhere to be found.

Worried, she rolled off the mattress and ran into the hallway.

Mama was in the kitchen, humming while she cooked breakfast. Papa was in the hallway, talking to the doctor from the morning before. "I don't know how... it's a miracle," she heard the doctor whisper as she moved into the kitchen.

The young girl enveloped her arms around her mother's waist.

"Aha, there you are! I didn't want to wake you up." Her mother hugged her back, giving her a kiss on the crown of her head.

The young girl looked up. "I'm glad you're better."

"Me too, little one." Her mother grimaced. "That's strange, I had figured that birthmark would never leave," she mused, rubbing a thumb across the young girl's forehead.

And just like that, her golden sun was gone.

But her mama was back. That's all that mattered.

And, despite that, they all lived happily ever after. And the young girl—well, she never moved her bedroom dresser ever again.

# THREE

# FOX

———

"I like that story, Mama," Adela sleepily exhaled, as her eyelids slowly closed, turning the room a faded black.

"I like that story, too."

The emanating heat from her mother's hands helped Adela to slip deeper into the down comforter and even deeper into a dream state. Her mother's thin fingers caught a falling strand of hair and wrapped it back around Adela's ear. The cottage was quiet and still. The wind screamed outside, whipping around the corners of the cabin, decidedly more hostile than it had been just an hour ago. Everything creaked: both the small, wooden bed and her mother's knees as they lifted off from the mattress and onto the hard floorboards.

All was still.

And then the noises began. Not the noises of an old house settling into the earth, but the organic ones of someone waking and rushing up the stairs. The sounds of anger and animosity. The bedroom door flung open, and so did Adela's eyes. The worn doorknob flew into the left-most wall with a ferocity. Weary from almost-sleep, Adela propped herself onto her elbows and flinched, readying herself for what was to follow.

"So you two have been up here, hiding and laughing to yourselves about how you embarrassed me today?"

"What are you talking about?" her mother asked.

"Everyone in Sunseree is laughing behind my back! Everyone is talking about my stepdaughter who steals bread, who runs around collecting rocks and pieces of *garbage* strewn on the floor," he roared, his unforgiving gaze moving side to side and finally pausing as he acknowledged the knick-knacks on the bookshelf. From the opposite side of the room, his blue eyes gleamed with excitement as—with a single swipe of a boorish hand—her prized possessions rained onto the rug below. Temporarily cushioned from damage were a trio of cave pearls rolling onto the floor.

With hate dancing in his irises, he brought his boot down. *Crack.*

That was the crack of the incisor. The delicate wildflower had been snapped in half, and the porcelain doll's face caved in. As his foot lifted up from the floor, the dust of a single cave pearl was left behind, the other two rolling to safety by the foot of Adela's bed.

Without a word, he retreated from the room, slamming the door in its frame and rattling the cabin from pantry to attic.

Adela tried to breathe, tried to swallow the saliva that had collected in her mouth, but couldn't. Sniffling, with every iota of power remaining, she fell out of bed and crawled on all fours over to the threadbare rug.

Her mama sat there already, holding the knick-knacks in her hand and collecting shards of porcelain into the nook of the doll's face. "I'll fix this. I promise. I'll fix all of it," she said, whispering as she turned toward the door. "Are you okay?"

Adela didn't know how to answer the question; this wasn't the first time she had been caught off-guard in this way, disrupted from deep sleep or deep thought. This wasn't the first time she had encountered one of Conrad's episodes. The corner of her eye found the canine tooth, and she collected the pieces closer to her legs. "I'm okay, Mama."

Her mother kissed her on her forehead, lingering longer than usual. "Into bed you go," she said, lifting Adela by her clammy hands and helping her in.

As her mother tucked her under the pillowy comforter, Adela rubbed a thumb over half the incisor that she'd swiped from the floor. Her mother placed both her hands at the base of Adela's throat, right over her collarbone, and closed her eyes.

The warmth pulsed through her upper body, spreading to her legs and her toes from that singular point. Her mother had this unusual ability to warm anything she touched. It was particularly useful on these cold nights, when the wintry weather would creep into the cracks of wood and escape into the bedrooms. Prompted by the smile spreading on Adela's face, Mama's palms lifted off her chest and Adela heard a whispered, "I love you," before the door closed and the room was enveloped in darkness once more.

"I love you, too," Adela responded, only seconds too late. Under the sheets, the two halves of the incisor found one another. In her mind, she pictured her fingers turning white in an attempt to keep them together, like invisible glue to seal the broken edges. She closed her eyes, thinking back to the memory that was tied to the incisor.

And then it began.

Adela had transported only a handful of times before. Earlier, in the field, had only been the fifth time. Right now, the sixth. While the process in its entirety took seconds, inside her body, time felt drawn out. On its own, it was painful, both emotionally and physically. Her breath caught in her throat, like all the oxygen had rushed out, thick and dense. Adela labored to inhale and exhale. Everything slowed. The clicking of clocks like dripping molasses and the creaking of the house dragged on, emitting a low groan.

A rush of emotion bottled up in Adela, as if she were a balloon slowly filling up with air, mixing with fear and anxiety, growing large and intense until it released.

*Who am I? How did I get here? Why can I do this? And when will it be over?*

A single tear rolled down her cheek, involuntarily, as her heart threatened to beat right out of her chest. Around her, the world became a blur, colors melting together as cold and warm sensations equally fought for dominion. She squeezed her eyes shut, more tears escaping their ducts.

And then it became easier to breathe, and she inhaled and exhaled and inhaled and exhaled. The air grew thin and clear. She knew where—and when—she stood.

Opening her eyes, Adela took in the earthy, sweet smell of conifer trees. In this stretch of land, fir and juniper stood like soldiers, crowded on top of one another. Her breath clouded the air as sunbeams found their way through the maze of branches and pinecones, landing on the packed earth of the forest. Inching closer to the sunlit areas, her eyes opened wide in awe of this now-foreign sight.

The faint clanging of pots and pans behind her brought her back to the present—or past, in this case. She remembered the task at hand and, keeping the halved tooth clutched in one hand, knelt to gather the purple-black juniper berries into the deep fold of her skirt with the other. As she raced back home, a couple of adventurous berries escaped from the crease and forged a path back to the small haven, like breadcrumbs leading the way.

Adela skidded into the kitchen and lifted her skirt slightly, allowing the berries to fall on the counter. It was only too late that she felt the presence of someone behind her, just out of sight.

"What a mess," he said.

It was a curious moment, living in the past. Despite her desire to say—or do—anything off-script, the story and scene had been written before. She'd experienced this before. And so, Adela's next actions were instinctive, following the script of the past, no matter how intensely she wished to change it.

"I brought the berries."

"Excuse me?"

"I brought the —"

"Who said you could talk back like that?"

A lone juniper berry rolled from the counter onto the floor, as if attempting a grand escape from what would happen next.

Adela searched for her mother, though the future version of her knew that her mother was not in this memory. She had been at the store all morning, and it was unlikely she had returned by now. The two figures in the room were the only two people in the house.

"I'm sorry," she whispered and stepped back, a juniper berry bursting under her bare foot.

Conrad's gaze softened for a moment. "It's okay," he said, beckoning to her. "Come here."

Adela obliged, though again, she knew this memory was not a happy one. She found herself face-to-face with his splotched face, holes bored deep into it from years of work as if the dirt and sweat burrowed into his pores and then escaped, leaving behind pockets of emptiness. Both on the outside and the inside. She sensed a shift in the atmosphere. With a flick of his arm, he grabbed Adela's empty hand and twisted her wrist back.

"Ow," she cried out.

His grip lessened but still held firm. The pain was bearable but sharp, bones grinding together from the pressure, which had evolved into a dull throbbing. Tears began to build in her eyes and her nostrils flared, fear and anger intertwining. He kept his hold as she squirmed, still firmly grasping the incisor with her other hand. Adela needed to stay in this moment, needed answers to the questions still skipping in her mind.

*Who am I? How did I get here? Why can I do this? And when will it be over?*

Still trying to escape, she finally let out a sob. In response, Conrad let go, and Adela fell back on the floor, scraping her elbow on the tiles as she tried to soften her impact. Her wrist was red and swollen. Lines of blood began to pool on the skin of her elbow, and she rushed to her feet to run it under the sink, wincing as her tears dried on her cheeks.

Conrad sat in the corner, the sun setting behind him and emitting a soft orange glow that made him more frightening than she had ever seen. He had never acted as ill-tempered toward her as he did now. Ever since he had returned from his most recent expedition, he had changed. Adela stood in shock.

"Nobody likes you," he said, spitting in her direction.

Something in Adela broke, like a dam that suddenly gave way. A rush of emotions built up inside her and then were quickly tamped down, collecting in a place that was inaccessible with dark feelings swirling in their own purgatory. Stumbling away from the kitchen and into the outside world, Adela held her elbow close to her side. She didn't even close the door behind her before following the path of juniper berries back into the forest.

And at that moment, entering the enclave, her body lifted those emotions from their purgatory and let them overtake everything. She fell forward, palms to the dirt in an effort to ground herself. Adela wept, rocks and roots crunching under her hands as she bunched them into fists. Her tears soaked the ground, fueling the forest floor with a dull sadness. The air began to whistle, and the sun disappeared behind the South Mountains that overlooked the village. She shivered. At once, the flames of anger warmed her body; she had only disdain for the cruelty brewing in her home, fear for her own well-being, and—scariest of all—absolutely nothing. Her emotions were frozen once more, as if trapped under a layer of ice in the abyss they called home.

The snap of branches behind her made her head snap too. Balancing on the tips of her toes, Adela slowly turned around. Bright amber eyes blinked back at her.

She had never encountered a fox before.

Her grandmother told stories of their cunning and mischief, purporting that they couldn't be trusted. But the Fox stayed still, watching her. His large ears were on alert, twitching every so often to swat away the lightning bugs that buzzed about whenever the sun dipped low. Whiskers blew in the light breeze, and his silver-tipped brick red fur was full and dense, readying itself for the cold even now in the midst of April. His mouth was slightly agape, and his pink tongue peeked through his slender jaws.

"H-hello," Adela stammered.

The Fox smiled, his amber eyes squinting from joy and becoming two black slivers on his rosy face. "Hi."

She gasped. Her grandmother once told her that foxes could speak, but Adela had never been able to prove—or disprove—that theory. Adela had attributed it to the musings of a mysterious woman who believed in evil and magic concoctions, princesses and brooding witches.

"You can talk!"

"And so can you."

"I just... I've never... I mean... I'm Adela, what's your name?"

"My name isn't important."

"Why not?"

"Didn't you know? Telling someone your name gives them power over you."

"But I just told you mine."

"Precisely."

Though her future self remembered this moment, she navigated it with the blindness and naivety of the girl who had stumbled into the forest months ago.

"Why were you crying?"

"I wasn't."

"Come now, how can we be friends if we can't be truthful?"

"Why would you want to be friends with me?"

"Very well." The Fox inched closer, the claws on his paws retracting with each step. He settled next to Adela, his bushy tail swatting her in the side every so often. With this small action of sitting down, Adela towered over the Fox, and he bowed his head in deference. "My name is Alby," he yawned. He opened a single eye. "Now, will you answer my question? Truthfully?"

Adela looked past the openings in the trees, above the treetops until she pinpointed the plume of smoke escaping from her cabin's chimney. "Something happened."

"You encountered a monster."

"Is that what that was?"

Alby moved his head, mimicking a nod.

"I couldn't even fight back."

"You feel powerless."

"I feel powerless," she parroted.

Alby sighed, licking his paw and eyeing an earthworm that had wandered over to his position. "I'll tell you what, why don't you come back to my den?" He swatted at the earthworm and gulped him down in one motion. "My partner lives with me. But she's harmless, wouldn't hurt a fly," he said, his eyes twinkling.

"I don't know. It's getting late. I should really get going."

"I promise it'll be worth your while."

As much as Adela-in-the-past was wary, Adela-of-the-future tried everything in her powers to urge her on. This was the moment, after all. The one where everything changed.

"I have to be back before nightfall," she said, the position of the sun in the sky telling her she had about fifteen minutes before it would be dark as soot outside.

"Yes, yes, follow me. And hurry!"

She trailed the Fox, tripping over branches that tore into her knees and broke skin. The low gurgling of the nearby, slow-moving stream complemented the chirp of owls that pierced the night sky. Adela shuddered as the wind grew colder, biting at her face—until finally, they stopped at a small cave.

"This is your home?"

"Yes," the Fox said, wiping his paws on the grass before he stepped foot inside. "Come in before you freeze to death."

While the Fox disappeared farther into the outpost, Adela entered the refuge and took in the environment. The rocky walls were covered in moss and two holes were set deeper inside the home, one filled with insects, frogs, and berries, and the other emitting screeching Adela could only imagine came from smaller red foxes, sounding eerily like cries for help. A pile of leaves and feathers created soft bedding, a brief respite from the cold, hard dampness of the cave.

"Here, look at this." Alby emerged from the murky shadows, poking forward three smooth, iridescent cave pearls.

"Wow," Adela exhaled.

With a glimmer in his eye, Alby nudged them closer to Adela. "Take them."

"Me, but why?"

"You know, I'm not from Sunseree. I'm from Western Wilerea. They say that's where magic began, where regular folk—like you—began to experiment with herbs, spices, plants, fire, what have you. And they began to develop a form of earthly magic."

"I know about that place. My grandmother was born there. She lives there now."

"Yes, yes, that makes sense," Alby said, a sly smile settling on his face. "In Western Wilerea, you can solve any problems with magic. Isn't that the dream? To be able to, with the snap of your fingers, make everyone love you? Escape the darkness? Defeat your monsters?" He gave out a short, quick succession of barks, his eyes squinting again as his tail passed in front of Adela's face.

"Yes," Adela answered, mesmerized, repeating the word that would change her life forever.

"Well, then, take the pearls. They're yours."

"Really?"

"Yes, really. And keep them safe. You'd be surprised at their purpose, if only you keep them with you."

"What do they do?"

"Anything your heart desires. With all three, your desires are at their most powerful. With two, less so, and with one even less than that."

Adela knelt down to grab the glossy pearls.

"But wait! Before you take them, tell me about this afternoon. Tell me what happened."

She hesitated. "I was gathering juniper berries."

"No, no. I'm terribly sorry to interrupt. Tell me how you felt, what you wanted."

"I felt scared. Powerless. I wasn't brave or clever enough to escape. And that's exactly what I wanted to do. I wanted to escape. I would have done anything to escape that moment. To go anywhere in the world." She thumbed the tooth in her left hand as a familiar tingle rushed up her spine, reaching the base of her neck and spreading to the tips of her fingers.

Alby nodded and placed a small paw over the pearls before pulling it away. Adela picked them up as a peculiar haze took over, her fingers charged with static electricity. She tried to drop the pearls but couldn't. Instead, she sank into the pile of feathers and leaves she had taken notice of mere minutes before. Alby's mischievous eyes softened with a kindness that she hadn't seen all day, and then she closed her eyes.

"Adela! Adela!"

Adela began to awake, groggy with sleep. She was in the Fox's cave. But it was cold and dark, and the screeching den of foxes had quieted, the place evacuated.

The voice grew closer, shrill and coated with worry and fear. "Adela! Adela, are you here?"

"Mama?" Adela answered weakly. "Mama?" Her voice gained strength, echoing off the stone walls and in the outside air.

"I hear you, keep calling!"

"Mama!"

"Adela!"

"Mama! I'm here!" Footsteps grew louder, and a large shape filled the entrance to the cave.

"There you are!" Her mother rushed to her, bumping her head amidst the low clearance but barreling forward in desperation. "Why did you run off? I've been searching for hours!"

"I—I don't know," Adela lied.

"Let's go home. You're freezing. We should get you in front of the fire." Her mother turned around, her back to Adela as she maneuvered back outside.

The cave pearls were still clutched in her hand, and she glanced around for the fox tooth—the whole version of the halved one she held in her other hand. Tucking all the keepsakes into her shoe and pulling her socks up to cover her ankles, she followed her mother through brambles and twigs, keeping an eye out for Alby and his family to no avail. After some time, her mother lifted her into her arms, carrying her the rest of the way home.

As they approached the cabin, the sky had turned pitch black. Entering the home, her mother placed her in front of the fire and brought her a mug of tea to warm up. Conrad was nowhere to be found.

"What time is it?" asked Adela.

"Near sunrise."

"But the sun isn't rising."

"What?"

"The sun isn't—"

"Please go to bed. I'm exhausted." Her mother's eyes were tired and sad.

Adela chose not to press the moment further; she gulped down her tea and shrugged off the blanket her mother had wrapped around her shoulders earlier.

"You can go to bed, Mama. I want to take a quick bath."

"Call me if you need me, okay?"

"I will."

Her mother retreated from the living room.

Adela hurried up the stairs, glancing behind her. She shut the door to her bedroom and raced over to the window. This was it, of course. The day of the Last Sun. Turning toward the empty bed, she opened her hand, letting the remnants clutched in her palm fall on the floor.

Her breath caught in her throat. Adela exhaled as the ticking of the clocks sped up. She was back in bed, firmly in the present. She crawled out and reached under her bed for the two glossy cave pearls, reminders of Conrad's cruelty. Tiptoeing to the windows, she knelt forward and picked up the tooth halves she had dropped. She took inventory of everything as she sank to her knees on the threadbare rug before finally peeling back a loose floorboard and depositing the items in their new home, safe from the terrors outside.

She lay in bed after tucking herself in and reminisced on the memory from mere months prior. Adela thought revisiting the memory would provide clarity, but she still didn't quite understand what had happened that night.

All she knew was that afternoon, the villagers awoke, dazed and reeling. The sun would never rise and the moon would take its place for a long time. That same day, she touched a wildflower in a vase in the kitchen and found herself in a flower field, a mile from home, the very place where she picked the wildflower weeks before.

Adela had a gnawing feeling the events of the Last Sun had something to do with these adventures, but that wasn't something she could dwell on now. She had figured out a way to escape the monster in her home.

# PART TWO

# FOUR

# TRAIN

—

She fell deeper and deeper and deeper.

Shifting, sinking. The bed creaked under her belly. Morning pried at her eyelids, though in front of them was only darkness. Slowly, Adela opened one eye and then the other. The room was pitch black. In the hallway, the tick-tock of the wooden grandfather clock and a faint clamoring climbed up the stairs, rounding the corner into her room. Outside, stars beamed, cradling a full moon.

Adela got dressed, slipped on her wool-lined slippers, and walked to her bookcase. She carefully observed the trinkets in front of her before tucking one into the band of her skirt. Before leaving the room, she pulled up the floorboards, securing the remaining two cave pearls into her socks before lumbering into the bathroom to wash up. She emerged soon after, like a mouse scurrying out of a hole in the wall, darting down the stairs as she made her way to the front door.

"No 'good morning'?" Her mother was in the kitchen, a wooden spoon in hand as she stood guard over a pan of eggs that were beginning to catch color.

"Morning, Mama." Adela exhaled, nervously anticipating an unwelcome addition to this conversation if she did not leave the house soon. "I promised Milo I'd watch the trains pass with him this morning."

"It's too dark out."

"But, Mama, it's a full moon."

Her mother frowned, inadvertently creating harsh lines right between her unkempt eyebrows. While her mother deliberated the veracity of this claim, Adela picked at her fingers, catching a corner of her fingernail and ripping it in a straight line, dangerously close to the sensitive pink flesh of her nail bed. As the stinging sensation set in, Adela continued to stare down her mother, willing her to let her out of the house.

Too much time was passing.

"Go. Be back by lunchtime, and—"

Adela was out the door, leaving her mother's sentence unfinished. The full moon cast a faint luminescence on Sunseree below, and she raced down the hillside, picking up speed and stumbling over her own feet with momentum, only stopping to catch her balance before continuing on.

The hillside was slippery this time of year, and its wet surface reminded Adela that the coldest seasons would soon be upon them. That meant Conrad would be home more, not just a handful of breaks here and there. She shook her head, hair whipping her in the face, as if attempting to knock the thought out of her head by force. Eying the faint amber light at the base of the hill—beckoning to her—she made a beeline, her eyes locked ahead.

She kicked up dirt as she galloped, imagining disheveled insects and their homes in disarray, trampled wildflowers with bent stems, and woodland animals stumbling out of their evening hiding places.

Almost there.

The door swung and Adela slammed into the shadowed figure emerging from the doorway.

"Oof," Milo gasped, clutching at his chest in an attempt to catch his breath, both figuratively and literally. His eyes widened as his chapped lips formed an "o" shape to facilitate the passing of breath in and out, in and out.

"Sorry." Adela brimmed with adrenaline, the escape from her cabin filling her lungs with mountain air that burned with each new breath. She would be sore, but for now, she observed Milo as he doubled over in visible pain.

Milo was Adela's best friend but only because nobody else wanted to be friends with either of them. They had a quiet understanding of one another. They rarely talked, rationing words and sentences as if they were precious currency. As she waited for him to compose himself, Adela took in the house around her, one she had taken inventory of many times before, quaint but lit in an amber glow. Outside the front door, flickering gas lanterns complemented warm bulbs housed within vibrant, abstract glass bowls.

Milo's dad was a glassmith. He moved his family to Sunseree after the Last Sun, hearing tales of a picturesque town suddenly descended into darkness. They arrived in the middle of the night, like drifters appearing out of thin air, fashioning sculptures and lamps out of molten glass and earthly chemicals that added vibrant colors near indistinguishable in the dark. Their cluttered home was constantly lit, and the front door was nestled under an elaborate stained glass panel depicting a wooded sanctuary, filled in with glimmering grays, greens, violets, and yellows.

"Ready?" Adela bit at her lips and peeled off the topmost layer of skin as a grin stretched out on Milo's face.

"I don't hear—" Milo started, though his thought was immediately cut off.

The thundering sound broke through the early morning's silence. It started low and rumbling, and the earth vibrated, prompted from miles away. Treetops shook, emptying their feathered inhabitants into the night sky.

"Run!" she yelled.

Adela led the way, lungs filled from her earlier endeavor, as Milo stuttered to a start in the same direction. From behind them, his mother emerged to lecture them about leaving the door open and taking off without warning.

Sunseree was transcendent in the moonlight. The town existed under the shadow of the South Mountains, a range that inexplicably split in two to make way for a lake peppered with small rocks that poked their tops out through the mirrored surface. Houses and cottages dotted the water and, in warmer months, people swam in the lake, drawn to its mysterious beauty.

When cold, it was not uncommon to see children skating on the transparent ice. With a sharp eye, one could see fish swimming underneath the thick slab separating the overworld from the underworld inhabited by salmon, trout, and perch. This natural haven gave way to a stretch of grassland, peaking at the precipice where Adela's house lay. That stretch of land, in turn, led to the woods.

Where Adela first met Alby. Where everything changed.

But today, they ran past the split mountain range and lake, curving up toward where the other edge of the forest lay, the side Adela had never explored. It would take her hours to traverse from one end to the other, getting perpetually lost in the fog and brambles and circling until there was nothing left to do but lose hope.

On this side of the woods lay untouched nature. But in the light of the full moon, she could make out faint beams of light as the train approached, still minutes away.

She and Milo paused and settled down into the dewy grass, breathing heavily and knowing they had been waiting for this moment all week. Her ankle was red and raw, and she bit her lip in anticipation.

"Sometimes," she said to no one in particular, "I look out the window at the train and picture myself in that seat. Nine rows behind the conductor—close enough that I can anticipate the curves of the road ahead, but far away enough that I can sit in my own thoughts for hours at a time."

Milo sat silently. Adela didn't expect him to answer. In the distance, wolves howled, still confused at the darkness in which they awoke. It had been two months since the sun left, and they had yet to become fully accustomed to the changing environment.

"Are you planning to leave again?"

"Yes."

"Why don't you ever take me with you?"

"I don't know if I can, to be honest."

"But you've never tried it."

"And what does that have to do with anything?" Adela caught herself, her tongue slipping out of her mouth. The harsh words were fueled by negative feelings that lay dormant. She softened. "You don't understand what it's like."

"I could."

"No. You can't understand when you talk too much."

Milo sighed, leaning back on his palms as the early morning wind rustled his mousy blond hair. Like the constellations that emerged in the sky at all hours of the night, brown moles infiltrated the surface of his neck. His ruddy complexion paired with drooping cheeks, the remnants of a well-fed childhood.

"How long?"

"I don't know," Adela said as she pulled on the band of her skirt and let the ticket fall on the dewy grass, sections becoming dark with dampness. "My mom said I need to be back by lunchtime." Her voice could barely be heard over the bellowing train horn that signaled its approach. It was time.

"Make sure you keep watch," she said. "I'll be back in a few hours."

She fell back, smiling, and pushed the train ticket into her clammy palm.

Alby had been right. Her powers were diminished with only the two cave pearls tucked into her sock. Where the process before had been swift, completing within the span of a few seconds, Adela simultaneously felt both a pull and push from her reclining body, releasing her into the world yet wanting to keep her safe in Sunseree. Or perhaps she was imagining it.

But it passed. In a blink, she was wistfully glancing out a grimy window at her original body, situated feet away from Milo. He stared forward, eyes blank and hair blowing in the breeze; Adela never could fathom if he saw her when she escaped, but she sensed he felt her presence. And part of her knew he was tracking her departure at this very moment.

Adela had found the train ticket in her maternal grandmother's belongings only four days ago. The destination was a town she had heard of only in stories, a kingdom called Nuimtree halfway between Sunseree and Old Kitfalls, which itself bordered New Kitfalls. She wasn't entirely certain what to expect in Nuimtree, though she heard it housed a sprawling castle that was situated in the heart of the Whitt Woods.

Long ago, Adela's mother admitted that she knew someone from Nuimtree. And, would you believe it, Adela discovered in her grandmother's possessions a ticket to the very
place! Just as she used her abilities last night to get answers
about how her powers came to be, she needed to go to Nuimtree to understand the mystery of why her grandmother went
there and who her mother knew from the reclusive kingdom.
It seemed like the one way Adela could better understand her
family. And, in turn, herself.

Adela had also never been on a locomotive train before.
She tucked the ticket back into the band of her skirt, pressed
against her skin to keep its properties securely in place. With
one of the cave pearls shattered, Adela had to be careful. On
the train, she took in the unusual environment. Plush red
seats stretched in either direction, each facing one way, like
a crowd of well-behaving schoolchildren looking forward.
They held the scent of their previous inhabitants, and Adela
scrunched her freckled nose in disgust as she caught the waft
of hand-rolled cigarettes. She rose to her feet, holding onto
the tops of the seats while inching to explore more, when her
fingertips faintly throbbed.

"Ouch," she exclaimed, sucking on her thumb. She had the
worst habit of picking at her fingers and, at once, she knew
she shouldn't have pulled at her nail earlier. Momentarily
distracted by the throbbing pain of the hardened keratin,
the presence of a dark shape caught her attention, and she
twisted her eyes to meet the black ones of a peregrine falcon.

The Falcon stared her down as Adela stood in the middle
of the train, her body swaying with the mechanical rhythm
of the steel carriage's movement. He blinked, eyes dotted
with a white fleck, like a paintbrush that had slipped, and
his neck bobbed to compensate for the energy in his short,

powerful body. She had seen falcons perching in the tree canopy, dive-bombing rodents and woodland squirrels in the fields below, but had never seen one up close.

Adela took a side step closer to the conductor's car, testing if his eyes would follow her. They did, but he remained perched on the side of the train, his flaxen-colored talons gripping the side of the window frame that jutted out. The two carried on with this charade for a few moments until Adela became annoyed. She edged closer to the grimy sliding doors separating the compartments.

Instantly, the cool forest air flew in her face as she opened the divider. The motion of the train made the platform holding the two compartments together rattle and her heart raced with the irrational possibilities of what could happen. She could fly into the air, whisked away by the clouds, never to be seen by her mother. The ticket could fly out of her skirt and she could be instantly transported home, which wasn't entirely awful on its face—but she needed answers. She needed a moment to escape. She shook her head once more, physically ridding herself of the toxic thoughts, and braced herself to enter the door in front of her.

Before she placed her foot on the platform, she lowered her gaze to see the Falcon, confidently perched on the platform and barring her from crossing forward. The train swayed as it hugged the small curves of the mountainside, and Adela once again braced herself—feet, arms, and all—to avoid falling over. She eyed the Falcon crossly, increasingly irritated that it was in her way.

"Go away," she mumbled, shifting her body and hunching her back to make herself appear larger, so as to scare it away. The Falcon, unperturbed, continued to survey her presence. Though his notched beak was downturned and covered with small keratin scabs, likely the result of battles with its mammalian prey, she sensed a troublesome glimmer in his eyes. With a blink, he was gone, flying forward with the train. Adela's stomach churned, a physical response to her discomfort, but she slid the door open and quickly latched it in place before taking in the new car's environment.

This train compartment bore similarities to the one she had transported to, but it housed an additional traveler. The sound of the door locking in place caught their attention, and they leisurely turned toward Adela and smiled.

"What's a little girl like you doing here?"

"I'm not little," Adela said, offended.

"Right, you're not. Come sit."

Adela obliged, shuffling down the aisle and dragging her boots along the dusty red carpet. She settled into a sectional across the aisle from the mysterious stranger. "Who are you?"

"You can call me Clara."

"Clara," Adela tried it on her tongue. It was a curious name, one she felt she had heard before but, at the same time, not at all.

"I come from far away," Clara added, picking up on Adela's confusion. "I'm traveling to visit someone."

"Where are you from?"

Clara laughed, and Adela experienced a sharp humming in her ear. Clara flipped her long, copper hair as she laughed. Her hair was the in-between of the deep red of blood and the golden hue of Adela's own, catching the light in places while darkening in others.

"I'm from Western Wilerea. I've been called for by someone very important."

Clara's eyes were a misty blue, mirroring what Adela imagined the sky looked like right before the rain began, and her lower lip was thin, but patchy in places. Adela assumed she had been biting her lips before this encounter, a telltale sign that she was nervous, for Adela had picked up the same habit from her own mother.

"Western Wilerea? You're a witch?" Adela blurted out.

Clara flinched and grimaced. "I'm not a witch."

"My grandmother is from Western Wilerea, and *she's* a witch."

"How do you know she's a witch?" Clara chuckled.

Once again, that same humming returned, and Adela's hand instinctively moved up, rubbing at her temples. The sound lasted for only a second before fading.

"Is something wrong?"

"I don't know," Adela answered. She was tired, though it was only early morning. "Do you know how much longer it is to Nuimtree?"

"We've been talking for a while. We have an hour left to go. Or longer."

"I've never been this far from my house."

"Really?"

Adela nodded, her thin hair bobbing in place. "I've never been to Nuimtree. Do you know what it's like?"

Clara sighed wistfully, settling into her worn seat. At that moment, a muslin bag tucked under the crevice of her arm creeped into Adela's peripheral vision and, as it shifted, the delicate clinking of glass jars that had gotten too close to one another rose to meet her ears.

"Nuimtree is unlike any place in the world. The train will drop us off at a small station a half-a-day's walk from the castle. In between the station and the castle is a lush forest—the Whitt Woods—and inside the forest live a few families. There's a deep well and a small brook where they fish, and the castle and its inhabitants watch over the entire landscape."

Clara continued, regaling Adela with great stories about the kingdom and its inhabitants, tall tales about the families that lived in the forest, the royal family that ruled with vigilance and wisdom over its small jurisdiction, and the verdant landscape that Adela supposed had been drastically changed by the events of the Last Sun. Adela sensed that Clara had visited Nuimtree countless times before, as she had an intimate knowledge of the area that few other travelers would.

Maybe Clara could help her find out the secret behind the yellowed train ticket hidden in the band of her clothes.

"That sounds magical," Adela said.

"It is. Are you going to the castle?"

"Yes, I think so."

"We can walk there together. I'll show you the way."

"Thank you." Adela's fingers throbbed with pain, and she picked at them again, biting at the calloused edges until they bled. When they hurt, this was the only way to achieve release from the pain, a series of anxious tics that never resolved the underlying problem. "Ow," she yelped.

"Now why would you do that?" Clara said, her brow furrowing as she dug in her peculiar cloth bag.

Adela took in Clara, her lithe, pale fingers picking up items just out of view. One of Clara's thick, red locks fell from its place behind her ear, and Adela could peek through the small window of hair to observe her more closely. Her left cheek had a thin scar, thickened with age and about the size and shape of a sunflower seed.

"Give me your hand."

Adela stretched her arm out, hand in a fist with her thumb resting atop.

Carefully and silently, Clara applied an acrid brown paste to her thumb, which eased the pressure at her fingertips. "How's that?"

"Better," Adela said, her voice rising. "I knew you were a witch!"

Clara laughed and the humming in Adela's ears returned, albeit for a brief time.

"Enough witch talk, we're almost there."

Adela looked out the window, cleaning the dirt with the crook of her elbow. She took in the strange new world around her. The train station stretched out ahead, glowing lampposts leading the way for weary travelers. Over the treetops, small blue turrets and a massive golden one proudly hoisted the flag of Nuimtree to all who passed by the kingdom.

The flag itself featured a red deer, its grand antlers holding a straw basket. Peeking over the basket were two small pink heads and two small pink hands each. Adela ventured a guess that the flag depicted babies, a curious image to put on a flag.

The tops of the approaching trees were unlike the ones in her home village: crimson, violet, and amber in color, mimicking the colors of the center of a flame, vibrant and bright and completely unlike the fir trees she was familiar with. Adela was awe-struck, mouth agape, at the new environment.

"Ready?" Clara said as the train screeched to a halt.

Adela nodded and pried herself away from the window. Before answering, she pulled the train ticket, damp from the heat of its hiding place against her stomach. Without lifting her fingers away from it, she tucked it safely into the elastic of her sock to accompany the pearls. She couldn't lose it now. "Ready."

"Where's your bag?"

"I'm here for only a little while," Adela answered, knowing she'd have to return to her original body, and Milo, and her mother, and the unspoken trepidation of her home soon. She shivered, wishing she could run away, stealing her mother and taking her elsewhere.

"Alright."

Clara grabbed her cloth bag and an even-larger one that had been laid on the empty row of seats in front of them. Clara apparently planned to stay in Nuimtree for a while, at least a week. She made her way to the front of the compartment and slid the door open, turning to rest her eyes on Adela only for a moment before appearing on the platform outside. She set off in the direction of the Whitt Woods, standing defiantly in between the station and the castle, and called out, "Are you coming?"

Excitement bubbled up in Adela's muscles as she rushed to her feet and ran toward Clara, clumsily stumbling over her own shoes. Tired, unusually so for this time of day, she had difficulty keeping up, especially as her ribs were sore from the earlier clash with Milo.

The station ran alongside the leafy forest, a small dirt path carved into it that allowed wandering folk to make their way to the kingdom's main attraction. Without words, the two stumbled a few hundred steps into the forest.

The bustling of the station was behind them, the train idling in place until it didn't. She yawned.

"Tired? You're right. It's getting late."

"What do you mean?" Adela asked, stretching her face back into its normal state.

"It's dark out," Clara chuckled.

Humming again.

"Yes, it's always dark," Adela retorted, wholly confused but following behind. As she followed, she took in more of Clara's physique. She wore a beautiful velvet cloak, in the indigo and silver colors of Western Wilerea; underneath she was clothed in a silk shirt that rose to meet her short neck, and a thick pair of pants allowed some give to her rounded shape.

Clara herself seemed bemused. "What are you talking about, girl? Watch out," she said and pointed toward the ground. Adela realized she had almost stepped on a snake, its brown body dotted with darker brown diamonds in a row. Clara led Adela into a small clearing, devoid of trees, and patted the ground, letting the soft dirt sift through her thin fingers.

A strange feeling bubbled in Adela's stomach; she was unnerved by Clara's behavior and wondering why she had followed a strange woman to the middle of the woods. She turned, cursing her instincts for not alerting her to danger earlier and determined to find the castle alone. Above the treetops, the blue and gold turrets peeked through, tucked under the cloud cover and the perpetual moon above. A full moon, just as she had left it.

Before she could step any farther, she nearly lost her balance to a disturbance, the ground rumbling behind her. Turning slowly, her chin dropped as a log home sprung out of the earth, like fungus poking out of its underworld hiding spot. Brown bugs leapt off the rising structure as windows and a door emerged.

Clara stood with her hands on her hips, admiring her handiwork. As suddenly as it had started, the ground stopped moving and the structure creaked into place. Clara stepped forward, brushing dirt off the doorknob before turning it decidedly.

"Are you coming inside?"

Adela nodded, as if in a trance. She followed Clara inside, dragging her feet to the small porch and taking her shoes off before entering the magicked cottage.

"I don't have a second bed, but I can sleep on the floor while you take the bed. We should rest for the journey," Clara continued, shuffling around the house and taking off her cloak.

Inside, the house was wholly charming. To her right was a quaint wooden kitchen with a stone countertop. Dried herbs—thyme and sage—and mushrooms and animals hung from a hook fashioned into the ceiling. A mortar and pestle for grinding the aforementioned herbs into a paste was tucked into a dark corner, alongside a blue tea kettle with a rusted handle. A rocking chair with a lavender-colored pillow had small down feathers that were peeking out, waiting to be plucked, while a stone fireplace housed a cast-iron cauldron and a pile of weathered logs next to it. In the back of the room was a recess with a humble bed covered with blankets that looked unbearably scratchy. Next to the bed was a straw mat that now Clara pulled into the room, picking up dust in the process.

"Are you hungry?" Clara huffed, picking up an armful of logs and hurling them into the pit. She grabbed the broom angled against it and glanced up the chimney.

"Shoo!" she yelled. "Blasted birds. Damn falcon, always sticking his beak in the chimney."

Putting the broom away, she rubbed her palms together and shut her eyes as she hovered her hands above the pile of logs. The fireplace glowed with the faint orange color of kindling catching fire, and Clara pulled her hands back, resting them in the crook of her pants. A small fire appeared.

Clara turned and winked at Adela. "No witch talk."

Adela stood in place, unsure what to do next. She nearly pinched herself to wake up. Whole houses rising from the ground, witches who could create fire with their hands, falcons that seemed to follow her from place to place. At least, she told herself, she knew she was firmly in her world and present time.

"Now then," Clara said, "what was it you said about it always being dark?"

Adela sighed and tilted her head, amused by the fact that Clara could not follow the topic of conversation.

"The Last Sun, just a few months ago. We've been under the dark of the moon ever since. How can you not remember?"

The air was still and musty, and time temporarily seemed to slow.

"Oh, girl," Clara cooed like a preening dove. "But that hasn't happened yet."

# FIVE

# SECRET

———

Early evening transformed into thick, dark night without pause. All night, Adela roamed the small hallway of the home, unthinking and inattentive. Clara had not investigated any further after their conversation, the Last Sun as the primary topic. Adela had ascertained—correctly, of course—that she had traveled in time. That alone had been a shock. But the bigger surprise was learning how long she had traveled: *decades.*

Clara had settled on the straw mat beside the fire, keeping it far away enough to not catch any popping embers but close enough to welcome the familiar warmth.

Readying herself for bed, Adela pulled her wool sweater over her head, flinching as she brushed her ribs; she was regretting greeting Milo earlier in the day. Her weathered skirt slipped to the floor, and she stood in her long-bottoms and thin undershirt.

She remained awake, even in bed. In time, Clara's breathing became relaxed and steady.

The cottage was still.

*The cottage is still.*

Adela lay, eyes wide open in shock. In her bed, the thin blanket itched against her arms. She scratched at her head, teeming with microscopic insects that had found their way into her hair during the brief moments she stood in the clearing. She rubbed her arches against each other, the ticket tucked inside one of her socks for safe-keeping. Her arm hairs stood vertically as her mind reeled.

She acknowledged that it was entirely possible, of course, to travel in space and time. But pushing the limits of her powers within Sunseree had been simpler. At first, she practiced transporting in space only. This was complicated, as two Adelas walking around town proved to be confusing to others. And she had to keep her distance—what if she ran into herself? Controlling two copies of herself with the same brain proved to be a feat in and of itself. If she let up for a moment, she'd lose sight of her original body.

Goosebumps ran up the back of her neck as she remembered the bakery incident. One moment, she was admiring the caves behind her house and the next, chased after smuggling freshly baked rolls in her pockets. Before she learned that she needed to keep her original body at rest and hidden, which came with its own challenges.

Adela bit at the corner of her mouth, a nervous tic she had developed over the last year. She had tested bending time in small intervals, practicing jumping backward ten or fifteen minutes at a time. She would spend all day in the field, covered with muck and rainwater. Holding on to grass and weeds that grew alongside the edge of her cottage, she ran to the top of nearby hills, hidden from sight, and practiced holding her tokens, closing her eyes, and traveling.

Of course, that new experience had taught her another important tenet: to keep her original body sheltered and secure. Away from others who may cause her harm. She could still feel the bruise on her skull from when she transported without finding a safe clearing, allowing her original body to rest against a tree, apples raining down on her head. Her traveling body always found the original one, forever retreating to its home. But if people found her—people who did not understand the magic that was afoot—they could very well mistake her motionless body for a dead one.

And then, of course, she jumped back in time, to the serendipitous meeting with Alby, that charming Fox. It had been such a vivid memory. But it was more than just a memory. Adela learned then that her mind remained in both places. She remembered what had happened, yet she was experiencing the moment anew. She had known what was ahead, but her traveling body still searched for answers to unspoken questions.

Over these few months with her new powers, she had learned those key rules:

*Don't run into your original body.*
*Maintain control of both bodies at all times.*
*Keep your original body safe.*

But this moment was different.

This time she had traveled to a time and place that she had never encountered prior. She panicked, heart racing and skin flushing with sweat. Nobody taught her the rules associated with this method of travel; her reclined, original body was with Milo. Surely, he was getting worried now. She had been gone at least half a day, and she had promised him she would return soon. She could just end the magic spell and pull the token out of her sock now, drop it anywhere on the stone ground, and instantaneously return to Sunseree.

But she had come so far, meeting the kind Clara, a witch summoned by someone important in Nuimtree. She was close to the kingdom, close to finding out why her grandmother had a train ticket to this place far from home. In the Whitt Woods, the sole inhabited area where her mother knew someone. The answers to simple questions were within reach, she felt, and she could not imagine rushing to return home. While her mother would welcome her with unconditional understanding, Conrad would fly into a rage, saving his wrath for when her mother wasn't around. The sting of his grip on her arm still bit on her skin.

She exhaled, her chest shaking, and the earthy cottage seemed to mirror her action, creaking as it settled. Adela briefly worried that the house would sink back into the ground, burying her underneath the cold, dark earth. She waited for what seemed like forever before pushing the thought from her mind.

The fireplace waned, small embers lit from within while a thin layer of ash blanketed the stone surface. Adela's stomach gurgled happily, bloated with the mouthwatering stew that Clara made to help her calm down: duck, potatoes, wood mushrooms, and fragrant spices that felt inviting and familiar.

Splayed out next to the fire, Clara released small snores, her body twitching on the floor while seeking to release the tension of the day.

Pressing down on her thumbs with her forefingers, Adela rolled out of the small bed. Clara snorted, stirring. Adela stopped, arms outstretched in front of her to balance. Seconds later, the snoring renewed, and Adela tiptoed to the front door. Stepping over the doorway, she noted that the air was slightly warmer than back at Sunseree. Or, more accurately, in the time of the Last Sun.

The balmy air blew past her, lightly toying with the hair that had been deftly braided and tucked into itself by Clara's fast fingers. She was weary but wanted to explore the Whitt Woods. They seemed to whisper, as if calling to her. The castle's turrets were just ahead, and she supposed the station was at her back. Foliage and flora here were dense, and she quickly deduced that if she wanted to explore properly, she'd have to find her way back. Creeping back into the house, Adela stepped over Clara as she slept. Slowly and quietly, she collected the light gray ash from the outer rim of the firepit into one of Clara's muslin bags. She hoped its light color would help guide her back to the cabin.

Slipping on the shoes left by the front door, she set out, dipping her hand into the bag to coat it in ash and wiping it on the nearest tree. Venturing a few steps forward, she turned to admire her handiwork.

Good enough. Her brain whirred into place, conjuring scenarios for how this could go wrong. The wind could blow the ash off the tree, or a squirrel could swipe it off with a flick of its bushy tail, or it could begin to rain.

Traveling from home instilled her with a false sense of courage, and she was determined to proceed, the forest calling to her like a magnet pulling her through the thicket of trees. Adela continued, keeping an eye out for stray animals that could venture into her path. She peered through bushes, conjuring images of ferocious brown bears and wild boars with great tusks lurking in the shadows, waiting for her to cross their paths before pouncing and devouring her whole. But the animals never came, and the most she experienced among the towering beech and redwood trees were blood-sucking ticks that tried to jump at her clothed legs, bouncing off to the ground as they failed and alerting Adela to their presence.

The trees gave way to her journey, bending and allowing space for her to crawl through their cover. She marked trees with an ash smudge, implementing a numbering system made of circles. Her first tree—the one just outside the cabin—had no dots, her second had one, and so on and so forth. She was up to nearly twenty-nine dots now, if she had counted accurately, and realized just how far she had ventured into the forest.

The wind had picked up by now, and she imagined it must be close to midnight, presuming this was a popular time for any mythical creatures of the forest to come out of hiding. Adela shivered, realizing Clara had never admitted whether these creatures were well- or ill-intentioned.

This deep in the woods, the trees reached inexplicable heights. Her inquisitive nature had led her to a dangerous place as the wind whipped around her, screaming ferociously. Sounds of woodland animals stepping on twigs and branches, and yellow glowing eyes in the bushes around her signaled to her that she should retreat. As she walked backward, in the direction of her smudged trees, a voice whispered, "Wait."

Adela stopped, dead in her tracks. She attempted to pinpoint the voice.

"Wait," the voice said. "How did you get on that train?"

"C-Clara?"

"No. I'm not Clara."

"How did you know I was on the train?"

"I saw you!"

The voice came from above.

Just out of reach, the Falcon perched on the highest tree, the midnight moonlight shining off his feathers. He must have been over a hundred feet above her, and yet—within seconds—he swooped down to rest just before her. It happened in a flash, and her breath caught in her throat.

"Are you the girl? The girl who can travel?" The Falcon's beady eyes shone, glassy with wonder.

"I think so."

"I knew it! I'd never seen you before."

"What do you mean?"

"I'm a peregrine falcon. I've traveled the whole world over at least twice before. And I've never seen you. That's why you caught my eye on the train. You're not from here. Place or time."

"You're right. I'm not," Adela admitted. "And that's all I'll say about it."

"Ha!" the Falcon squawked. "Alby told me you'd be trouble."

"Alby?" Adela shook her head in disbelief. "That's not possible." She scoffed. "If, to your point, I've bent time, it would be impossible for him to be living right now."

"My dear," the Falcon's deep voice became gentler, "is it not out of the realm of possibility that the same Fox who gifted you your powers would himself know how to bend time?"

Adela gasped, hanging on to the bird's every word. "Is he here?"

The Falcon shook his head, his feathers ruffling with the motion. "He's not here, but I get the feeling he's always watching."

The wind snapped at the trees and the various twigs and branches that peppered the forest floor. Forgetting about the eyes in the distance, Adela settled into the ground, bemused. Ensuring that her token was still safely in place in her sock, she eyed the Falcon, getting a close look at him. He had a lithe, muscular head, perfectly curling toward a hooked beak. While his eyes were large and dark, his feathers were tipped black with patches of brown and white on his underbelly. His feathers caught the moonlight perfectly; not shiny like those of a crow but mesmerizing all the same.

"You're very quiet," he said, interrupting her train of thought.

"I am. I like the silence." She picked up a rock and threw it against a tree just behind the bird.

"What do you think you'll find here?"

"Here?"

"In Nuimtree. In this time."

"Answers."

"To what?"

Adela kicked up a cloud of dirt with the back of her shoe. "The world is too big to stay in one place for a long time. I've been stuck inside the village for years, and then I discovered that I could escape to places and... things got better." She again kicked at the small stones and packed dirt in front of her, speaking in hushed tones so as not to attract any creatures that may be stumbling through this area of the woods.

"What are you escaping from?"

"Home."

"You seem happy and healthy and well-fed," the bird prodded.

Adela sighed, eyes growing heavy. She focused her energy on a stray, brown freckle she had found on her hand, picking at it as if she could pluck it off her skin altogether. "You wouldn't understand. You're just a bird."

"As I said, I've seen everything."

"I'm not sure. Something happened a few months ago." The air grew colder and she shivered, bringing her knees closer to her chest as goosebumps dotted her arms and legs. She had stripped down to her undergarments for bed, but the night had grown too cold for the thin items.

"Your powers?"

"In a way. People change is all. People discover new abilities and use them for good, use them to expand their world. And some people become bitter and callous and cruel." She recalled Conrad and touched her elbow, remembering the pain that lay imbedded in her bones. "Monsters aren't only in fairytales. They're all around us."

"I see. But don't you miss your mother?"

"Of course, I do! She's probably worried about me right now." Her eyes fell to her sock, the train ticket scratching against the raw skin of her ankle. "I suppose I could—"

"Shh!" The Falcon was flustered, glancing around. "Someone's coming!"

He disappeared into the canopy of trees, safely under cover while Adela lay waiting, in plain view, like a sitting animal. The duck stew from earlier threatened to come back up any moment, her underarms hot with sweat and feet clammy. She waited, closing her eyes and flinching.

"What are you doing?"

Adela wheezed, her arm yanked upward. Clara was irate, pale blue eyes darting back and forth. She was shaking uncontrollably. "Who told you that you could leave?"

"I just—"

"You are my guest," she whispered furiously. "I shouldn't have to wander the forest looking for you. It's good you had the sense to mark the trees so I could find you!"

"I'm sorry, I—"

"Stop! Don't talk so loud. You don't know who, or what, is listening."

She pulled Adela back in the direction of the cabin.

"What do you mean by that?" Adela asked, glancing backward. But the Falcon was gone.

"The woods are alive at night. They're in their darkest form. You never know what creature you'll encounter. And whether their intentions are good."

A shiver ran up Adela's spine, and she worried that she had spilled her darkest secrets to the forest, not knowing who had been listening. In the bushes, where yellow eyes had disappeared, green eyes appeared in the farthest corner, watching her retreat. She gulped. Was she imagining it all?

Adela let Clara lead her back to the small cabin in silence.

"Off to bed now. And I mean *now*."

Adela obliged, wondering if she had made a mistake exploring the woods. And wondering if the Falcon—or anyone who had listened—knew too much about her now.

# SIX

# SPIRIT

———

"Up, up. Get up, girl."

Adela peeled her eyes open and then, involuntarily, quickly shut them tightly. The sun was streaming in, finding the edges of the small alcove with its long, golden rays.

The sun.

She lay in bed, her heart beating quickly, as the tactile discomfort of the blankets scratched against her skin. Just as soon as the feeling rippled against her skin, they were stripped back, her small body exposed to the cool, musty air inside the cottage. It smelled like the pantry back home.

"No time to waste. It'll be a half-day's journey," Clara said.

Breakfast fried in the far corner, and Adela followed the sound of Clara's voice, stomach rumbling and eyes slowly adjusting to the light outside.

"Eat quickly so we can get on the road."

Prompted by Clara, Adela glanced down at the ceramic plate, two orange yolks and browned sausage sliced in half lengthwise, with a dollop of sweet ketchup pooled on the edge of the plate.

Clara slid two small bowls over, one filled with freshly ground black pepper and the other with sweet, mild, red paprika.

Salivating, Adela started devouring the food, forgetting to properly chew and coughing down eggs with a sip of water. "This is good. It's like my grandmother makes when she visits."

Clara smiled, her almond-shaped eyes becoming smaller with the motion. "It is a popular dish where we're from," she admitted. "When you're finished with that, gather your things and meet me outside. I'll be picking herbs just outside the clearing. If you can't find me, yell and I'll get you. Five minutes, quickly."

Adela wiped her mouth with the back of her hand and carefully dropped the dishes off in the sink, rinsing them with soapy water to run the yolk remnants down the drain. She questioned where the rubbish would end up if this house truly was kept underground. Perhaps even farther underground? She skipped to the alcove and put on her clothes, aware that she would be overheating in the sun.

Once fully dressed, she went to the small window in the back of the room. She hadn't seen the sun in months, and here it was, glinting off the grass stalks outside as bees—yes, bees!—flitted around purple and golden wildflowers. Adela could sit here all day, taking in the sun; but she knew they were to explore more of the kingdom this morning and time was of the essence. She patted her ankle, feeling the rectangular shape of the ticket, and wondered if she'd learn more about her grandmother after visiting the castle. Her mind raced with far-off possibilities. What if her grandmother was the *Queen*? Surely, she'd be able to recognize her as soon as she set eyes on her.

"Where are you?" Clara called.

"Coming!"

Adela raced out the front door, braided hair whacking her in the face as she ground to a halt at the doorway.

Clara walked over to her, holding a small rucksack over her shoulder. She crouched down to pat the earth, and the house began to sink into the ground. If Adela hadn't been watching it from the very beginning this time, she would have convinced herself last night was a trick of her anxious mind. But now she was fairly certain. Clara was a witch.

"You marked the trees nicely last night," Clara said. "Where did you learn to do that?"

"My mother. She gathers berries in the woods during the summer months. It's a trick she uses to mark where they're abundant so she can return to them."

"Your mother is very resourceful," Clara admitted. "We'll use the path you started to make our way to the castle."

They traveled for some time, stopping only when Clara wanted to share information about a cluster of seeds, a bushel of berries, or to show Adela animal tracks. "This here is a hoof print," she exclaimed at one point, not far from the small clearing where Adela spoke with the Falcon the evening prior. "That means a red deer is nearby!"

Adela kept close to Clara, who seemed to know the woods well. A few hours in, tired and sweaty, they stumbled upon an older man resting atop a rock by the base of a small pond, his clothes soaked from an early morning swim. Approaching slowly, Clara greeted the man by name and he by hers. But he paused when he saw Adela.

"I've never seen you before," he croaked, running his fingers through a long, brown beard. Adela took in the strange figure, clothes patched with various textiles, creating a quilt that clothed his thin body.

Before Adela could let out a word in response, Clara interrupted, "This is a court lady's daughter. She was helping me gather herbs while the lady was attending the Queen." She held the man's deep gaze, keeping her body in front of Adela. The air became still and thick, like honey, during the standoff.

The man broke the silence. "Why, of course, now I recognize the young lady." He laughed. "How silly of me!"

Clara echoed his jovial attitude, forcing a laugh while nudging Adela to do the same. She obliged—ears humming again—as the three collectively diffused the tense situation.

"Well then," the man interrupted, "I'm sure the court lady wouldn't mind if I welcomed you to my home for tea. Would she?"

Clara stopped laughing and smiled, but her body tensed, and her feet turned away from the rock. "We really should get going. We have a ways to go and the Queen is expecting us back."

"A cup of tea won't hurt anybody. Will it?"

"It's too much of a detour, really."

"Clara, come now, we're not strangers. Are we?"

The corners of Clara's mouth turned up, but her eyes remained still. She tried on a small smile in compliance. This was perhaps an unusual request from the man. "Lead the way! I'm sure a cup of tea won't hurt."

The man grinned, showing yellowed teeth, and climbed off the rock, bowing to both women. He grabbed a cane perched on the side of the rock, whistling and occasionally turning back to ensure he was being followed.

The direction was opposite of the one they were heading, farther even from Clara's cottage, driving them off the path to the castle. Large redwood trees gave way to dropped tree branches and dirt that was wet, transforming into mud that squelched beneath Adela's shoes.

Clara hadn't said a word since they left the pond, and Adela was fidgety. She looked ahead at the man, who continued his stroll into the vast emptiness ahead. There was nothing as far as Adela's eyes could see, and she worried this was a trap. That there was no house at all. She nudged at Clara's arm, trying to get her attention.

"Where are we going?" Adela whispered. "Who is this?"

"Speak slowly and low," Clara responded, slowing her steps to drop farther back from the mysterious man. "We're not in any danger, so long as you stick to the story."

"What danger? What story?"

"You're a court lady's daughter. Your mother's name is Elena, and she serves Queen Ada. Your mother is recently employed by the queen, which is why you seem unfamiliar to these parts. We're gathering herbs and food for the yearly Festival." Clara turned to Adela, her gaze steely and focused. "Do not forget any of that. I will not repeat it again."

"You didn't answer my first quest—"

"What are you two talking about?"

Adela stopped in her tracks. In front of her was a stone house, a functioning water mill attached to its side. Much like Clara's cottage, the house seemed to have sprung from the earth, and Adela thought how rich the earth must be, for its ability to sprout whole homes from nothing was miraculous.

"I'll put the kettle on. Come inside," he called.

Adela continued to tug at Clara's arm but found it was to no avail. Instead, Clara led the two over the threshold.

Inside, the home was slightly longer than Clara's single-bed home. Where you could walk the latter's length in twenty steps, this one stretched to the left and right and had a small staircase that led to an upstairs loft. What the home had in length, however, it lacked in depth and height. The walls were short and squat. Four people would not be able to stand behind one another without having one sticking out of the front door. Luckily, the house currently held three.

The man waddled to the back of the dimly lit room, rushing to clumsily light a wood-burning stove. "What type of tea? Chamomile?"

"Mint, please," Clara answered.

"Me too."

"Very well," he mused. "Clara, dear, any chance you've some freshly picked mint on you? I'm all out."

Clara approached the man, digging in her cloth bag for the requested item. With their attention elsewhere, Adela explored the home. A hallway led her to a dusty living room, with a seating area against the wall and a bassinet tucked into a corner. Adela frowned; she hadn't seen a small child anywhere, let alone a baby. The room smelled of water damage, and the water mill's clanking and clanging reverberated behind the stone wall. In the back of the room, a nook provided a second outlet to the loft above. It was dark, and Adela convinced herself to not explore any further.

That is, until she heard the whispering, hushed and low and indistinguishable.

She attempted to pinpoint the source of the voice. She peeked in the bassinet. Still empty. She moved closer to the other wall, the one near the nook that housed the wooden staircase.

There it was again—coming from upstairs.

Curiosity got the best of her, and she took her first steps to ascend. Upstairs, it smelled even more like stagnant well water, and she gagged at the musty scent. The ceiling was shorter and, even with her small stature, Adela had to duck to avoid banging her head against the roof. The only source of light was a sliver of sun coming from a boarded-up window that faced the front of the home. Adela stepped forward. Downstairs, the front door closed, and the blood rushed from her face.

She wouldn't.

She clamored to the boarded-up window and peeked between the wood to find Clara, outside, walking away from the house. Adela could hardly believe it. Though she had known Clara only a few hours, she could sense that her intentions were good and that her goal—just moments ago—was to protect her at all costs.

Adela slumped to the floor, unsure what to do next. Her fingers gravitated to her mouth, and she picked at the callouses, the sharp taste of blood spilling into her mouth as she picked deeper and deeper still.

*What went wrong?*

She had tried resisting her dark thoughts over the last twenty-four hours. There had only been a few occasions where these thoughts had taken over, warning Adela of all the things that could go wrong.

But now, everything had most certainly gone wrong.

For one, her only friend on this journey had abandoned her in a stranger's home. Adela was lost in a forest that she had no idea how to exit, not any closer to the castle or to finding her grandmother's secret. She was stuck in a different time and place altogether, far from home. As much as she had mustered up her courage, determined to leave the grasp of the monster in her home, at this moment she broke down.

Adela hugged her knees and quietly sobbed, sitting in the dark and hoping with all her might that she could live in this attic forever, undiscovered by the man downstairs. The ticket in her sock rubbed against her ankle, and she picked it up, keeping it in contact with her skin. She turned it over in her hand, edges yellowed with time and slightly damp from the trek over here. Adela should have known when she picked it out of her grandmother's belongings that it was old; at the time, she wondered why her grandmother was planning a trip to Nuimtree. Now, she knew the trip had been taken long ago, and it was possible that Clara and her grandmother had even crossed paths.

Clara, who had abandoned her.

She readied herself to release the ticket, to release the spell from her traveling body, when she realized the tea kettle had settled. It no longer whistled. The man downstairs no longer hummed.

"I see you've found your way upstairs."

Adela jumped, almost dropping the ticket in surprise. "I'm sorry, I thought this was the way back to the front room."

"What did you say your mother's name was again?"

"Elena," Adela lied.

"Lady Elena," he said. "I don't recall the Queen having a court lady of that name."

"We just arrived in Nuimtree."

"Well, that explains it!" He chuckled, keeping his green eyes fixed ahead, unblinking.

But he didn't believe her explanation. The outline of his body stood out against the small sliver of light coming from the window, and he was situated so that he was blocking the entrance to the living room. More sounds of movement sounded from the back wall, short scuffles and soft whispers.

"What's over there?" She motioned with her head, trying to divert attention away from herself.

The man followed her gaze and smiled. "Damn lightbulb, it always gets a bit dislodged." He reached above his head and turned his hand counter-clockwise, screwing the bulb back in place. A dim light filled the attic space.

Adela exhaled the breath she had been holding as the dark wall was lit up.

Teapots. Hundreds of them, of all shapes and sizes. Some embellished with ornate designs of blue and gold—the colors of Nuimtree—and others in red and emerald green. Others were plain and cream-colored with scalloped edges or upturned spouts.

"What do you think?"

"I love them," Adela breathed. She stepped forward, keeping an eye out for any deer mice that may have made their way to this section of the house; she had heard scuffling and small noises after all, and a mouse could have reasonably made them. "Why do you collect teapots?"

"It's a funny thing," the man started. "I sit by the rock every day and they often wash up on the land—perfectly preserved! Travelers, I tell you. They overpack and start dumping their unwanted possessions in the lake just like that."

Adela laughed, directing the mood of the conversation. "That makes no sense. For one, you sit by a pond, not a lake."

"And the pond feeds into a lake."

"Even if that was true, I can't imagine people taking teapots with them when they travel."

The man's voice became cold and dark. "Really? You don't believe me?"

The mood in the room shifted once more, and the man stepped closer to Adela.

"I just meant—"

"Why don't you open one of them?"

"Why would I?"

"You don't believe me! Maybe you'll see a frog inside or some lake water, to help you believe."

"I don't hear a frog."

"Why don't you check?" He grinned, showing off yellowed teeth that appeared green in the dim light.

Exasperated by the conversation and wanting to oblige in order to get the man to stop bothering her, Adela grasped the hook of a teapot and readied herself to lift it. She was certain she would prove the man wrong.

"Put that down," Clara's voice rang out. She was positioned on the top of the stairs, entering from the front door's side. With a rush, she ran over to Adela and pried her fingers from the porcelain cover.

"Ouch!" Adela exclaimed as Clara pushed her toward the staircase.

Clara turned toward the man. "It's best we be going now. I picked some fresh mint for you, like you asked, but it's going to get dark soon, and we need to return the young lady to her mother before night falls. Thank you for your hospitality."

Before the man could object, Clara ushered Adela out of the cottage and into the humid air outside, buzzing with flies and other insects. She grabbed Adela's hand, nearly crushing her fingers. Without looking back to exchange further pleasantries or close the door behind her, Clara pulled them back into the dense canopy until they reached the redwood trees and farther still, to where they first encountered the man.

Clara looked up at the sky. "We've lost an hour from that detour," she complained, her brow furrowing.

Adela stood firmly in place, hands balled into fists. When she didn't answer Clara, she caught her desired attention.

"What's wrong?"

"You left me behind."

"I returned."

"But you left. You left me with him."

Clara sighed, eyebrows turning up in their corners with worry. "I know. I'm sorry." She knelt down to Adela's height, resting her warm hand on her shoulder.

Adela took in Clara in more detail now: the wrinkles of age imposing on her body. Her face was sun-damaged, browned by years of living in Western Wilerea, of trekking the warm landscape that was abundant with the inputs required for its inhabitants' brand of practical magic. Her eyebrows were bushy, growing every which way, hairs criss-crossing one another. Her nose sloped to a point, though her nostrils were large, making her nose as prominent as the rosy lips on her face. She was pretty, in an unconventional way, and Adela was comforted by the warm hand on her shoulder.

"I forgive you."

"I'm glad," Clara said and smiled. She got up. "That wasn't a man, though," she clarified.

"What do you mean?"

"That was a water spirit. Around here, we call him Father Vodnik."

"I don't understand."

"Remember when I told you that creatures lived in these woods? Water spirits are one of them. They take the form of humans," Clara began, leading Adela back in the direction of the castle. She pushed thick branches away as they ventured farther into the dense covering. "But they belong in the water. If they are approached by an unknown person, they are known to lure them out to sea and drown them." She grabbed Adela's clammy hand. "That's why the story was important. You were unknown. But you seemingly held special value, as a child connected to the Queen."

Adela's mouth became dry, as if a large rock had been lodged in her throat. "But he didn't try to drown me."

"Oh, but he did. Only, in his own way."

"I don't understand."

"The water spirits capture and trade in spirits. A soul for a soul. He was willing to exchange your soul for another. Perhaps, he realized that you were special. Perhaps, he wanted a shiny addition to his collection. Who's to say?" She shuddered. "I'm glad I came when I did."

"But you said they capture spirits," Adela said, her confusion superseding the nausea. "How do they do that? How would he have taken my soul?"

Clara paused, refusing to meet Adela's inquisitive eyes. "Didn't you see all the teapots?"

# SEVEN

# NUIMTREE

---

"Are you alright?" Clara's lilting voice broke the silence, gently prodding for an answer. Nearly an hour into their walk, the monumental turrets of the castle peeked over the treetops like homing beacons.

Adela had been characteristically taciturn, her mind ruminating over what had transpired the last day. She grew nervous and considered what was likely transpiring back in Sunseree, twitching her nose in deep thought. She had left her original body with Milo, safely reclining in a meadow far from civilization. Adela knew Milo well, and by now, he had most certainly grown worried and run to find an adult. Her imagination conjured images of her mother stumbling across her body: unmoving, eyes clamped closed, breath indistinguishable.

Yes, she had yearned for a moment of adventure, but she did not feel up to this. With each passing second under the cover of these majestic trees, sunrays beat down on her pale skin—which was unaccustomed to this new climate— burning her neck to a crimson shade that grew warmer and warmer. Adela was increasingly exhausted, forcing her little feet to continue their forward motion.

"I've noticed you're very quiet," Clara added.

"Everybody says that."

They ducked under a sturdy tree bough that had crept too low to the ground, Adela clumsily and Clara acrobatically, for she had ventured this path many times before.

"It's not a bad quality, you know?" Clara said.

"What isn't?"

"Being quiet."

"Really? Kids at school pick on me," she said, kicking at the packed forest floor and sending a small cloud of debris into the air.

"That's mean. From my perspective, we have too many people talking these days. It does us a world of good to look internally for a second, to gather our thoughts, to think before we say something."

Clara was perceptive, seeming to inexplicably understand Adela's inner thoughts.

"I have a question," Adela said, avoiding eye contact and maintaining focus on the trodden path ahead. In front of her, a prematurely dead leaf drifted aimlessly in the air, and she waited for it to land on the ground before stomping on it with a resounding *crunch*. She waited for Clara to answer, anticipating her reaction and allowing the silence to grant her the avenue to ask the question she had been musing about all day.

"Go on."

"How do you know about the Last Sun? If, to your point, I've traveled decades into the past?"

"I'm a witch. Remember?" She grinned, pulling back her rosy lips to display the straight, white teeth underneath.

"Yes, but a practical witch. Herbs and medicines, removing evil curses and that stuff."

Clara sighed, grabbing the strawberry-colored hair at the nape of her neck and deftly twisting it about itself to pull her hair out of her sweaty face. She blew at a single strand that fell loose and maneuvered around a boulder that lay in their path.

"You're traveling with a witch," Clara said, "is it not within the realm of possibility that, as a witch, I may encounter someone who can see the future?" Her eyes twinkled at this suggestion.

"All of this seems out of the realm of possibility." Adela's brain nudged her attention back to the ticket in her shoe. She realized how insincere her statement was before it even left her lips.

"Right. But a time-traveling little girl isn't?"

Clara pushed a handful of foliage out of the way, and the two travelers found themselves in a small field. Here, the sun reached every section, showering the meadow with rays of warmth in every direction. As far as Adela could see, there were delicate ivory dandelions, swaying gently in the breeze and releasing their seeds to glide on the air like lightweight umbrellas.

Directly to their left was a compact stone well, attended solely by a wooden bucket for travelers to quench their thirst after a half-day journey. Ahead was a small body of water, quick-moving, with jagged rocks jutting out of the riverbed. The water was perfectly clear, and it reminded Adela of the lake by her home, transparent enough to see your toes wiggling at the bottom.

Fish as long as her forearm jumped out of the water, flexible tails twisting left and right and mouths agape before they descended back into the water. They had big hazel spots and sections over their mouths that resembled mustaches, like the one Milo's father sported. She stifled a giggle with her hand.

"Trout," Clara interrupted, "delicious when cooked."

"Ew."

Clara pointed toward the wooden walk-bridge connecting the land parcels. "Over that bridge is the castle."

Turrets towered over them, beckoning. They crossed the bridge with care, making sure not to fall over and join the lively school of trout waiting below. Adela wondered if they, too, could talk to her—but that was something she could spend brain space thinking about another day. For now, the sun was beginning to set, and she tried to memorize the details of the darkening sky, not knowing when she would see a sunset again. Its illustrious oranges, pink, and purples were like colors mixed specially by her mother as she tackled one of her paintings. A pang twisted in her stomach as she remembered her mother and how far she had ventured from home.

"We're here."

Outside the castle was a manicured garden filled with flowers Adela had never seen before and had only imagined in her mind's eye: salmon-colored tulips, crimson poppies, with their spindly black centers, violet peonies, with their fluffy, overlapping petals, and even simple daisies, like the ones that ran along the edges of the forest near her home. She had never seen such a wide variety of flowers and had only encountered them in her grandmother's diaries, poring over the details of their medicinal properties.

Bees and iridescent hummingbirds with long beaks flitted around, and the air was alive with the sound of living beings. The garden stretched out for ages.

Behind it, two soldiers sat on horseback, guarding the entrance gate to the courtyard. Each horse was majestic, outfitted in clothing fit for royalty: cobalt blues paired with gilded gold. They snorted and whipped their tails about while the guards atop matched them in color; the guards, like the horses, were clothed in the finest equipment, including swords tucked into their protected sheaths.

Clara made a beeline for the guards, and Adela hastily ran behind.

"Afternoon, my name is Clara. I'm the healer called for by the Queen."

"Credentials?"

"You must be new here," she joked. "I've a letter. Somewhere." She dug in her cloth bag, her voice trailing off as she pulled out jars labeled *Feverfew* and *Ginger* and *Chamomile*.

"Aha, here it is," she said and thrust the letter toward the main guard, who carefully observed its seal, opened it, and read its contents. The other guard appeared uninterested in the conversation, and Adela was amused at this apparent contradiction between his duties and behavior.

"Very well. And who is this?" The first guard beckoned toward Adela.

"My daughter," Clara lied. "I couldn't find anyone to care for her on such short notice. When the Queen calls, one drops everything and comes running."

Adela smiled, going along with the plan. She had told a lot of lies in the last day.

"Go on then." The guard whistled and shouted, and the gates began to creak open, screeching wide like the calls of a golden eagle.

The gates were grand, towering over Adela and even Clara like the redwoods they had encountered on their journey here, and decorated with ornate imagery. Suns and moons intertwined themselves into abstract shapes and figures, melding together until their original outlines were indistinguishable. Behind them was the stone courtyard, bustling with fervent activity. Children laughed and ran around, bumping into market stalls while their parents traded coins for fruits and vegetables.

"Come, girl," Clara said.

Adela walked slowly behind Clara, who seemed to be growing impatient. But she had never seen Nuimtree's castle before and likely never would again. Just outside the main entrance was a vast linden tree, its greenery sprouting thin flowers, capped with golden pollen that gave the tree a glowing demeanor. Underneath it, a young man rested in the shade, reading a well-worn book.

The royal residence sported a white-washed, beige exterior and smooth stones complemented the gold and blue roofs. Small square windows dotted the top-most floor, carefully laid out and repeated across the length of the building, itself divided into a main building and multiple, shorter wings. Beneath the square windows, rectangular ones allowed its inhabitants more access to the outside view. Occasionally, a stained glass window broke the pattern, encased in ornate stone that matched the outside.

The smaller, blue turrets were equal in size, the golden one more substantial, topping the main building where Adela assumed most of the castle's activities took place. She blinked, half-expecting the castle to disappear.

It didn't.

Clara passed the threshold to the main hall, and Adela promptly followed, the sounds of the rushing fountain and chatter of the outside world falling away.

Soaring ceilings were prominent in the great hall, with ornate tin squares depicting the same mysterious imagery of the gate outside. There were nooks, crevices, and areas where the gold dripped down the plastered walls, and Adela imagined the tons of gold that were spun to fill this room.

The walls featured carved panels that circumvented the room, and Adela moved closer, touching them gently with curiosity. From far away, these panels gave the room a muted look. But up close, the maroons, emeralds, and sky blues could be observed individually. In one scene, gold was inlaid with a sky blue to simulate sunrays spreading across a hilled landscape. In another, inlaid gold and bone became the stars in an indigo sky.

Overhead, see-through crystals were bundled inside the casings of a grand chandelier, hanging like the jagged stalactites Adela had once stumbled upon in the Ceprith Caves.

With a small whistle, Clara called to her. She rushed to the center of the room, her skirt twirling as she spun around and her head tilted toward the ceiling.

"I'm here the see the Queen," Clara said.

"Her Royal Highness is not accepting visitors at this time," an emphatic voice responded.

"I've been called for specifically. From Western Wilerea."

Clara's words hung like chandelier crystals, suspended mid-air.

The guard grunted, recognizing Clara and motioning for another guard to hasten over. "These two," he started, turning to look at Adela, "have been summoned for by the Queen. See to it that they make her acquaintance. And that nobody follows you."

The latter guard nodded, beckoning for Clara and Adela to follow. He led them through a door at the far end of the hall, which closed in place and met with a steep wooden staircase, ascending and descending in either direction. They climbed for minutes, and Adela soon lost count of what floor they had passed.

When she thought she would not be able to walk any farther, they stopped at a landing and the guard opened a door, ushering them into the small alcove. Another hall, this one smaller than the one downstairs, was outfitted with a long, hand-knotted rug and a gilded mirror nestled atop a wood-burning fireplace itself protected with an iron grate to prevent embers from escaping onto the polished wood floors.

In the center of the room was a small seating area and a bouquet of the outdoor flowers, freshly picked and infusing the air with a floral scent, collected in a vase on a low, wooden table. Adela was unsure which wing of the castle they were in, though she assumed it was the one punctuated with colored stained glass from the exterior.

"Please, take a seat," the guard said and motioned with his hand outstretched. He had a gentle demeanor, kinder and more soft-spoken than the ones they had encountered to-date. When he smiled, a small dimple formed in his right cheek, and his eyes shifted between hazel and brown depending on the amount of light streaming into the room. "I'll let the Queen know you're here."

Clara and Adela obliged. Clara placed her hands on her lap, staring ahead as the guard retreated. She sighed, hugging her bag of jars close to her stomach.

The guard returned. "She's ready to see you."

Passing through an intricately carved double door, Adela stepped into the room.

The Queen stood in front of the open, main window in the bedroom, her side profile to the door. She wore a simple blue embroidered gown, a lightweight skirt billowing away from her body in the warm breeze. When the door clicked shut, she turned to face the visitors. Her hair was a soft, muted brown that was pulled to her left shoulder, and her skin was slightly browned from days sitting in the beating Nuimtree sun. She had long eyelashes that curved toward the ceiling, covering gray eyes; her nose was imperfect, the tip leaning slightly to the right. She smiled, and her shoulders relaxed.

"Clara."

"Your Highness."

"Please, call me Ada. You know that."

"Ada."

"And who is this young girl?" The Queen motioned toward Adela.

"My sister's daughter." Another lie. "She had never seen your kingdom, and I wanted to bring her along this once."

"I see," the Queen said as she beamed down at Adela, her eyes crinkling at the sides. "Welcome."

"Thank you," Adela said.

The mood shifted, and the Queen sighed. "I'm at a loss, Clara." She reclined on an embroidered settee, tapping the space next to her for Clara to settle.

"What happened? Your letter—"

"Yes, my letter. It didn't provide much information. I know. For a reason. It could have been intercepted."

"I understand."

Queen Ada hesitated. "The twins, they're not doing well."

"Where are they?"

"Just in the nursery." The Queen pointed toward a door at the far end of the room. "I'll take you to them."

Clara and Queen Ada made their way to the back of the room, to the right of the main doors. Against the wall was a canopied bed, down comforters and covers askew. Adela crept behind, increasingly curious about why Clara was summoned here.

Through another door was a small nursery, two bassinets with canopied covers below a vast skylight laid in the ceiling, casting shadows on the environment. The room was dark. Night had fallen quickly since they set out on their journey.

A second night away from home.

Clara stepped over the bassinets, resting her hand on the shell while gazing past the canopy. She paused and then whispered, "Girl, bring me my bag. In the next room."

Adela returned with the cloth bag, handing it over to Clara while maintaining arm's reach.

Clara balanced the cloth bag on her knee, quietly digging and coming away with a luminescent paste in a round, light blue glass jar. She nudged the bag in Adela's arms.

"Can you hold her?" she asked the Queen.

"Yes, of course." Queen Ada rushed to her side and pulled the newborn out of the bassinet while Clara held the canopy and then released it.

Adela leaned in, trying to get a better glance at the baby. She smelled freshly bathed, and she had thin, blond hair and plump cheeks. Adela caught her breath when the gleam caught her eye, a symbol on the baby's forehead—a golden sun.

The baby's chest moved up and down at a glacial pace, and her eyelashes fluttered. Underneath, her eyes moved furiously in their sockets, and her breathing slowed.

"She's been like this for too long. She hasn't woken up in weeks," the Queen wailed.

Clara nodded, her face softening in empathy for the Queen's despair. "I'll fix this. I promise," she said, grasping the Queen's trembling hands between her own. She pulled a dollop of the paste out and rubbed it between her fingers, her brow furrowing.

With her thumb, she gently swiped across the baby's eyes, coating her thick lashes. With an index finger, she brushed a line down the bridge of her nose. With her third finger, she hovered across the tip of her nose, allowing the baby to slowly inhale the paste on the edges of her nostrils. Her last two fingers smoothed the paste over the baby's small, pursed lips. Clara paused, waiting, her palm outstretched, still sticky with the paste. She observed the baby girl's breathing, waiting a few moments to see how she was responding to the magic concoction.

"Hmm. Getting better." She firmly pressed her palm to the baby's forehead, her fingers curving to envelop the golden sun. They waited and waited and waited.

Within minutes, the baby's cheeks flushed and her breathing became stronger. Clara removed her palm and walked over to the other baby. While the Queen held the girl, Clara cooed at the baby and picked it up. He was a boy, that much Adela could see, for he was naked from the waist down. And he was identical to the baby girl, except for one distinct difference—a silver crescent moon imprinted on his forehead.

Suddenly, the solar and lunar symbols throughout the kingdom were clear.

"Who's a good baby boy?" Clara asked, bouncing the boy on her hip. He was alert, staring intently at Clara, eyes blank and blinking. He babbled, realizing his sister was out of the bassinet, and reached for her. Clara pulled his small fingers away.

"No, not yet." She placed the boy back in the bassinet and opened her arms for the baby girl. The Queen obliged, and Clara held her briefly, gazing intently at her slumbering face. "She'll be fine, I'll send more of this," she motioned to her cloth bag, "when I return to Western Wilerea. Every night.

Thumb to the eyes, forefinger to the nose, middle finger to the nostrils, ring and pinky fingers to the lips, palm to the forehead until her breathing improves."

Queen Ada nodded, presenting a clean rag to Clara.

"He's pulling energy from her. Isn't he?" the Queen asked.

Clara wiped her hands clean of the paste. "I won't venture to guess what—"

"Be honest with me, Clara. We're friends."

Adela was having difficulty tracking the conversation. The Queen and Clara were friends. The twins were magic. And one of them—the boy—drew energy from the baby girl who gasped for breath beside her.

Supposedly.

The newborn appeared to be sick, eyes closed. Adela wondered why and what magic was behind this. And how, specifically, Clara was involved.

"I'll figure this out," Clara promised. "I'll send herbs. I'll visit more often." She shook her head and dropped the rag on a side table. "That should be washed, with gloves," she added, motioning to the towel.

"I don't care about that, Clara," the Queen said as she threw her hands in the air, exasperated. "You see she's weak. She can't live happily with me."

"I don't understand."

"She'll thrive in Western Wilerea. She needs someone who will protect her, hidden from here. Very few are special like her."

Clara's eyes met Adela's for a split second. "I don't know anything about taking care of a child," Clara retorted. "She's yours, and she's better suited here."

Outside the windows, the wind began to pick up, and the screeching calls of golden hawks and falcons hunting sounded in the night.

"Clara," Adela whispered. "Are we leaving tonight? Where will we sleep?" A shiver ran up her spine as she thought of the harsh elements awaiting them outside the walls.

Queen Ada broke in before Clara could muster an answer. "Here! Of course, spend the night. There are plenty of rooms." She touched Clara's cheek, capturing her attention. "And please, think about what I said. Sleep on it."

Clara sighed, looking at the newborns who cooed in their bassinets. "I will. I promise I will."

# EIGHT

# BALANCE

———

That evening, a brutal storm raged outside the vast room where Clara and Adela slept. The court attendants' footsteps reverberated through the halls as they rushed to close shutters before they flew off the facade of the building. From across the castle, newborn cries were carried by the wind into the indigo night, turning to enter Adela's corner of the world.

Clara snored in the opposite side of the room, and Adela was comforted only by the crackling fireplace, occasionally flickering when a gust of wind flew over the chimney: a melodious accompaniment that filled the room with whistles and chimes, melding in the air alongside the screeching cries.

A shiver erupted down Adela's back, and she shut her eyes, pushing them closer and closer until stars popped behind them. With the cacophony of noises around her—footsteps, cries, the wind and the raging storm outside battering the windows—she began to cry.

It was as if, in a single moment, the emotions she had kept burrowed inside, deep in the recesses of her mind and body, were awakened by the deluge of water collecting outside and in the corners of her eyes. She ducked under the thin covers, worried that Clara—or the attendants—would hear her. Her chest heaved as she tried to keep her sobs quiet, internalizing them and, in turn, causing herself to hyperventilate. Creating a small cavern in the covers to allow for the stale air to stream in, she cried. And cried.

"Stop crying."

Adela's eyes resurfaced from below the covers; she glanced at Clara's reposing body.

"Just as before. Not Clara."

Her eyes met the black ones of the Falcon, who was perched on a small window that had escaped the attendants' attention. His body was slick, damp from the storm just outside the room, and he ruffled his feathers in an attempt to flick off the droplets.

"It's you. What are you doing here?"

"Simply paying a visit. Our conversation was interrupted last night so I found it fitting to continue."

"This isn't a good time," Adela said, her tears drying on her face.

"What are you doing here? In the castle?"

"We're visiting the Queen."

"The Queen? Why?"

"I'm not sure," Adela admitted. "Clara and I met the Queen and her babies tonight. They seem to be sick."

"Babies? Yes, I had heard that the Queen had twins," the Falcon replied, his eyes gleaming in the moonlight as he appeared to lean forward in the window frame. "What are they like?"

"It's the most curious thing, one has a golden sun right on her fore—"

"Who are you talking to?" a sleepy Clara murmured, interrupting Adela's excitable whispers.

Adela jolted, looking in her direction as she heard the flapping of wings retreating from their hiding place.

The Falcon, again, had been startled and left. Clara's snores started once more, her question left suspended in the air, never to be answered. Wondering if her encounter with the Falcon had been a dream, Adela slipped into sleep.

The sun woke her at dawn, the light-tinged blackness giving way to deep ember oranges and vibrant yellows, like the shades of calendula in her grandmother's garden. Her grandmother would pluck the bright heads off the flowers and dilute them with hot water, using them to coat compresses that she would then press against Adela's sunburns. How she wished she had one of those compresses now. Her scalp was burnt from her journey here, and Adela fought every urge to scratch.

She pushed the covers off. In front of her, Clara's bed was empty, poorly made. Her traveling bag was gone, and Adela began to worry. Clara had left her!

Anger flushed in her cheeks, heating her body even more. Hands clenched into fists, Adela rolled out of bed and gathered her things, quickly changing into her outside clothes. She emerged from the room, leaving her bed unmade, and ventured to the other side of the building in the direction of the Queen's quarters.

"It happened again when you went to bed," the Queen cried out.

"You're being hysterical. Calm down." Clara's firm voice rang out, attempting to steady the Queen's emotions. The dual cries from last night had condensed to a single one.

Adela walked faster, moving in the direction of the voices. As she approached the guards stationed outside the room, they recognized her and allowed her to enter. Inside the bedroom, Clara balanced the baby girl on her outstretched arm, streaking the paste from last night—which was candy blue in the daylight—across her face.

In the corner, the Queen was backed against a wall, her pupils dilated and eyes wide, heavy dark bags indicating that she had not slept all night. The other twin—the young boy—wrestled with his mother, throwing himself around and screeching as his pudgy arms reached for his sister. The moon on his forehead was a deep indigo color in the daylight, glinting briefly. His voice was hoarse. He must have been crying for hours.

"There," Clara said, as a small gurgle erupted from the child in her hands. "All better." She grinned at the Queen, but her smile waned.

Queen Ada was terrified, shaking. On the verge of tears, lip quivering, she breathed deeply to avoid calling more attention to herself. "King Leon," she started, placing the boy in his crib with a small rattle, "has granted his permission to re-home our daughter." She paused, awaiting Clara's response.

"And where is—"

"On a hunt," the Queen interrupted. "He left before she fell sick and has been on his way back since. His messenger delivered a note last night." She stepped toward Clara and dug in her skirt's pockets for a small envelope, sealed with wax imprinted with the royal seal.

Clara took the letter and read it for what seemed like a lifetime. The room was quiet, the only sounds the small sobs calling out from the boy's bassinet and the girl's soft cooing in Clara's arms. "Very well," she finally answered. "The instructions are clear."

"Please, keep the letter. Maybe you can give it to her one day. To remember," the Queen said.

Clara nodded, looking down at the floor.

"I asked the night nurse to pull together a small bag of necessities for the journey to Western Wilerea. Whatever you need, we will send, you will not want for anything." The Queen called out and a small, older woman bustled in, holding a satchel of items that she carefully draped over Clara's shoulder, atop Clara's own satchel.

The woman had silver hair pinned into a bun, strands loosened from the clutches of baby fingers. Her smile was kind but sad as she caught Adela's eyes. She bowed slightly toward Adela, followed by a deep bow to the Queen, and departed from the room as quickly as she had arrived.

"Clothes, milk—only enough for a couple days' journey, I'm afraid—bottles, and her favorite toys," the Queen said.

"Thank you."

The Queen grasped Clara's hands, tears welling in her eyes. "I knew I could count on you." Silence permeated the air again, as Clara refused eye-contact with anyone in the room.

"You should all leave soon," the Queen said, glancing over at Adela. "I know the journey is long and harsh, and you'll have an infant with you now. I almost forgot," she said, burrowing again in her pockets and emerging with two train tickets. "Set for Western Wilerea but with a few stops in between. Sunseree, Al Ainab, and the Isle of Vila."

Adela's ears perked up at mention of the Isle of Vila. She had heard the name before but couldn't place it.

"The Isle of Vila? Are you insane?" Clara whispered furiously, grabbing at the tickets.

"Excuse me? I will forgive your insubord—"

"I do not owe you respect. I am not your subject."

Queen Ada flinched, surprised by the harsh reaction. "That was the quickest route out of Nuimtree. I trust you will be able to protect her?"

Clara glared ahead, clearly upset. "Very well."

The Queen glanced in Adela's direction. "I only have two tickets. I didn't know you'd be bringing your niece."

Clara's mouth twitched into a small grimace. "We'll figure it out," she promised, as if both to the Queen and Adela. "You're right," she said, looking out the window as the sun had now nearly emerged from behind the trees. "We should go."

The Queen stretched her arms out, tears pooling in her eyes. Her face was red and blotchy, as if unable to hold in the fury of emotions welling inside. "Can I have a moment alone? One last time?"

Nodding, Clara handed over the girl and ushered Adela out of the nursery and into the corridor where the guards stood. She knelt to Adela's left, her knee popping.

"We'll have the baby with us, and we're all going to set out in the direction of my cabin. It'll be a tiring walk, but I trust you to be able to take care of yourself."

Adela nodded.

"When we get to the cottage, we'll figure out a way to get you back home. Back in your bed, safe and warm."

Adela flinched, anticipating the cold, frantic reaction when she went home. "But what if I want to stay? I still didn't figure out why my grandmother had—" She motioned down, her ticket tucked snugly under the bands of her socks and held in place by the tight fit of her shoes.

"That is not important," Clara exclaimed, the displeasure on her face clear.

The doors opened and the Queen emerged, nuzzling the baby girl. With her arrival, Clara fashioned a small hammock from the satchel the night nurse had draped over her shoulder. She contorted the fabric, creating a secure harness that would wrap around the infant's belly and tightening the loop around her shoulder to ensure it would not drop and risk harming the child. Confident that the setup was secure, Clara nodded at the Queen.

The Queen helped tuck the baby into the carrier and gave her a single, small kiss on the sun atop her forehead. She pulled away, the corners of her eyes wet and glistening.

"Very well, my guards will see you out," the Queen said. "We'll send more items in a few days, when the King returns. Please visit when you can."

"Of course, Your Highness. We'll be back soon." The infant grasped Clara's finger, which now wiggled in front of her face, and popped it into her mouth, her eyelids softly lowering.

"I just fed her, but she'll be hungry in a few hours. Hopefully, she can sleep during most of the journey."

Clara nodded. "Goodbye, Your Highness," she said, as the guards left their posts to escort the three of them outside the castle walls.

Adela trailed behind Clara and the baby, looking back only to burn the picture of the Queen in her mind once more. By the fourth time she looked back, the Queen was gone, like smoke dissipating in the wind, having retreated back into her room with her remaining infant to keep her company.

Outside the castle walls, Clara trained her eye to the sky and rushed past the fountain, past the linden tree giving shade below, and past the garden scattered with various colors, back to the edge of the forest and the wooden bridge that led to the field of dandelions.

"Keep up, girl," she called. "We need every inch of daylight to make it back safely. I'm going to take a new path too, to avoid running into anything."

Adela nodded, remembering their run-in with the water spirit the day prior.

Crossing the bridge, they happened upon the field again, glistening with rainwater from last night's storm. Pausing by the well, Clara took out a small canister and, unscrewing the top, topped it off with well water.

"Here," she said, pushing the canister into Adela's hands.

Adela drank, realizing she had not eaten nor showered nor drank anything all morning. Her stomach emitted a growl, suddenly aware of her hunger.

"We'll eat when we're home," Clara said, acknowledging the noise. Grabbing the canister, she drank, draining and then topping it off once more before tucking the container into one of her many bags. She looked like a traveling salesman, bags hanging off her hips and shoulders, a precious package nestled just under her chest, squirming here and there.

"This way," Clara said and gestured, pointing opposite of the direction from which they came. "We'll circle around the pond, staying close to the rocks for balance."

Up ahead was a strange rock formation, vast and towering. Over the redwood trees and in the twilight, it had been difficult to spot, but its jagged facade was clearly seen in the emerging daylight. Adela tripped over her feet, trying to keep up with Clara's hurried pace.

They traveled this way, silently, for nearly three hours. The sun was approaching its apex in the sky and Clara seemed content that they would make it to the cottage before nightfall, even with this longer detour. They had stopped only once to drink water and feed the baby, about an hour ago, and Clara was now singing to the infant in an attempt to lull her to sleep once more. Around them, the forest creaked with noises and, as the treetops shook, rainwater would fall on them, giving Adela respite from the beaming sun. Where possible, she hugged the tree trunks and used the rocky wall to balance, trying to stay in a sliver of shade.

"Damn."

Adela crawled over the small rocks like an insect crawling over the landscape to safety, making her way over to Clara, who was clearly discontent. "What's wrong?"

But Clara didn't need to respond. In front, trees were upturned, clearly affected by the raging storm from last night. The jagged rock facade that had provided them with balance and protection on one side gave way to a massive crack in the earth, where the land had split in two and created an uncrossable canyon. Uncrossable except for a suspended bridge, though posts once staking it into the ground had dropped to the bottom of the canyon due to the eroding earth on either side.

There was no way to cross.

"Damn, damn, damn!" Clara shouted, and the infant awoke, beginning to fuss in preparation for a drawn-out wail. "Hush," Clara whispered, giving her pinky finger to the newborn to chew on in an effort to calm her down. It worked.

"Now what?" Adela asked.

"Now we find another way forward." Clara peeked over the felled redwood trees and glanced back at the path they had been forging. "We could go back," she ventured, lifting her face to the sky, "but we've wasted far too much time." Irritated, she blew a strand of hair from her eyes.

A stone crumbled off the wall to their left and bounced, settling in front of Clara's feet. Her eyes lit up as she ran over to the wall, feeling along its surface and brushing the greenery away.

"Come here!" she called out to Adela.

Adela rushed over, finding Clara scratched and bloody from the thorns she had cleared. Opening her mouth to say something, to draw attention to Clara's disheveled state, she saw it—the mouth to a cave, nondescript and tucked into the greenery. From inside, faint dripping noises echoed off the damp limestone walls, and Adela wondered how she had not noticed the noise as she was brushing her hand across the outside, the dust of the rocks settling into the creases of her palm.

At Adela's side, Clara fidgeted with the bags, unhooking the one holding her clothes and belongings and wrapping it around Adela's body.

"There. That will allow me to crawl through the space," she said, gesturing toward the cave entrance. "I'll carry the baby and her things and the herbs. When we get through the other side, I'll take my bag back." She smiled. "Are you ready?"

"I've never been in a cave this big," Adela responded, her voice trembling.

Clara knelt, carefully cupping the baby's head in her hand. "There's nothing to be scared of—this is Curling Cave. It'll loop around the canyon and bring us back on the path to the house. It'll only be another hour, but you need to follow me. There's no time for wandering around. Do you hear me? No time."

Clara emphasized the last few words, holding on to Adela's shoulders and squeezing tightly, her warm hands releasing some of the tension held in Adela's little body.

But Adela was terrified. Blood rushed from her face as her small hands trembled. She knew she would need to squeeze her body into the small opening, that she would encounter a steep incline that she would likely stumble through—or, even worse, fall down. And jagged rocks would threaten to impale her, or Clara, or the baby, at every turn.

Clara grasped her clammy hands, smiling and nodding. "You can do it. I promise."

Adela nodded, inhaling deeply. She hugged Clara's bag to her side and watched as Clara hunched forward, disappearing into the cave's deep darkness. Adela followed, falling on all fours to maneuver through the tightly packed walls. She was right. The floor of the cave had begun to slope downward, and she crawled over sharp rocks and mossy algae on her way through. Around her, the cave continued to loudly drip with the sound of rainwater seeping through the layers of sediment, becoming softer echoes.

She breathed in a musty smell, like wet and dust. Goosebumps formed on her arms the farther down she went and the air became damp and cold. Coming to a small cliff, she carefully leaned over the edge, trying to balance her body to avoid falling.

Below, Clara looked up and broke into a grin. "I told you that you could do it! Jump. I'll catch you."

Clara had unclipped the baby from her shoulder. The infant was safely tucked behind a rock, eyes wide and glancing about. Her golden sun was dimmed in the inky dark.

Adela gulped. Fear coursed through her veins, and she again imagined all the ways in which she could fall to her death. She could land awkwardly, falling on her leg as a single bone pierced through her skin, or she could fall on her face, injuring her brain and never awaking again. Adela took a deep breath and, trusting Clara—and herself—she jumped.

Clara caught her, as she had promised.

"This way."

Clara rushed over to the rock and picked up the baby, securing her to hang around her chest again. She pulled her hair back, away from her face, and turned to face Adela, motioning for her to follow.

Adela fell in step as she marveled at the underground world around her.

The jagged rock formation from outside sloped and curved into a rocky dome, enveloping its inhabitants as it made way for smooth limestone, gradually lightening as they continued. The curves of the cave were perfectly rounded, the walls shiny and glimmering. Adela pressed her hand to a wall and shivered from the brisk air.

There was no clear path forward. To their sides was a small underground lake, still and dark, unknown dangers hidden below the surface. From above, jagged stalactites hung from the ceiling, like the chandeliers that draped from the ceiling of the great hall in the castle. They varied in length and size, some thinner and shorter, like small icicles, and others large and thick, threatening to break off and come crashing in front of Adela's path. Or on her head.

Adela carefully leapt over flowstone and moved out of the way of stalagmites that rose from the ground. They were a beige color, white in some places but blue closer to the ground, where the sheen from the water would color them slightly. On one side, the cave wall sloped upward. From a crevice in the ceiling, a well of water gushed through, landing on the floor and making the surface slippery.

"Careful," Clara warned, one hand gripping the wall and the other gripping the baby at her chest.

Adela climbed onto a plateau, following Clara as they ventured farther into the cave. The limestone walls here ranged from smooth to jagged. The rugged sections were often dotted with veins of orange, gleaming and glinting in the small beams of light that poked their way inside. The plateau was mirrored, reflecting the stalactites down below, as though they were in the mouth of a toothy monster.

She giggled, the sound reverberating off the walls, and adjusted Clara's bag on her other shoulder. It was becoming heavy. They continued like this for a while, not taking many breaks in an effort to make good time. As midday approached, the cave grew dim and gloomy, and the dripping sound intensified as if it were surrounding them.

Adela grew tired. She hadn't slept well last night, and her steps were clumsier, affected by the lack of sleep. Not to mention, she had experienced her second run-in with the Falcon, which had entered her dreams. Or had it been real life?

Worried she would fall into the water at her side, she called out to Clara, "Can we stop?"

Clara hesitated, worry spreading across her face, touching the corners of her mouth and her nostrils and the expanse of her forehead.

"We're going to run out of daylight soon. We have to keep pressing on," she warned, rubbing the baby's feet to keep her warm. Small cracks in the cave's ceiling allowed light to spill through, providing them with a path out. Adela could see that that light source was dwindling, becoming purple as the moonlight threatened to take over.

"I'm just a little tired. Can we stop for a moment only?" The baby fussed and Adela seized her opportunity. "Look, she's getting hungry too."

Clara paused, finally obliging and seating herself on a small, smooth outpost. "Just a moment," she mirrored back. She reached into the baby's bag and pulled out a glass bottle with a small rubber nipple. The bottle was half-full of a white liquid that had a yellowish tint. As soon as it came out of the travel bag, the baby reached for it and drank, thin arms grasping the bottle tightly.

Adela walked over to the two, thirst setting in. She always preferred the light over the dark and the damp mustiness of the cave made her feel shut in. The space, despite its cavernous size, felt small, like it was shrinking with time. It was unnerving, and she now understood Clara's insistence to hurry through it.

Clara gave her space to sit and passed over the canister of water. "Thirsty?"

Adela nodded. When she had gotten her fill, she screwed the container's cap back on and handed it over to Clara. In the quiet—the dripping of the cave and gulping sounds coming from Clara's chest—she asked, "Why did you agree to it?"

"Agree to what?"

"To take the baby."

Clara paused, trying to find the right words to say in response.

"The Queen was right," she started, slowly. "The other twin was harming her. Unintentionally, of course. Even if I visited every month, bringing that paste with me, it would be only a matter of time before she became fully unresponsive, even to my magic. They needed to be separated."

Adela waited for Clara to continue. But she didn't, and so Adela filled the silence.

"How was he pulling her energy? They're just babies."

"They're just babies, yes. But also, special. Kind of like you," she said, flicking at Adela's nose playfully with her thumb and forefinger.

"Special? How?" Adela responded, scratching at her nose.

"I'm sure you've noticed the symbols on their foreheads."

"Oh yes, it reminds me of a story my mother read to me, about a little girl with a golden sun who could paint and enter magical worlds."

Clara shot Adela a funny look, curiosity spreading to her eyes. "What a fantastical story! Will you tell me all about it tonight?"

"Of course, I will. But this baby has a golden sun too," Adela said and pointed, brushing the baby's birthmark gently. "Where did it come from?"

"I don't know," Clara admitted. "I was first called to Nui-mtree months ago, before the twins were born. I specialize in maternal medicine, and the Queen heard that I had medicine to aid with childbirth. She sent a letter, explaining that she was due to give birth, but that there had been complications. When I came, she was ready to pop—and that night, I helped deliver two babies into the world."

She flicked off a drop of milk that had dribbled down the baby's chin. "I had noticed the birthmarks right away and asked the Queen what had happened. She refused to tell me more, asking me only to help heal her body and care for the twins. Two more months I returned, staying for a week at a time. During my last visit, I noticed one of the twins becoming weaker, thinner and paler with each passing night. The other twin, the little boy you met, seemed well-fed and happy, rosy-cheeked and round as a button."

Clara shifted slightly in place, allowing Adela to lean closer.

"By now, the Queen and I had become good friends. We spoke every evening, with the guards stationed outside, and stayed up talking about living in Western Wilerea and how it differed from her castle life. I told her about the young children in our city, how they had an affinity for plants and botany and the arts. My own mother had tried—unsuccessfully, I might add—to get me interested in painting. She pushed a paintbrush into my grubby fingers early on. But no," Clara said and laughed, "I was interested in the garden outside. We planted marigolds, sage, aspen, vervain. All these fragrant, colorful plants and herbs. At night, my mother would teach me how to mix them to create concoctions and pastes to heal stomachaches and dampen fevers. The Queen was captivated, just as you are now."

Adela closed her mouth, only now realizing that it was agape. Clara was a fantastic storyteller, almost as great as her mother. "Then what?" Adela asked.

"That night, I asked the Queen how the babies had gotten their birthmarks. And with the strength of our friendship urging her on, she told me a sad story. She and King Leon had been trying to have a baby for many years. But they had no luck. Many doctors and nurses came through, yet they couldn't figure out why they could not have a child. They had all but given up hope when, one winter day, King Leon set out on a hunt. On his journey back home through the Whitt Woods, he came across a witch. Welcoming the King into her home, she showered him with food and drink while he confided in her their troubles having a child. The old woman listened and admitted that she could help. She would cast a fertility spell on the Queen.

"The King was overcome with excitement and rushed home with the old woman in tow. When he arrived at the castle, the Queen was overjoyed at the plan and allowed the old woman to cast a spell on her. And so she did. That evening, the old woman set out to leave, gathering her things.

But she was stopped by the Queen. 'What if,' the Queen asked, 'I can't have any more children? What if this is my only chance?' The old woman replied, 'You're right. This is your only chance.' The Queen was horrified. She knew at that moment that she would have an only child. The King jumped in and asked if it would be a boy. The old woman replied, 'You will have a beautiful baby girl.' That caused even more discomfort, for how was a King meant to pass his kingdom along to a woman?"

Adela grimaced.

"Tell me about it," Clara said and laughed. "Kingdoms aren't too quick to realize how powerful girls can be." She winked. "The King and Queen, fraught with worry, begged the old woman to give them another child, a twin brother to accompany the young girl in life. The old woman advised against this, urging the couple to reconsider. There could be unintended consequences. They insisted, however, threatening to keep the old woman in the castle until she obliged. And so, the old woman granted their wish. But there would be, as she mentioned, unintended consequences. You see, the old woman lived far from the castle, where the weather rarely changed and the days and nights were perfectly balanced all year-round, even in the cold months.

"She gave the royal couple a warning. She would grant them twins, a girl and a boy. But, like the day and night, they were to stay balanced. When one cried, the Queen should pinch the other, to make sure their cries were in sync. When one fed, the other needed to be fed at the same time. The old woman had disrupted the balance of the universe in order to grant the Queen a child. All the creatures in the world would be aware of a new, magic soul that was birthed. To hide the second twin, all aspects of life needed to be balanced.

Otherwise, they would draw attention to the other's presence when together. If they became unbalanced, the old woman warned, there would be earthly consequences.

"The Queen and King obliged, not understanding what they were agreeing to, and nine months later, I appeared. I helped deliver two healthy twins, one with a sun on her forehead and one with a moon on his. The very manifestation of balance. That night at the castle, I quickly realized that the Queen had not heeded the old woman's words, had not pinched one when the other cried. She had been separating them, caring for them individually. And the twins were imbalanced. In fact, one was feeding off the other. Not maliciously, no—unbeknownst to them. But when you come from magic, you have little control over your abilities. The Queen was never meant to have a child. But she had two, and she didn't understand how to stop the old woman's prophesy. As the girl grew weaker, the nights became longer."

Clara pulled the bottle from the baby, who was beginning to settle into a deep slumber. She got up, and Adela followed, struggling to catch her balance on the icy plateau.

"Because I'm a witch, I know why it's important for the earth to stay balanced. You know as well as I do, in fact, considering you're growing up in the Last Sun," she mentioned, looking over her shoulder at Adela. "Careful, it's slippery here."

"I'm being careful. Your story doesn't explain why you agreed to take the baby."

"She'll have a better life in Western Wilerea, learning the magic arts. And this way, things stay as they should."

"What do you mean 'as they should'?"

"The storm raging last night, do you think that was a natural occurrence? Of course not. The Earth was angry at the abomination living and breathing inside the castle. With the girl in Western Wilerea, the twins are kept separate. They appear distinct and not of the same, singular magic soul. The world can be in balance."

Adela's head hurt, reeling from the various superstitions and magical creatures she had both encountered and learned about during this short journey. When her mother had read her the story of a girl with a golden sun on her forehead, Adela imagined it had been so, just a story. She never thought she'd one day meet an infant that resembled the young girl. But then again, she never thought she'd meet talking animals and have the power to transport from place to place. Deep in thought, she slipped and caught herself on a rock that was jutting out from the wall, mere steps from falling backward into the water.

The baby cooed.

"There, there, Lulu," Clara whispered, tickling the infant under her chin.

Adela stopped in her tracks. "What did you call her?"

"Lulu, why?"

"What is that baby's n—"

"Watch out!"

The rock Adela had been leaning against broke, sending her momentum backward. She had a split second to pinch her nose closed and shut her eyes as she fell.

"Girl!" Clara's screams echoed off the walls, becoming more faint as Adela sank.

But Adela wasn't sinking; she had floated to the top, buoyed by the big breath she had taken before splashing into the murky water. Emerging, she gasped, scanning the cave for Clara.

"Clara!" she shouted, her voice bouncing off the walls.

It was much darker than the moment before. Clara was nowhere in sight.

"Clara!"

No answer.

Adela treaded water back to the edge of the cliff, pulling herself back up on the platform. It was unbearably cold, and she shivered, wet and covered with the scum and slimy particles from the water. Around her waist was Clara's bag of belongings, and she unwrapped it from her body, letting it dry off separately. She gasped for air, wiping her face on the cloth bag. It was dark.

Clara had been right; the night was quickly approaching. There was no use in venturing deeper into the cave, trying to find an outlet. Outside were predators and ungodly creatures, ready to cause Adela harm. Though the cave was cold, Adela was hopeful she could find dry clothes in Clara's bag to help her pass the night. She had become inexplicably tired, her bones and muscles aching from the long hike to this cave and her feet tense as she had tried, unsuccessfully, to maintain her balance.

Adela settled herself in the underground cave, lulled to sleep by wind howling through its nooks and crevices. In the morning, when the dangers outside would pass, she would follow the sound of the train to try and find Clara's underground home. Or Clara would come back for her. Regardless, the sunlight would reveal the path forward. The dripping of the rainwater from the storm had stopped, and Adela was grateful. It would be impossible to sleep with that sound echoing through the cave. And so, Adela hugged herself, positioning her body close to the far wall of limestone, digging in Clara's bag for a small, wool coat that was only slightly damp, having been cocooned by all the other items as it fell into the pool of water. She worried about Clara and the baby. They were all she could think about, so much so that she hardly noticed that the ticket in her sock had become damp, torn in half from her fall into the water.

# NINE

# SYBIL

———

Stirring and rising from the cool cave floor, Adela wondered
how long she had slept in the pitch black; it must have been
a full day, for it was already dark again.

But she couldn't stay much longer. She had to move. She
packed Clara's belongings into the satchel, draping it over her
shoulder. A rush of cold air came from the direction Clara
had turned toward before she lost her.

This must be the way out.

Adela set out ahead, holding on to the limestone wall
for balance. She ducked under stalactites, jumped over the
cloudy puddles brought on by stagnant cave water, and
maneuvered around the columns growing from the ground.
As the air became cooler still, she sensed she was close to the
outlet, yet wholly unsure as to where the cave would empty
her out, like a captured net of fish emptying out into the sea.

The exit to the cave opened in front of her like the smallest
of eyes, perfectly encircling the dark night sky above. Stars
twinkled from behind the looming redwood figures firmly
planted in the earth. They seemed to have desaturated slightly.
Adela hadn't realized the impact last night's storm had on
the flora in the Whitt Woods. But she couldn't think about
that right now. She needed to get out and find a path back

to Clara's cottage. She had even more questions—thoughts unanswered—and yearned to speak to her.

And after that, she needed to get back home. And quickly.

She ran toward the exit, skidding across the dry earth and letting momentum drive her forward. Emerging from the cave, the air smacked her in the face and her body involuntarily shivered. The seasons were rapidly changing. The air bit her face, much colder than it had been that night spent talking to the Falcon.

Below her feet, a small path wore its way into the forest floor, which forked in many directions. Above, a crescent moon stood dominion in the sky, watching over the lands. She recalled what her grandmother had once taught her, a way to navigate using the horns of the moon. She knew Sunseree was west of Nuimtree, and determined that the cottage must be westwardly, in between the castle and the warmth of home and her mother's embrace. Adela shivered again. She needed to begin her journey.

In her mind, Adela drew a line from one end of the horn to the other and followed its path to the ground. This was the southmost direction. To that path's side would be west, which is where Adela now set out, walking softly and quietly so as to avoid disturbing the wildlife of the evening.

She traveled like this for nearly an hour, eyelids slowly drooping, heavy with sleep and exhaustion. Her hands bore cuts from grabbing at branches and swatting them away, and mosquitos began to land on her arms, drawn to the ruby red blood that had made its way to the surface of her skin.

Her eyes shut, as if suspended from hinges that creaked open and closed like a door swaying back and forth from a breeze, allowing her feet to guide her through the forest. Her brain had shut down, unwilling to deal with the revelations that she had arrived at the evening prior. She continued laboring forward, swatting away at the blood-sucking mosquitos. That is, until a faint crackling broke through the silence.

Adela was wide awake now, foot poised over the forest floor but refusing to take a step, clumsily wobbling on one leg as her ears stretched to meet the noises around her. Someone was nursing a fire nearby. Adela tiptoed forward, to a small evergreen bush alongside violet fairy primrose flowers. The smokiness and smell of the campfire began to billow above the tall trees in this opening. With her fingers, she grasped at the bush and created a small hole whereby she could take in the scene.

At the fire sat a hooded figure, balancing a whole, spotted small fish on a branch over the fire and turning it over to roast. The figure crouched, hiding their features, other than a small hand that wrapped around the branch itself. The figure began to hum, and Adela recognized the melody from one that she'd heard Clara sing during their long journey to the castle. Was this Clara? And if so, where was the baby?

Uncertain about the woman by the fire, Adela took a step backward in an attempt to get back on the path, but she lost her footing and stepped firmly on a long branch that splintered beneath her feet. The sound echoed through the forest, bouncing off the canopy above and weaving its way through the barren tree branches before finding the woman in her clearing.

"Who's there?"

Adela held her breath, immobile; she dared not answer. The woman's face was still cloaked and dark. Adela could not make out her features.

"Announce yourself."

Releasing her shaky breath, Adela crawled through the opening she had made in the flora.

The woman stood still, taking Adela in. She did not feign surprise to see her standing there. Rather, she turned toward the fire, twisting her fish while continuing to hum that melodic tune.

"Where is that song from?" Adela asked, remaining in place, rampant curiosity superseding her fear.

"Are you going to speak to my back? If you have questions, come ask them to my face. I don't bite." The old woman pulled the fish off the fire and tore at it, stuffing the crispy skin and white, fragrant flesh into her gaping mouth. "Wrong choice of words," she chuckled, mouth full.

Adela took a wide berth to the fire, staying far enough away from the woman to run at a moment's notice but obliging the woman's request. She carefully observed the figure: this woman was older, at least as old as Miss Sona, their neighbor in Sunseree, with a strong resemblance to her as well. Her skin was darker, generously kissed by the sun, and she had a large white scar that covered the entirety of her forehead, spreading down to cross over her eye. She had a broad, round nose, and thin, chapped lips. Her eyes were brown, but her left eye had a milky center. She positioned the right side of her face toward Adela, and Adela realized then she was half-blind.

"What are you doing here, child?" the old woman asked.

"I was looking for someone."

"Ah," the old woman replied.

Silence spread to the corners of the clearing as the old woman continued to eat, notably refusing to offer Adela any. Some time passed before she was finished, leaning back on the jagged log where she had been sitting. She continued to make eye contact with Adela, intense and unyielding, and it reminded Adela of the way in which the Falcon had looked at her the other night, in her dreams.

"Where is that song from?" Adela repeated.

The old woman smacked her lips and dug between her tooth with her pinky nail, sucking her teeth. She found a piece of fish that had escaped the journey to her stomach and picked at it before swallowing and clearing her throat.

"What if I told you that someone taught it to me? Years ago?"

"Was it a woman?"

"Yes, a woman. Her name was Clara."

"How do you know Clara?"

"She passed through this area of the woods a while back."

"She lives here. Doesn't she?"

The old woman shrugged. "Hell if I know. Excuse my language," she laughed. "She passes by here often. Retracing her steps. Trying to find something—or someone—she's lost."

"How many times has she come here?" Adela asked. Her palms were clammy with sweat and her heart beat harder, the sound making its way to her head along with the dull drone of the woman's hums that were like an interlude to her speech. Adela's head spun with unease.

Was this the same uneasiness that rushed over her when she transported? Or was it different?

She looked down at her ankle to the ticket. It had been torn in half and was wet, clinging to her skin. Before the old woman could give her response, she knew the answer to her question.

"Many times over the years and decades. Who knows exactly?"

There was the answer. Adela had traveled forward.

*But is it my own time?*

A chill overtook Adela, as she shivered and grasped at her shoulders with her hands. "It sure is cold tonight."

"Of course, it is, girl," the old woman said, eyeing her suspiciously. "The Last Sun has dipped the entire world in darkness. Why do you think I have this fire going in the afternoon?" She pointed toward the flames that jumped at the center of the pit, flickering when a strong gust of wind forced its way through.

"What do you mean? How long has it been?"

"Two months, I reckon," the old woman responded. "You're asking a lot of silly questions."

Adela was back in her own time. It was no use finding Clara anymore, for she would surely be gone from here, raising the girl in Western Wilerea. The plan for Adela now was to return to Sunseree. Her mind raced with frightening scenarios of what awaited her back home. Was she still in the field with Milo dutifully watching over her body? Or would her mother have found her? Was she in bed, being poked and prodded by doctors, medicines and fluids flowing into her body in an attempt to nudge her awake?

"Snap out of it!" The old woman clapped her hands together in front of Adela's face, like the school erasers that emitted a plume of white chalk whenever Adela beat them against the board.

Adela, surprised, fell backward, over the log she had been positioned on, her legs flailing. She rested up on her elbow, the old woman above smiling and with an outstretched hand. Adela grabbed it, hoisting herself back on the log with ease.

"Thank you."

"Eh," the old woman said and waved away. She limped back to her log, "You shouldn't be out in the woods alone. Where is home?"

"I live in Sunseree," Adela volunteered.

"Sunseree?" The woman lingered on the name for a moment. "That's very far away."

The wind whistled through the bushes that stood guard alongside the clearing. Adela leaned into the fire, desperate for warmth. Its heat seeped into her bones. Her stomach loudly protested, hungry from what seemed like an eternity without food.

"What's your name?" Adela asked.

"They call me Miss Sibyl," the old woman replied.

"Miss Sibyl, can I ask you a question?"

Miss Sibyl grunted, lying lengthwise on the log and shutting her eyes.

"What do you remember about Clara?"

"What do I remember? You mean all those years ago? She was carrying a wee one, and she was distraught. She had come from the same direction as you, likely from the Curling Cave. Her voice was hoarse from yelling, and the baby was hysterically crying. She told me she had lost a little girl." She paused, opening her good eye and glancing toward Adela, who refused eye contact.

"I had seen Clara only once before, in the castle," Miss Sybil continued. "But now I was trying to get myself out of these woods. You see, the King had brought me here, desperate to find out if a witch's curse had befallen his children. You can never trust a witch," she admitted, her toothy grin sinister.

The old woman pulled herself up to sit on the log across from Adela. "Story goes that the Queen was infertile and had asked a witch for twins. The witch had granted it, though she opposed it, and in turn put a curse on them. Months before the babies were due, the couple grew frantic. They called every magical creature from across the lands to come to Nuimtree. That's how I suppose Clara found her way here. And the King, well, he scoured the forest, looking for every magical creature in sight that could help him make sorts of his predicament. And then he found the fortune teller, of course." She did a mock curtsy.

Adela gasped. This was surely the fortune teller Clara had met, the one who had told her about the Last Sun.

"But I told him what he wished not to hear. That the witch's curse was final and that his wife had been silly to force a witch to do her bidding. Ha!" Miss Sibyl cackled, her harsh voice fighting with the wind that whistled through the trees.

Adela inched closer to the fire for warmth, both literal and figurative. The air, and the company, were frigid.

"The King ordered me out of the Whitt Woods. I packed up my things and set out, trying to find the way out of here, wandering for months, until I grew enchanted with the place and decided to live a nomadic life here among the redwoods. And one of those days, I stumbled upon Clara and the baby, both of whom I recognized from my time in the castle. And she told me about the magic girl she had lost." Miss Sibyl's eyes gleamed, hungry for validation.

Adela pressed on, terrified of admitting the truth to a stranger. "Clara mentioned a fortune teller. You told her about the Last Sun. Didn't you?"

Miss Sibyl laughed again, showing teeth yellowed with age, like the golden paints her mother kept locked in her room. "I do admit, a little tea liquor will get me talking. And it's hard to stop," she said, winking. "But that's the case for Clara. Some liquid courage to calm her nerves and she told me all about her magic girl that evening. She asked me where that girl was, and if she would see her again, and if the girl would turn out okay. And now my question... are you that girl?" She smacked her lips together, rubbing her calloused hands against her upper arm for warmth.

Adela stretched her hands in front of her, letting the flames delicately lick at her fingertips, ignoring the line of questioning. "What did you tell her when she asked about the girl? What were your answers?"

"I told her the truth. The girl was still here but in a different time. And that she would see her again, many times."

"And the last question?"

"That I can't answer. It's dangerous to know your future."

"How do you know that girl was me?"

"I know."

"Why won't you tell me the answer to that question then? You told the King about the twins."

"I told the King that the curse was real. I did not provide the answers he was seeking. Whether his children would be happy and healthy. Whether they would survive past their first birthday. Those were all questions left unanswered."

"How do I even know you're telling the truth?"

"Cheeky one." Miss Sybil paused, eyeing her. She turned, digging in a small knapsack by her foot.

The fire grew strong, popping and crackling from the larger logs the old woman had added for fuel. Around Adela, the trees rustled and the wind reared its head, threatening to put out the fire but kindly fanning it so Adela could stay warm.

"Thank you," Adela whispered to the glowing fire and to the vast, towering trees that protected her from the terrors of the world. She chewed on her cheek, her tongue running along the inside of her mouth as she waited for Miss Sybil to speak again.

"Here we are," Miss Sybil squawked, holding a small jar with a brown paste inside, and Adela's moniker—Girl—ceremoniously scrawled in ink and left to dry. "Clara asked me to give this to the little girl, if I ever came across her."

Adela reached for the jar; of course, she recognized it and the medicine held within, for Clara had used it on her fingers not long ago. So the old woman did meet her.

"Does Clara ever come back?"

"Occasionally, yes."

"With the baby?"

The old woman laughed, a barking laugh that caught Adela by surprise. "She used to. But the baby is not a baby any longer. She's grown now and with a child of her own."

Adela's stomach dropped. This conversation was careening toward a dangerous cliff, and Adela chose her next words carefully, hoping she would not tumble off. "Do you know why I came to Nuimtree?"

"I do," Miss Sibyl admitted. "You were running away. And, at the same time, searching for the truth." She motioned toward Adela's ankle, her good eye tracking Adela's reactions, surprised—and also not—at the fact that the old woman knew about the train ticket.

"Miss Sybil, I learned the secret behind my grandmother's train ticket. Didn't I?"

Miss Sybil nodded, quieting down. Where she had seemed terrifying moments ago, her gestures now felt familial and warm, encouraging Adela to continue. The fire crackled with bits popping off the flame, the ground singed at Adela's feet.

When her mother had told her the story of the girl with the golden sun, the setting so familiar, Adela had an inkling.

Feeling the power of the sun's warmth behind her mother's fingers. Using her grandmother's ticket as her token to meet Clara, the witch from Western Wilerea. Hearing the mystical humming in her ears each time Clara laughed, alerting her to something amiss. Clara calling the baby "Lulu," her mother's nickname.

Clara was her grandmother.

The baby was her mother.

No wonder she had felt close to Clara, safe and protected. No wonder she had found the train ticket in her grandmother's belongings. It had been a special token, a reminder of when she picked up her newborn daughter. And that meant her mother was the girl in the story. The girl who painted and entered the Isle of Vila. The girl with the golden sun on her head.

"I have many questions," Adela whispered, only to herself. Looking down at the ground, she realized the halved yellowed ticket had dried up from the fire. It had peeled off her ankle and was now lying on the ground.

This was surely how she was able to revert back to her time, even if in an alternate place. The token had lost its magic. Perhaps the cave pearls had seen to that. She slowly picked it up, but nothing happened.

"What is that?" Miss Sybil asked, feigning curiosity, for Adela knew she knew everything.

"Nothing," Adela whispered. "Just a stupid token." She kicked at it, partially burying it in the musky earth. She bit the inside of her cheek, willing herself to not cry in front of a stranger. A panicked state was the last thing Adela wanted Miss Sybil to encounter.

"You know," Miss Sibyl said, standing up and hobbling over with her good leg. "I have a sister in Sunseree. A goody-two-shoes, if you ask me. The children call her Miss Sona."

"I know Miss Sona," Adela exclaimed. "She's our neighbor. She raises bees—or, used to, at least."

"What a small world!" Miss Sybil said, edging closer. "Would you tell her that I miss her?" She set her wrinkled hand on Adela's head, fingers picking at her fine hair.

"I don't—"

Miss Sybil pulled back her hand, dropping the other half of the token, which had seemingly found its way into Adela's hair and had dried up by the fireside. It joined the first half, the sock's half, on the ground as the old woman smiled and waved her fingers individually. "I'm sure we'll see each other again soon."

The valediction seemed eerily sinister, and Adela was uncertain as to the fortune teller's true intentions.

But with that, Adela was transported back to Sunseree.

# PART THREE

## TEN

# THE DEATH

———

Adela squeezed her eyes shut on the journey to her original body, her stomach lurching as nausea rolled over her, like the children who rolled down the hills of Sunseree in the summertime, joyful and giddy. Yet Adela was not giddy; the effect of traveling was worse than the journey to the train. Much as she had never transported this far in time before, she had never transported this far in space before either. She grasped at her body in hopes that nothing would inexplicably fall off, stomach heaving with emptiness. She hadn't eaten in nearly two days.

With eyes clutched, the acrid scent of earth hit her first. The air was thick here, and she coughed involuntarily, prying her eyes open to the darkness. She had stopped hurtling through the universe, and her stomach somersaulted before finally settling in place. Her journey had ended. She was lying down.

Adela moved her head in the pitch black. This wasn't her bed. She presumed she was still in the field. But the surface beneath her back was hard and firm, not the pliable softness of the prickly grass and spindly wildflowers where she had last left her body, guarded by Milo. To that end, Milo was nowhere to be found. She could not hear any murmurs, nor snores or breathing. She was alone.

Utterly confused, Adela spread both hands at her sides and realized, at once, that she was in a confined space. Behind her back was a solid mass, at her feet was the same solid mass, and on either end were walls. Reaching in front of her face, her hands skimmed along the edges of her environment. She pulled them away, bringing a grainy substance to her face; she licked it and grimaced.

Dirt.

A box.

She knew where she was: underground, in a coffin.

Panic set in, and her body wasted no time in its response. Her chest tightened and throat constricted, threatening to cut off valuable airflow. Her palms and armpits became wet, clammy from the sweat that had been triggered by an involuntary fight or flight reaction. Her nails scraped at the bottom and side of the box, digging in, while her hands balled into fists, pounding at the sides until she became dizzy.

Her nails snagged on a splinter and she flinched, pulling away and inadvertently driving a sliver of wood deep into her palm. Yelping with pain, her face warmed with intense heat, tears cooling her cheeks while she gasped for air, playing a fatal tug-of-war with the confines of the box. Intrusive thoughts rushed into her mind. What if she died in here? Or was she dead already? Did she suffocate? Or had she been eaten alive by the nocturnal creatures that inhabited the cool earth?

Of course, this was bound to happen given how long she had stayed in Nuimtree. That was one of the rules, after all, to keep her original body safe until she could return. Nobody, other than her and Clara, knew where she had been the last seventy-two hours. She had stupidly left her original body behind—immobile and limp. And she had promised Milo she would return within a few hours' time. While she was not surprised that he had not waited for her return—she had been gone for days, after all—an irrational anger welled within her. She had been too careless.

She imagined Milo's scrawny body, his face screwing itself into a grimace of concern, gradually shifting to worry, and then unbridled fear. Adela could trace his hurried footsteps retreating from her unmoving body, as he yelled and flailed his arms for attention after she had not returned that evening. She could picture the village lights turning on and dotting the dark landscape, neighbors awaking to the ruckus and peeking their heads out of windows and doors to console Milo.

And, saddest of all, she pictured her beautiful mother in a nightgown, racing down to the field, distraught and screaming, her face fixed into a wail of hysteria. All while she had been selfishly exploring. Adela choked up, ready to cry again. She hated herself for leaving.

But hidden beneath the earth, she could not waste another second, for she had already wasted too many. It was time to muster up any courage remaining in her bones and conjure up an escape. Her arms trembled, and she cleared her throat of the dirt that had settled there, thinking of her options. She did not want to die down here.

She first checked the folds of her clothing, wondering if she had mistakenly—and by a stroke of luck—brought another token with her, one that could transport her from this danger and elsewhere. But her powers would not help her in this instance. Only sheer determination could.

Adela willed herself to calm down, to slow her breathing. She knew the more erratic her breath became, the quicker the air would run out, and she needed time to think about her next steps. Blood rushed in her ears, and her heartbeat sounded at her temples, though she ignored it in order to lull herself into a false sense of security. It worked.

Stretching her hands over her head, she first tried pushing on the small square above her head, willing it to pop open by sheer force. But it simply gave way for a second and shifted back into place, refusing to budge. She then directed her attention to the wooden panel at her feet and, within the small space of the coffin, pulled her knees and slammed with all her force on the block. But after six stomps, Adela grew weak and stopped. Exerting this much energy was not sustainable with the state of her empty stomach.

Unseen creatures crawled up her shoulder, their long spindly legs making Adela ticklish, and she flicked them off, her hand settling on the soft cloth of Clara's satchel. Adela turned her attention to this bag of mysterious wonders. It was still pitch black, but she pulled at the drawstring that held the bag closed and allowed her fingers to brush over the items, feeling for something that could help her out of her current predicament.

The pads of her fingers found soft wool and cotton, undoubtedly Clara's change of clothes for her visit to Nuimtree, slightly damp from Adela's dip into the cave river hours ago. A book was nestled within the clothes, and Adela was careful as she brushed her hand over it, not wishing to get any paper cuts. A sack of what seemed to be fungi was next, and it took everything in Adela's power to not eat the mushrooms right then and there; her stomach grumbled, as if announcing its presence. But first, she had to get out.

And then she felt something: a mass of metal with a long, tapered but firm edge and a robust head with pointed, dull tines. Her fingers brushed over the top of the object, tracing blank spaces, raised edges, and ornate tracings of flowers. A hair comb, one she had never seen Clara use. Perhaps she had worn it when getting ready for bed? She pulled it out, holding the pointed edge away from her chest.

Once again, her free hand perused the cracks and corners of the coffin, this time searching for a small section where she could dig the hair comb in, creating separation between the edges to pry open the top of the coffin. She scooted down farther, breathing softly but working quickly to find an opening. And finally, she found it.

A small section of the coffin had not been properly sealed. Adela could just poke the sharp end of the comb into the nook of the opening. She pushed it forward with the palm of her hand, allowing enough traction so the hair comb would not simply snap.

Closing her eyes tightly, she cemented the comb firmly in the opening and used as much might as she could conjure to pull her weight downward, effectively nudging the pointed end of the comb up, willing the lid to follow its lead. A creak let out as the comb gave way, edging closer to a *snap*. But there was no such sound. She continued, resetting her position and nudging the comb even farther into the crack, which had expanded from her efforts. Again, she pulled her weight downward and, this time, when she heard the creak, continued pushing and pulling, pulling and pushing until the lid popped up half an inch and settled back in place. The lid was freed.

A new fear overtook Adela.

*What if it's safer in the box?*

If the dirt outside was wet, or if she had been buried here a long time, there was no way she could escape with hundreds of pounds of dirt packed atop her body. She would be crushed. Adela's chest heaved again, panic setting in.

But she needed to be brave and so she poked a finger out of the box and felt the earth outside. It was soft and loose. That meant she hadn't been buried for long. This coffin was freshly interred.

Adela tucked the comb back into Clara's bag, closed her eyes, and took a deep breath. Pushing the lid off to the side, she felt loose dirt fall on her face. Sitting up, it continued to fall in her lap as she tried to slowly worm herself out of the box. This proved more challenging than anticipated, as the dirt was soft and refused to hold her weight properly. Inside the earth, creatures made contact with her nose, her face, and her hair, but she kept moving upward until finally, her head broke out of the dirt.

Cold air hit her cheeks. She let out the stale breath she had been holding and blew out of her nose, forcing any bugs that had taken up temporary habitation in her nostrils to evacuate. Adela pulled herself up and remained hunched over, on all fours, catching her breath and relieved to have made it out alive.

If anyone had come across her at this moment, they would have seen a small girl covered head to toe in dirt, hair bedraggled while ants crawled over her arms and through her strawberry locks. Clara's satchel had let out its contents at her side, having been unfastened and thrown off her shoulder during the escape. Adela coughed, spitting up dirt that had made its way into her mouth, mixed with saliva and mucus. The taste of dirt would stay forever in her mouth.

Time stood still as the soft howls of wolves and cooing hoots of owls danced and mingled in the wintry air. Adela was not sure what to do next. Should she find the nearest house, announce her presence to the inhabitants? Should she go home, hoping her mother would understand why she left? How she came back?

The villagers had understandably presumed she was dead, having come across her body only days before; delving into an explanation for anything to the contrary would be impossible. No, she needed to lay low until she knew she could trust someone to keep her secret.

First, she would need to find her mother.

If the story was true, her mother had special powers as a child. She'd only need to explain what had happened. The two of them would be able to get Adela out of this situation. And if they couldn't explain it to the villagers, they would leave forever and never return. They could go live with Adela's grandmother in Western Wilerea.

Adela's next steps needed to be careful. The only comfort she had at the moment was knowing she was alone in the graveyard, offered the opportunity to pause.

"Adela?"

# ELEVEN

# SUNSEREE

———

Adela followed the voice, hair caked with sweat and dirt falling over her bloodshot eyes. Almost immediately, she locked eyes with a small shadowy shape sitting underneath a barren tree mere steps away. She could not make out the facial features, nor the shape of their body, but she knew the voice.

"Milo?"

She pulled herself to stand, knees cracking with pain in response to the confined space she had just escaped from. She tested a few steps forward until she could no longer hear her bones pop and approached the figure.

"Don't come near me!" he yelled, scrambling away, the palms of his hands serving as his single source of movement.

"Why? It's just me," Adela said.

"I-I watched them put you in the ground." His voice cracked slightly, emotion catching in his throat. "You promised you'd return. But you didn't."

"Milo," Adela cautioned, coming nearer still, "I can explain."

"Don't touch me!" he screamed as Adela rushed forward, clamping her hand over his mouth.

"Shh!"

Her eyes darted back and forth, fearful not only that someone would hear and come to the graveyard to investigate, but even more so that someone would not be understanding of the grave situation.

"I'll explain everything," Adela offered. She crouched low, trying to stay hidden in the shadows while the moon shone above, threatening to reveal her hiding spot among the withered trees and dead bushes. Around her, the hooting of an owl sounded and she wondered if it, too, was trying to uncover her position.

Milo's eyes were wide. A large grave marker towered over the both of them, a rectangular mass nestled in the hill that was covered with a thin layer of frost. The stone was chipped in places, the result of blatant carelessness on behalf of neighborhood teenagers who roamed the graveyard during evenings, looking to encounter a ghost. It was unmarked.

Adela wondered who lay there.

Milo refused to move, as if frozen in place like the gravestones around them. Adela grabbed his arm, letting her fingers rest there in an attempt to calm him down and hoping the physical contact would convince him that she was real. A few seconds passed and then he nodded.

Side-stepping together, they crouched behind the marker, hidden from the houses beyond the field. The graveyard was suitably far from town. The people had been superstitious and had chosen this burial place, away from the majestic South Mountains and Ceprith Caves and lazy lake that beckoned to voyagers, away from the village and the farmland that they plowed for sustenance, away even from the woods.

No, this landmark was on the edge of Sunseree, sitting atop barren soil and dead flora. Only the occasional barn owl, curious fox, or midnight crow ventured here, lured by the quiet. Adela had never been here, not even when her father, Fritz, had passed away; she watched from afar as he was lowered into the ground, the owls and foxes and crows guarding over the ceremony.

As such, there was a clear line of sight for any villagers who deigned to look in this direction. They had to be careful not to attract attention.

"Why are you here?" Adela whispered, raking calloused fingers through her hair in a last attempt to dislodge the most stubborn of dirt. "Why aren't you home?"

Milo hesitated, looking at Adela with awe and disbelief.

Adela rolled her eyes and grabbed Milo's hand again.

"I'm real, see?" She pinched him and he yelped, dropping his arm and rubbing the area where her fingernails had squeezed together. "Will you answer me?"

"I come here at night, to think..." he started, his speech halting.

"Why?"

"Because I saw you die."

"I didn't die," Adela hissed impatiently. She had moved on to pulling the dirt out of her hair, which had resulted in strands dislocating themselves from her scalp and scattering loosely around her lap. "I traveled and now I'm back."

"You said you'd be gone a few hours. You were gone three days."

"I guess I underestimated."

"How did you survive?" Milo asked, looking behind him. With the mountains and lake in the way, he would not be able to see the unblemished woods behind them, the area where the train would have been passing through on its way to faraway lands. But Adela knew that was where he was looking now, and she could picture the field where she had left him perfectly.

"I found my grandmother."

"Your grandmother?" Milo asked, raising his voice and turning his head toward Adela again. "Doesn't she live in Western Wilerea?"

"Quiet, you're too loud. Yes, my grandmother. And yes, she does."

"Did she help you return home?"

"She didn't know it was me. She didn't know I was her granddaughter."

The air danced around them, playfully teasing Milo with the revelation that Adela was confiding.

"You time traveled. Didn't you?"

"Yes."

"What happened? Why did it take you so long to get home?"

Adela sighed. "It's not important. I found my way back. That's the important part." She bore her gaze into his face. Uncomfortable, he looked away.

"What are you going to do now?"

"What do you mean?"

"Everyone thinks you're dead. How will you explain it?"

Adela bit the inside of her lip in thought, her brow furrowing as she flicked a spider off her forearm. "I don't know. Either way, I need to see my mother."

Milo began playing with his socks, folding them over and unfolding them as if temporarily possessed.

"What's wrong with you?"

He murmured, avoiding her. Crickets chirped around them.

"Speak up," Adela warned, raising her voice, becoming increasingly annoyed.

"Your mother... well, she... you should see for yourself." Milo's words stumbled out of his mouth, like the flow of a river that had gained momentum and was unable to stop before spilling over the edge of a cliff.

Adela paused, letting her gaze fall on the field, the one from which she had watched her father's funeral proceedings years ago. Questions circled her mind, fighting for attention. What did Milo mean? Was her mother okay? What had she done?

She fastened her remaining items to her body and wished she could tie her hair back, the scent of the earth permeating her skin. She could smell it deep in her nostrils.

"You can follow me, or you can choose not to," she cautioned.

Milo nodded, running his hand through his mousy hair. "I'll come with you."

But Adela was off and running, sprinting in the direction of the cottage. Her skirt rustled as she pushed forward, her limbs sore yet converting the pain into pure adrenaline. Milo huffed behind her, out of breath and laboring, but she would not slow down. She needed to get home. She needed to see her mother.

Then, she remembered and stopped. Going home meant facing Conrad again, and she didn't feel strong enough to do that. His cruelty had no bounds, and she could imagine a world in which he was more, not less, unkind to Adela given the circumstances. He would not be happy that she was alive after presumed dead. In fact, she imagined he would be furious that she had returned, magicked alive by some unseen force.

She flinched, remembering his hands clenched around her upper arm, the pattern of his fingers still visible hours later in bruises that she meticulously hid from her own mother.

"Thanks for waiting," Milo panted, finally catching up to her.

Adela shook her head, willing herself out of her train of thought. She was fearful of Conrad but needed to understand what Milo had alluded to earlier.

The house was just ahead, and Adela turned to Milo and motioned for him to be quiet. Shushing him, she crouched low, waiting for him to fall into position. Lights were on in the kitchen, a beacon of amber glow that beckoned to her.

This time, she ignored the kitchen window completely, lit from inside but quiet and devoid of all its usual activity. Instead, hugging the facade of the home, she maneuvered past the front door, all the way to the other side of the house. Above Adela's head was the windowsill, filled with flowers from the garden just out the back. The frosted panes usually kept anyone from seeing inside, but today, the window was open to the cool mountain air around them. Her eyes crept past the ledge and peered inside the room, mirroring her movements from days before.

The room was lit by a handful of candles, wax dripping onto the floor and the nightstand upon which they were perched. The door to the hallway was open a hair, enough for a small beam of light to permeate the room, bringing attention to the dust bunnies that had accumulated by the entry. Adela heard only breathing, and she squinted her eyes to make out the shapes in the room more easily. Lit by the hallway light and the flickering glow of the candles, she made out a figure on the bed.

Her mother, lying on her back, arms gently folded over her stomach.

Adela's breath caught in her throat. She needed to make her way inside the room, to see her mother. She crouched again, turning toward Milo. "You need to prop me up so I can climb inside."

"Are you crazy?"

"I need to get inside that room, Milo," she replied, waiting for him to concede.

He thought for a moment but then nodded. She knew she could count on him to go along with her plans. He stretched his arms out and folded his fingers together, creating a net on which Adela could balance before being pushed up to the ledge.

She stepped on his fingers as he muttered under his breath and, within moments, was clutching the ledge, perilously close to falling one way or the other. She paused for a moment, trying to keep her ears and eyes open for any sign of Conrad. Convinced he would not interrupt her, she lowered herself into the room.

The air here was stale, despite the window being open. The floorboards creaked quietly under her feet, and she flinched. There was no new activity beyond the door, no threat of Conrad barreling through with his hand raised high. Adela kept her arms outstretched to keep from bumping into anything and strode toward the bed. Kneeling to avoid detection, she placed her hands on her mother's arm and gently shook.

"Mama," she whispered.

Nothing.

"Mama!" she urged, still keeping her voice soft in fear of being caught.

Nothing again.

Adela placed her ear near her mother's belly. Her stomach rose, slowly but laboriously. She was alive, but barely.

"Milo?" she softly called out, inching to the windowsill as she attempted to stay in the shadows.

A grunt from behind the wall affirmed that he was listening.

"What happened here? While I was gone?"

His head poked above the windowsill, and Adela met his eyes in the inky night. The whites of his eyes were bright and his pupils dilated, constricting only when hit with the soft light of the candles.

"After they found you, she fainted. My mother and father came and helped carry her home. She was weak and needed rest, so Conrad shooed us all away. My mom insisted she stay, so he let her sleep in your room. He spent all night down here, but in the morning, my mom came down and your mom was like this," he said and motioned with his head. "Breathing, but unmoving. She hasn't woken in days."

A plate of food and a mug sat untouched on the floor next to the bed. Adela left Milo and crawled forward, staying low. As she neared the plates, she noticed a small drawing etched into the floor with a white paste, like chalk mixed with water. It was the rectangular outline of a door, without a doorknob, positioned right under the bed, right under her mother's reposing figure. Adela touched the paste. It stung, as if a hundred bees had descended on her fingertips all at once. Biting back tears, she wiped the material on her skirt, leaving a white smudge behind.

Leaves lay crumpled in the bottom of her mother's mug. They weren't mint leaves or like any other muddled ingredients Adela had used to prepare tea. Her mint leaves were small with jagged edges, yet these ones had smooth edges.

They were significantly larger and nearly the length from her thumb to her pinky finger, dull in color and not as vibrant as the greens of mint.

As she examined the leaves, thundering footsteps sounded from across the hallway, and she turned to the sill. Milo was gone, either on his way back home or simply hiding behind the wall of the house, not making a sound. Adela had no place to hide, so she quickly lowered her body fully and crawled under the bed, careful to avoid the milky paste in the shape of a door.

The door creaked open, its sound deafening as Conrad stumbled in the room. He spilled water on the floor, which splashed with a *plop.*

"Damn it all," he muttered under his breath.

Adela froze, mentally begging him to leave it. If he knelt down to clean it up, he would surely see her under the bed. But Conrad was not one for cleanliness lately, and he walked to the bed, setting down the plates he had balanced in his hands on the nightstand. Adela knew all this, for behind the door was a mirror that had been hung years ago. With the door partially closed, she could make herself and the far corner of the room out as well. The angle was wrong and had its blind spots, but she had regained her sense of sight.

"There you are, sleeping beauty," his muffled voice said, but Adela knew from the sound of the clinking dishes that he was directing his attention to her mother. Conrad blew on the tea to cool it down and Adela would have thought it compassionate, if not for the words that followed.

"Who would have thought it'd be that easy to be rid of you both," he asked and chuckled to himself. "There now, up you go."

Above, the bed creaked. Conrad was positioning her mother up on the bed, leaning her head against the headboard. He waited until Adela's mother's eyes began to flutter open. Propped against the surface behind her, her head sloped forward but she appeared to be semi-conscious.

"Ade..." her mother murmured, voice trailing off.

"Yes, she's gone. Good riddance, too."

Her mother let out of a soft wail, cut short by the clanking of dishes and Conrad's brash voice.

"Don't worry," he interrupted. "You may just see her again soon."

Adela could hardly believe what she was hearing. She knew Conrad had grown cold and calculating. He had certainly hurt her in the past. But she never imagined he had the capacity for murder. She remembered early on, how kind he had seemed and how he had brought her gifts from his travels. Her eyes filled with tears, and she bit her bottom lip to keep from crying out.

"Hold still."

Conrad's voice brought her back to the present, and Adela focused on the mirror, trying to make out what was happening mere inches above her head. The bed shifted as Conrad pushed the teacup to her mother's lips. Her mother tried to move her mouth away, clearly weakened from sleep. And something else. But Conrad was not having it. He grabbed her chin and pried her mouth open, pouring the cooled tea down her throat.

"Drink it all," he said, and Adela's mother gulped it down. "Good. I don't have time to spend here with you. Eat your food. And quickly. If I come back and I find you haven't eaten it, I'll feed you myself. And I won't be as careful," he threatened. He left Adela's mother propped up and exited the room, oblivious to Adela's scared reflection on the back of the door. As he walked upstairs, all was silent.

Carefully, Adela pulled herself out from under the bed, her elbow grazing the white paste that stung her skin. She flinched yet knew she needed to talk to her mother before she lost consciousness.

"Mama?"

This time, Adela's mother slowly moved her head to the side, eyes widening.

"No..." she moaned.

"Yes, Mama, it's me."

"Dea... dead."

"I'm not dead. I'm not a ghost. It's me. It's Adela." She tried to keep her voice low and soft but loud enough for her mother to comprehend. It worked.

Adela's mother closed her eyes, tears escaping from behind her lashes. She reached one hand out to Adela but was able to lift it only slightly before it sank back on the bed. Grabbing her mother's hand, Adela kissed it, eager to feel the warmth of her touch. But her hand was cold. She focused her attention on the mug on the end table and its curious contents.

She acted quickly, opening the clasp of Clara's bag and looking for an empty jar she could dump the contents of the mug into. Adela finally found one at the bottom of the satchel and scooped the tea leaves out with her fingers, making sure to leave some stuck to the bottom of the mug so as not to arouse suspicious from Conrad. Bringing her fingers to her nose, she could smell the subtle fragrance of flowers but could not otherwise place the herb. But she knew who could.

"Go," Adela's mother whispered.

Her mother's eyes had widened even more, this time from fright rather than shock. Adela listened for the creaks of the house. Conrad was walking toward the staircase above and making his way back downstairs, back to the bedroom. She felt pressure on her wrist; her mother had placed her hand there.

"Take." She motioned across the room with her head.

Against the wall was a dresser, with hundreds of drawers jutting out from all directions. It was a work of art, intricately carved generations before Adela was born. She loved the dresser and knew her mother took great pride in its craftsmanship. On the surface, Adela's mother kept her perfumes and creams, as well as an ivory jewelry box carved from bone. The box had belonged to her grandmother and was filled with a collection of knick-knacks and keepsakes kept safe over the years. She had gifted it to Adela's mother and made her promise that Adela would receive it upon her twentieth birthday.

"Take!" Adela's mother urged again, as the lumbering steps drew closer.

The box. Slowly, Adela strode to the side of the room and grabbed the box, holding it just under her armpit. Heading back to the window, she froze. Conrad had reached the bottom of the steps, and would be here in a matter of seconds. He would see Adela climbing out of the window and pull her back into the room, for there was no way for her to hoist herself up and vault herself over in time. Adela would need to find another way out of the house.

She thought quickly, taking long strides to the door that let out into the hall, the one with the mirror on its back. Inhaling and holding her breath to make her body even smaller, the door lightly pushed on her tensed stomach and then stopped.

Conrad walked in, his back to the door.

"You moved," he said, bewildered. "And you didn't eat. What did I tell you?"

Adela's mother grunted, her speech deteriorating by the second.

Conrad stood at the base of the bed. "You seem to be progressing nicely either way. Maybe we can skip the formalities just this once. See how nice I can be?" He chuckled to himself.

As he moved closer to the nightstand, Adela seized the opportunity. With the box under her arm, she glanced back at her mother and communicated a sad smile. Her mother nodded and returned her own small smile, as her eyes fell into peaceful slumber.

Emerging from behind the open door, Adela made a run for it, moving into the hallway and straight for the front entrance. Without hesitating, she threw the door open, hearing it slam against the hallway, and stumbled down the hill in the direction of the woods that enveloped the area. The only sound that escaped her mouth was the screech of "Milo!" to alert him that she left the home and was careening away from it, calling for him to follow her.

She did not look back; if she had, she would have seen Conrad stepping outside the front door, accompanied by the roar that escaped his vast belly. She would have also seen Milo tumbling down the hill, only a few dozen feet behind her.

Adela kept running, even when she knew she was safely out of Conrad's reach and even though she could only hear the patter of a single pair of footsteps behind her. She continued this way for a while.

Finally, confident she had put enough space between her and the house, she slowed and stopped. Minutes later, the breathy sighs from Milo caught up with her. She held the box out.

"What happened back there?" he asked.

"Something strange is happening."

"What do you mean?"

Adela shook her head, unwilling to share more. There were more pressing details to discuss.

She thrust the box closer to Milo, her eyes widening and a frown forming on her face. Conrad was doing something—something bad—but she didn't know *why*. The leaves in the tea and the makeshift door at the bottom of the bed meant something, but she didn't know *what*. Her mother was sick. She needed to help her escape from Conrad's clutches, to ultimately save them both.

But she didn't know *how* just yet.

"What's that?" Milo breathed, keeled over with his hands on his knees.

"A box."

"A box? What's so special about it?"

"It's my grandmother's." Adela sighed. "I don't know why, but my mother wanted me to have it."

She slowly undid the clasp and took inventory of what was inside: a menagerie of tokens, ones that, at another time, Adela would grasp between her fingers and use to transport herself elsewhere. But there was no way her mother could know about her abilities. And there was no way her mother would have urged her to take this box and use them. Or was there?

Adela brushed her fingertips over the items of the box until one caught her eye—a beautiful brooch in the shape of a snake, its silver body lithe and curvy, eyes marked by pristine sapphires. A snake was the symbol of Western Wilerea, where her grandmother still resided.

Her grandmother. She would be able to help. Adela was sure of it.

Fingers trembling with excitement, she held the brooch in one hand and stretched her arm toward Milo. "Take it. Take my hand."

"Are you sure this is safe?" he questioned, his voice quivering slightly.

"No, but it's the best lead we have. We need to help my mother."

Milo hesitated, and Adela readied herself to leave without him, her fingers curling even tighter against the cool metal of the brooch.

"Fine, stay here. Just make sure my body doesn't get hurt." She glanced around the clearing where they had rolled to a stop, tucked away from civilization yet on the outskirts of the forest, where wolves and bears were not apt to venture toward. Still, that was no guarantee.

"No, I'll go with you. I want to see what all this fuss is about."

"Then grab hold and close your eyes. This won't be pleasant."

Milo obliged, resting his clammy hand in Adela's and closing his eyes. Adela followed, firmly holding onto the brooch and the box.

And they were both transported.

# TWELVE

# SYMBOL

———

This time was different. This time, the colors blended together from behind Adela's eyes. Pops of white erupted, like stars fizzling out, and the smell of smoke and a blend of fragrant spices wafted through the air. Beside her, Milo let out of a groan as he squeezed Adela's hand tighter, likely overwhelmed with the feeling of traveling. When Adela first began traveling, the feeling was not unlike being ripped apart. In a way, it made sense, her traveling body leaving its original one. Searing pain would originate in her stomach, shooting up her back until it escaped, oftentimes rather violently, from her mouth. But this time was more painful still. Perhaps with two people traveling, the magic would be divided equally.

She covered her eyes not only in fear that they would be ripped from her body or turned about inside her head, but from the nervousness of not knowing what was in the air around her. She longed for the original rush of excitement and power, both exhilarating and uncomfortable.

Finally, the two stopped, feet firmly on the ground and spinning slowly to a halt. Adela opened her eyes, first laying them on Milo, who had let go of her hand and was now clutching his stomach. Milo doubled over on the paved brick of the ground below them. He would be groggy and nauseated from the journey, much as she had been so many times before. She paused.

*Brick?*

They were in a small, dark alleyway, with quaint shopfronts peppered on both sides of the street. Bright, gleaming signs bore only symbols of what they carried within: a steaming mug for what Adela presumed was a coffee shop; an open book for what was surely a bookstore; a vine of tomatoes and a bunch of bananas on a store the citizens would surely swarm on Sunday mornings, packing their shopping baskets with goodies for the rest of the week.

The air filled with a smokiness that Adela had smelled only seconds before, during her journey. Ahead of her, the brick street was riddled with nooks and crannies within which rodents had taken up residence. From a nearby grate, a small mouse scurried across the road heading for the market. It paused, taking in Adela's shadow, before completing its journey and squeezing its furry body into a hole in the closed door.

Around her, angry shouts and classical music floated down on the air with the lightness of a feather floating among treetops. It was cold. Adela shivered as icy rain fell all around them.

This was not Western Wilerea.

Kneeling on the ground while Milo composed himself, she stowed the ivory box in Clara's satchel. Turning over the brooch in her hand, Adela only now noticed a faded inscription that had been carved inside.

*To Clarissa—*
*Yours, George*

Adela turned the brooch over, looking for even more clues as to its origin but finding nothing. Beside her, Milo let out another groan, this one stronger and more robust. He was getting better.

"We should try to figure out where this came from," she said, holding the brooch up so Milo could see it.

"What? We should go home, Adela," he replied, pushing up on his palms so he could kneel alongside her.

"There's a reason my mother told me to take that box," she started, "and a reason this brooch was in there." She sighed. "I need to find my grandmother so I can help my mother. And she must have been here. This place is important to her, and I need to find out why." She ran her thumb over the brooch and, maintaining her grasp on it, pinned it to the inside of her sweater, facing inward so it could keep contact with her skin.

"Where should we go?"

Milo rose to stand beside her. They both looked in opposite directions. On the right was a series of homes, standing side by side like soldiers. The lights were on in a few rooms, but otherwise, the street was filled with a cacophony of noises, proof that life continued on here, even after the events of the Last Sun.

Adela peered over Milo's shoulder, to the left, where a stone fountain capped the end of the street, in turn snaking to what appeared to be a paved courtyard. Beyond that, Adela could not see any farther, as the alleyway continued to narrow until she could no longer peer into any corner without needing a light source.

The two locked eyes and determined to walk left, continuing on the path of storefronts that lined the streets in hopes of finding a central area from which they could regroup. Or find someone to interrogate. Adela needed to know who George was, how he knew her grandmother and, more importantly, where she was.

They walked for some time, the cooing of pigeons filling the air at each section of the street. Some of the storefronts had been boarded up, closed for the evening, while others were bustling with a semblance of activity, small crowds of three or four huddled around to check out the various wares. After walking for some time and peering into shops that lined the street, Adela had nearly given up. Ahead was the fountain with a small ledge to lean on, and she determined to find some respite from the tiring walk.

Sitting, she bent forward, cradling her face with the sounds of the evening echoing around her. Milo sat beside her, trying—but failing—to comfort her.

"It's going to be okay. We're going to save your mother."

With those few words, Adela began to quietly sob. Milo must have been scared or shocked—or both—for he became instantly mute, though he fidgeted beside her.

"You don't understand," she cried, desperate to share her thoughts with someone.

"I don't understand what?"

"You have a father who loves you, who wouldn't hurt you or dare to see you sad."

"I don't understand."

"Well, of course, you wouldn't, your father is alive," Adela spat, instantly regretting her words.

Milo was unfazed, nodding while lowering his head and joining her hand with his. "Do you remember your father much?"

Adela looked forward, eyes unblinking. Of course, she did. At least, she thought she did. Fritz had been well-known in Sunseree, and he had loved her mother deeply and dearly. When Adela was born, he would attach her to his back and go into town to work, whistling as he went. Her father owned a bookshop in town, and he would often open for the day and place Adela on the floor to crawl around as he attended to customers.

As a small toddler, she was amazed by the towers of books around her, the vast volumes that dotted the shelves, some brand new and spotless while others were coated with a thin layer of dust, untouched for years. There were picture books and fairytales and children's books, too.

As Adela grew, Fritz built a Children's Corner in the lofted area upstairs, where she would hide during the day, nestled into a cozy armchair whose feathery filling had begun to escape the tufted cloth, poking Adela in her elbows and back. But she didn't mind; this was where her love of learning had grown, shaped and nurtured by the authors who lived in the shelves, calling to her and teaching her about new places. While her mother painted and her grandmother tended to her garden back home, her father had taught her the power of words.

When he died, Adela shut down, losing sight of that precious power. Closed off, she pushed away everyone around her. Like she had done with Milo many years later, when they first met.

"What are you thinking about?" Milo asked.

"Books," Adela answered.

"Books?"

"Books." In her mind's eye, she pictured one of her favorite books back home, tattered with love. The pages were well-preserved, and she took care not to bend them, as her father had taught her. How she wished she could run her hand over the embossed cover. She fought back tears, preventing Milo from seeing them.

"What's your father like?" she asked.

"My dad? He's a glass blower, and I like watching him work. But the best thing is that he makes the tastiest chocolate pie you've ever had in your life. I'll tell him to make us one when we get back to Sunseree."

"Is he kind?"

"Of course, he's kind. But he's firm. In fact, I don't think I've ever seen him cry. When he raises his voice, he apologizes right away, and he—"

"Has he ever scared you?"

"What do you mean?"

"Answer."

Milo hesitated. "What's wrong, Adela? What aren't you telling me?"

"Today, when I heard Conrad speak, he sounded... he sounded not well. It sounded like he wanted my mother to die."

The sentence hung in the air, heavy. Milo was the first to break the silence.

"That's ridiculous, of course. He loves you and your mom."

Adela broke eye contact, turning her head away from Milo and refusing to speak.

"Doesn't he?" Milo asked.

"I think he loves my mom, or used to, until recently at least. And maybe he loved me once, but he stopped a while ago."

"What do you mean a while ago?"

Adela's eyes welled up, and she brushed tears away with the back of her hand. "Conrad was nice enough at first, when my mother met him. Back before you came to Sunseree, it used to snow a lot. He had these great, big cooling trunks and he'd trek along the countryside, selling snow and ice to places that were under watch of a beating sun. He'd be gone for months at a time and bring back small tokens from his travels. Sometimes a handwoven plush toy, more often books. I pored over the books every evening, and he and Mama would come tuck me in at night, and everything felt right."

She didn't know if she should continue her story because, as she told it, anger rose inside her, her stomach and chest tightening with indifference.

"And then?"

"And then," Adela continued, "he took a trip far, far away. And he wouldn't say where. And when he returned, he was still Conrad, but he was different. Mean."

She kicked at the base of the fountain, allowing herself to lean backward ever so slightly, her head resting against the smooth stone behind her.

"Mean how?"

"It doesn't matter how. What matters is that everything is his fault."

"What do you mean?"

"Don't you see? He became cruel, and I stopped wanting to be home. And I ran into the woods time and time again, sitting among the insects going about their days. And one day I ran into someone, and they showed me how I could escape." Adela lowered her gaze.

"Is that how you received your powers?" Milo asked softly.

"I think so. But it's also when the Last Sun began."

"Why?"

"I don't know," Adela admitted, "but it ruined the entire world. And it was my fault. Conrad's fault, too."

"I don't think you can blame it on—"

"I knew you wouldn't be on my side," Adela scoffed, crossing her arms across her chest.

"I *am* on your side. I just think you need to approach this logically and think through the consequences of your actions."

"I don't understand the consequences of my actions? My mother is lying in a bed, unable to move, while *he* is plotting against her life, all because I left. All because I left her." Adela stood now, facing the fountain, fists clenched in fury at Milo's callous response. She had told him her story, she had spilled her emotions into the night, expecting comfort or empathy. Instead, he had told her she was confused. White rage overtook her vision.

Milo began to muster a response as he remained seated, likely trying to compose his balance after the journey. But Adela was not paying attention. Instead, by a stroke of luck, she had begun to piece this world together.

The fountain portrayed a strange scene. Amid the tiered steps of the fountain, where water spilled over the sides, was a long trunk in the middle. It took the shape of a barren tree, the top of which began to twist and curve outward, branches turning out into the sky. Small stone leaves dotted the branches, harkening a spring renewal that felt so distant in this wintry weather.

But the most curious part of all was the imprint of two snakes, intertwined. Each snake had a lithe, curved body, stone scales textured and catching the light from the lampposts on the street corners next to Adela. Their stone eyes looked toward the heavens, unblinking. From here, Adela could tell this was the same snake design on the brooch in her grandmother's box.

*But what does it mean?*

At this point, Milo stopped talking.

"What is it?"

"There's something about this fountain," she answered.

"It's just a regular fountain."

"No, it's not."

She walked over, climbing onto the stone ledge and dropping into the cool water below to get closer to the depiction that had been carved into the stone. The water was refreshing and Adela chuckled, realizing it was the first bath she had had in a long while. Her hair was caked with dirt from her graveyard escape, and the icy falling snow only served to further ingrain the granules into her hair. It would take forever to wash out. As she stood in the water, it turned brown, softly taking on the grime of the last few days.

Milo stepped in after her and they stood, shoulder to shoulder, looking at the snakes.

"There's something here," Adela murmured, brushing her hand against the fountain as water rushed from above. She ran her fingers over the snake's eyes and the eyeball slowly gave, depressing into the wall.

*Why would the fountain have a section that could be pressed?*

Curiosity and courage growing, she could not resist the urge to continue her investigation and so, she pressed down with all her remaining strength.

A deep mechanical grumbling sounded from within the fountain, and Adela grabbed Milo and quickly climbed back on the ledge to safety. She had made it in time. Within moments, the water commenced draining into a hidden grate. Where the water had, only moments ago, pooled at their feet, a trapdoor had now revealed itself, a small, rounded handle embedded into the stone around which a child's hand could naturally fit to grasp and pull.

Adela scrambled forward on all fours and pulled.

"Help me, please," she called out as Milo ran to her, grabbing onto the handle and pulling with his remaining strength.

It worked. The trapdoor opened and revealed a small stone staircase below. Adela took the first step forward, lowering herself into the ground, unsure where this was taking her but knowing in her gut that it had something to do with her grandmother. She turned, preparing to scold Milo for not hurrying after her, only to realize that he was fast on her heels, lowering himself into the ground. The stone here was musty, and the corridor was dark, lit only by a single source farther down the small tunnel beneath the trapdoor.

"We should close the door," she whispered. "So nobody can follow us."

Milo laughed nervously. "Who would follow us?" he asked but obliged.

On the other end of the trapdoor was an identical and opposite pull handle, and he pulled the door closed, gravity working in his favor while Adela protected him from tumbling down the stairs. Though it was a short fall, it would surely be a painful one. Out of the corner of her eye, the snake symbol again tested her theory; its eyes depressed into the wall and, nearly at once, the fountain filled up again with a rush of water. Small drops of water crept through the corners of the trapdoor, and she knew their tracks would be covered. Nodding to Milo, she descended into darkness.

From outside, a single peregrine falcon sat perched on a lamppost, feasting on a dove while it watched the two go farther into the earth.

Down, down, down.

Only two pairs of footsteps reverberated through the damp darkness, punctuated by the dripping of fountain water around them. Adela's nose twitched from the smell prevalent here, a musty scent that reminded her of the rotting vegetables her grandmother would scatter in her garden as fertilizer. Behind her, Milo's breathing was becoming increasingly loud, and she grew annoyed at the sound, jerking her out of her thoughts.

"Can you stop that?" she snapped, skipping over a puddle in their path.

"Stop what?"

"Your breathing. I can't hear myself think."

"I can't stop breathing, Adela," Milo exclaimed incredulously.

The two continued on. The journey in front was singular with no forking paths in sight. At times, the main path curved or looped around, seemingly taking them in a zigzagging motion farther underground. The walls were lined with thick gray stone, cool and wet to the touch.

Occasionally, they stumbled upon a mischief of mice huddled against a corner and feasting on slippery worms or the fungi that formed at the base of the stones. Their fervent squeaks sent shivers up Adela's spine, but she continued on, watching her step for any underground holes. She feared she would not return if she fell in.

Milo had taken it upon himself to stretch his arms out, letting his fingertips brush the sides of the corridor they were traversing. Every so often, he would let out a small yelp or groan as his fingers brushed against something gross that had lodged itself into the stone's crevices. He tripped on a small piece of string suspended a few inches above the ground and, by the force of propulsion, found himself only feet behind Adela.

She turned around, raising her eyebrows at his clumsiness, while he cleared his throat and promptly attempted to change the course of conversation.

"What's it like?"

"What's what like?" Adela answered.

"Traveling. Doing whatever it is that you do."

The scene around them began to change, muted paint splattered on the stone walls while the air became warmer and drier, allowing the damp coldness to slowly dissipate.

Adela continued on, leading the way. "You just did it with me."

"Yeah, but..." He sighed. "But you've been doing it longer. And this last time, you were away for days. Weren't you scared?"

Adela thought for a moment, remembering her encounters with Clara, Father Vodnik, the Queen and her guards, and the babies. She never yearned for home. More than anything, she yearned to be free and rid of the feelings that home meant for her. She enjoyed escaping the world from which she came. Most of all, she missed her mother.

Her mother. They needed to keep going.

"I wasn't scared," she finally answered.

"Really?"

"Really," Adela lied.

"What was it like being dead?"

"I wasn't dead."

"But how did you escape? Did you use your powers?"

Adela stopped in her tracks, allowing Milo to catch up. He nearly bumped into her. She hadn't thought about that, that she had become dependent on her abilities, allowing them to take her from place to place, letting her close her eyes and be transported by simply holding onto an idea. But in that moment, the moment when she needed to escape to save her life, her powers had failed her. The thought gave her pause and threatened to spin knots in her stomach. She needed to be more prepared next time.

"Adela?"

"I'm thinking."

Milo shook her shoulder, his movements becoming frantic. "Adela!" he hissed.

"What is—"

But she didn't need to finish the question, and Milo didn't need to answer it. In front of them, a small stone door filled the width of the wall. From the cracks under the door, a soft yellow light spilled out, stretching all the way down the length of the hallway to touch the tops of their shoes.

"Should we knock?"

"Shh," Adela hissed, straining her ears to any sound coming from behind the door. She could make out a sort of humming, low and deep, but could not determine if it originated from a living, or non-living, entity.

What joined the humming was a scent that wafted under the crack in the door and climbed up to reach Adela's nose. The smell of food: roasted chicken and mashed potatoes, and a savory gravy that made Adela salivate. In response, her stomach began to speak to her, calling out for sustenance.

Summoned by the smells within and pushed forward by her grumbling stomach, she took five quick strides to the door and, before Milo could stop her, knocked.

The humming stopped. At once, the light under the door was snuffed out and a small panel opened, just above Adela's head. A face poked through, looking around until spotting Milo a few feet ahead.

"Now, how did you manage to knock on the door from way back there?" the voice asked.

"I'm down here," Adela answered, as the face finally locked eyes with her own.

It was the most peculiar thing. The person at the door towered over her, but his face was child-like. Long, black hair spilled over his ears and his eyes were a light brown, almost gold when seen by the light of the room. He had a crooked nose that curved like a winding path over his face, and small, thin lips. Right under his left nostril was a small dark brown beauty mark. He looked like all the adults Adela had known, but when he finally smiled at her, baby teeth filled his mouth.

"Who sent you two here?"

"Where is *here*?" Adela returned the question.

"You don't know where you are? This is the Forgotten City."

"Forgotten City? I've never heard of it."

"Well, unless you have, it's no wonder you haven't. That's why it's forgotten."

"I don't quite understand," Adela admitted as Milo slowly made his way to her side. With the small panel open, the food cooking inside met her nostrils and she became light-headed. "Can you please let us in? I haven't eaten in days and whatever you're cooking in there smells delicious."

"I *could* let you in. But you haven't given me the secret password."

"The secret password?" Adela gasped. "How would I ever know what the secret password is?"

The person paused, looking up at the ceiling in thought, and spoke:

"What lies within is forgotten,

Dead and atrophied, downright rotten.

There are secrets here that have been buried,
Love unreturned and justice miscarried.
You may not like what you find inside,
But that's for you—well, you two—to decide.
So if the password is truly what you both seek,
Then look up to the stars and see what to speak."

Adela looked at Milo, confused and unsure what to do next. She shrugged and turned back to the figure at the door, but he was still looking up at the ceiling. Following his gaze, she let out a small gasp. In the ceiling were small, rounded holes, allowing for the moonlight above to spread downward. While it was dark, no light shone through, but the moonlight revealed a phrase meticulously carved into the earthen ceiling.

"I can't make it out," she said.

"You have to try," the figure at the door responded.

Adela needed to get closer to the ceiling to see what words had found their way above, and the ceiling was just high enough where she could be boosted up to get a closer look.

"Hoist me up," she said to Milo.

"No way."

"Why not?"

"Are you crazy? Why do you want to know what's on that ceiling?"

"So we can go inside." She motioned over to the door. "I need to see what's in there."

"And why do you care what's in there?"

"It has something to do with my grandmother. I just know it."

"This feels like a silly treasure hunt. Just because you found a snake symbol on the fountain doesn't mean this is the same snake symbol as the one on your grandmother's brooch."

"Really? You think this is all a coincidence? That the brooch that transported us here happened to do so somewhere that has an identical symbol, curiously hidden in a fountain, and that pushing on that symbol led us down this corridor, and that this door at the end of the corridor now has nothing to do with my grandmother?"

"Yes?"

Adela sighed, dropping to the ground in frustration. The metallic coolness of the brooch on the inside of her clothing brushed against her skin, and she thought back to her mother. Exhausted and hungry, she pleaded to Milo one last time.

"We need to follow this lead. My mother... you saw her yourself. She's not well. The whole world is not well. I have a hunch, and it's just a hunch, but I think my mother is the key to figuring out what happened. I think she's the key to ending the Last Sun. And right now, she needs us. Both of us."

Milo stared back at her, his blue eyes dark in this section of the corridor, like the deepest depths of a lake. The moles on his neck seemed, in a sense, to mirror the dotted ceiling above, and Adela brought her attention back there, to the words that seemed just out of reach.

"Not to mention," she added, "I'm sure you're hungry."

That would do it. Milo always had an appetite, from his early childhood days all the way up to his last birthday celebration, when his mother had made a large chocolate walnut cake for his ten closest friends and he had gobbled the entire concoction alone in three days. By the time Adela had come around to his house for the party—to which nobody but Adela had come, as expected—there were only five thin slices to be shared among the partygoers.

Milo paused and nodded. "What do you need me to do?"

Throughout their conversation, the person at the door watched them with beady eyes, his fingers rapping against the wooden door in feigned impatience.

With minimal direction, Milo positioned himself against the wall to boost Adela up. As she stepped on his hands for the second time in the same day, she acknowledged how much easier it was to have someone traveling with her, at her side. She looked forward to their possible future travels together, exploring the world around them, perhaps with Adela's mother to chaperone.

Nearly eight feet in the air, Adela began to feel queasy; had she always been scared of heights? What if she fainted and fell? What if she simply fell? She had to act quickly or risk injuring herself—and Milo—in the process, with nothing to show for it. Milo himself wobbled, his hands surely stinging from holding Adela up. She stuck one arm out at her side to regain balance, grasping the stone walls for support.

It was just there, within her fingers' reach. If she could only lean forward a bit more. She squinted, using her free hand to brush at the dirt and clearly make out the scratches in the stone. One word down, then two, then... she stood on her tiptoes to gain length as Milo shouted out below. Within seconds, her net had disappeared and she was falling, arms and legs flailing and suspended in mid-air, barreling toward the ground.

Adela slammed to the ground and managed to keep her head from bouncing against the hard surface, winter clothes cushioning much of her fall. Her tailbone stung, and she had landed on her wrist in a strange way. She was certain it was sprained as it limply hung from her arm. Her elbows were scuffed, pin drops of blood forming where she had braced for impact.

Around her, underground creatures scurried away from the commotion. House mice with their long, pink tails racing with spindly centipedes and shiny, brown cockroaches that swept the dirt floor with their antennae.

"Wow, that looked like it hurt!" the boy behind the door called out.

Adela winced, breathing in and out to make sure none of her ribs were broken or bruised. For the time being, she seemed to be alright. Milo knelt to offer her a hand, apologizing profusely for letting her drop. She brushed off the dust from her clothes, knowing the action was futile since she was coated in a thick layer of grime from her earlier escape.

"It's fine," she said, slapping Milo's hand away as he tried to help her.

"Maybe we should turn back," Milo suggested, eyes drifting to the area where he had seen Adela attach the brooch. "Maybe this was too much, too quickly."

"Maybe."

"Maybe if we return back home, things will be better. Maybe your mother will be awake again, and you can go see her, and everything will be back to how it was before."

"Maybe," Adela lied.

"And—and maybe the Last Sun isn't so bad. You know? Or maybe the sun will come back one day, and all it needed was a break from everything. We all need a break from life sometimes!" Milo began walking backward, in the direction from which they had entered the long, winding corridor.

"Maybe."

"Adela? Are you coming?"

Adela turned toward the door, watching the figure intently. He had locked eyes with her, a sly smile on his face, as if waiting for her to say something.

She obliged.

"What did you mean when you said we might not like what we see inside?"

"Did I say that?"

"In your poem, you did."

"Oh, that's just an old poem. It doesn't mean anything." His eyes twinkled.

"Do you know George?"

"Hmm," the figure mused, tapping a stubby finger on his chin, "that name might ring a bell."

"Is George there?"

"What are you afraid of finding in here?"

"I'm not afraid," Adela admitted, her heart beating faster.

Beyond that door, she hoped to find the answers to the questions she was seeking. Behind that door, she would understand the mystery of the brooch and be one step closer to reaching her grandmother. To figuring out the mystery that had plagued Sunseree and its surrounding towns and cities for months now. Milo would be nervous—he had a propensity for that—but she would need to muster up enough courage for both of them.

She could either follow him or go through the door. She had, after all, managed to read the entirety of the words carved into the stone.

"*Inter spem et metum*," she said.

A pause, and then the person disappeared. Seconds later, the sound of a door unlatching bounced off the stone and dirt.

"Come in."

# THIRTEEN

# NINE

———

Adela could not have been prepared for what she saw next. She stepped into a small stone enclave about seven feet tall and lit from within by a large hearth in the corner of the room, with candles placed about the wall. From this corner she'd smelled the delicious feast from before, and it took every bit of strength to keep from running over and gobbling all the food up. Adela began to salivate and quickly swallowed for fear of drooling all over the stone floor like a crazed animal.

Around the room, keepsakes dotted the walls. Broken picture frames were cobbled together with string, pencil drawings and finger paint masterpieces featured within. The walls were adorned with scraps of metal, pages from books, and dried plants pinned up with rusted nails. On one shelf was a robust collection of rocks and gemstones, seemingly unimportant and mundane to the untrained eye, but Adela assumed they held sentimental meaning.

In the same vein, the rough stone walls were sanded and smoothed, childlike nicknames spelled out with chubby fingers: *Tumble, Ember, Cook,* and *Little Mouse* forever etched into the walls. A rug covered the floor haphazardly, its colors undistinguishable due to the dirt on its surface. It was now a permanent shade of brown.

The room was lit with candles, their bases shoved into the nooks of the stone wall; they were hooked up to a vast system of strings and metal caps. She traced the path of the strings to a small device near the front door, where they were affixed. After some contemplation, she realized a simple tug would set off all of the metal caps to come barreling down, spurred on by the force of gravity to extinguish the candles.

Before she had a chance to open her mouth to ask a question, the figure at the door provided her the answer.

"It's to make the room dark, all at once. In case we have unwanted visitors."

"Unwanted?"

"Sure, not everyone who comes across our door has good intentions. We stay hidden from the outside world but only mostly. We need to leave to scavenge for food or medical supplies here and there. If we're followed and if we're found out, well, that's the best way to alert everyone to danger. Turn off all the lights in the complex and all the kids know to stay silent. We've been lucky so far. We've only had three visitors—and you, of course. They usually are the kind that are dazed, out and about after a night of overconsumption. They become confused, unsure how they found their way down here, and stumble their way back up to the overworld," he said, chuckling.

"How can you tell if someone is coming?"

"Your friend," he said and motioned to Milo, who was poised above the stove and stopped in his tracks, "tripped over a piece of wire on the way here. That wire is rigged up to a system of signals up there." He pointed above the door. "Those signals alert me to the fact that someone is in the corridors. And, of course, I have a little keyhole in the door to see who's coming."

"Couldn't an animal trip the wire?"

"Oh, no, not any animals down here. Unless they grew seven inches tall overnight. We've had the occasional fat cat venture down here, excited by the prospect of mice to feast on. We usually take them in, until they sneak out of a hole in the wall and leave us for good."

"How come you didn't turn the lights off when we approached? We saw the lights from under the door."

"I watched you two come down the path. You seemed non-threatening. Not to mention, we never turn children away." He walked over to the stove, gently elbowing Milo out of the way and using a bent and stained metal spoon to slurp up the gravy that was simmering above the fire. "Almost done."

Adela's head spun, though, and she needed a place to sit. Overwhelmed by this new place, and starving for sustenance to warm her belly, she carefully eyed the room, finding a small bundle of pillows and blankets. Laboring toward them, she sank down, letting the scratchy warmth envelop her. She cradled her face in her hand and let out a low, slow sigh.

"Is everything okay?" the person asked.

"Everything is not okay," she admitted. "I don't know who you are. I don't know where I am." She paused. "Not only that, I have no idea *when* I am." Out of the corner of her eye, the person turned his head, his attention grabbed by the choice of words. Adela had said too much.

"Well," he began, "I'm Nine."

"Nine?"

He laughed and added, "I'm the youngest of nine. Or was, at least."

"What do you mean?"

Nine shook his head. "That's a story for a different time. I told you who I am. Who are you?"

"My name is Adela."

"That's a nice name. Can I call you Del?"

"I guess so?"

"And what's this one's name?" He jerked his thumb in the direction of Milo, who had taken it upon himself to dig through a trio of wicker baskets shoved into a corner. He froze, realizing he had been caught again.

Nine let out a loud, barking laugh, nearly doubling over from the sound. "When you live with kids, you start to grow eyes on the back of your head," he said and winked at Adela.

Adela let out a small laugh, only now realizing that Nine had a soft tone to his voice, still high-pitched and not the deeper voice of a boy who had gone through puberty. She was increasingly curious about this underground home, Nine's presence here, and what this all meant in the context of the brooch and her grandmother.

"That's Milo," Adela answered.

Nine nodded. "So how did you two find this place? You haven't answered my earlier question."

"You wouldn't believe me if I told you," she sighed. "The story is a little complicated. And weird."

"You'd be surprised how many kids find their way here. I bet your story isn't any more complicated than theirs."

Shouts erupted from just behind them, locked away behind another door. This one was bolted shut, with three locks at the bottom and five others inching their way up to the top. There was a clamor and commotion behind the door, and Adela's imagination swirled, trying to figure out who—or what—was on the other side.

*Was George there?*

"Did you say this was a city?"

"I tell you what," Nine responded. "If you tell me how you found this place," he said, motioning around his homely surroundings, "I'll tell you all you want to know about it. How's that? Deal?"

Adela pursed her lips. Milo was in the corner, waving his arms back and forth behind Nine's back, trying to catch Adela's attention. He kept mouthing "no" and motioned over to the door with his round head, indicating that he wanted to leave. Clearly, he felt uncomfortable. Maybe he didn't trust Nine. Or maybe he didn't want to spill the secrets about how they found their way here.

But Nine teemed with a childish innocence, and Adela was certain he wouldn't harm them.

"Deal. But first," she said, smiling shyly, "I'm starving. May I have something to eat?"

Nine turned back to the stove, lifting the food off the fire as he sighed. "I didn't really account for any visitors, but given the circumstances, I don't see why not. You're all skin and bones, either way."

He grabbed a small bowl, loading it with mashed potatoes and bits of meat before pouring on gravy at the end. The plate quickly transformed into a stew of sorts, the starchy potatoes acting like a bowl within a bowl, holding the savory goodness of the remaining ingredients within.

Adela's stomach again growled in anticipation as she reached out with both hands for the meal. Nine turned to grab a spoon, but Adela had already started eating with her fingers, sucking out the bits of potato that had lodged under her nails and getting the taste of dirt as well. But she didn't care; she was ravenous.

"Wow, you really were hungry."

"This is delicious," Adela murmured, spitting out bits of precious food while she talked.

Nine laughed as, within minutes, Adela had finished the plate of food. She walked to the corner of the room and set the bowl down on a counter before turning back to Nine. "So, you want to know how we found this place?"

"I do," Nine replied, showing his full set of baby teeth as he grinned.

"It's a long story."

"I don't mind. I like long stories."

And so Adela—with scattered interruptions from Milo—regaled Nine with the story of how they had come here. She started with the story of Alby, the Fox and then described the beginning of the Last Sun. She told tall tales of her adventures testing her abilities, which bemused Milo as well. And finally she dove into the story of her journey in Nuimtree.

"He had hundreds of teapots!" she whispered, gesturing with her hands. "And he used these teapots to capture people's souls, one by one. He tried to capture mine, too. That's what Clara—I mean, my grandmother—told me."

"Creepy," Milo said, grimacing.

"That's not *creepy*, Milo," Adela said. "It's *horrifying*."

She continued on, telling the story to both Nine and Milo, who had not yet joined her on this leg of the journey. She detailed how she had escaped the grave, her heart pounding from the unparalleled fear of dying; she replayed the scene of finding her mother; and she detailed how she had come across the brooch and escaped with Milo, aiming to find the person who had gifted it to her grandmother. And last, she detailed how they came here. How they followed the serpents underground.

"And that's all of it," she finished.

"Wow. What an adventure!" Nine exclaimed, clapping his hands together.

"It is, I'd like to think."

"I just have one question."

"What's that?"

"Why are you here?" Nine asked, a smile playing on his lips.

"I told you why. My mother needs help."

"But why do you think *this* is the place to get her help?"

"I didn't think I was going to be here. I thought I was going to Western Wilerea."

"Western Wilerea? Why?"

"My grandmother lives there. She would know how to help." Adela grabbed at her satchel and pulled out the jar into which she had scraped the dregs of the mug only hours beforehand. "She knows all about herbs and plants. She would be able to identify what this is and how to help."

"What is that?" Nine asked, reaching out for the jar.

"No," Adela said, turning her body to protect the contents, and shuffling the fragile container back in her satchel, tucking it under heavy pieces of clothing. "You never told me what this place is," she accused. "A deal's a deal, Nine."

He laughed, running his hand through his black hair and showing those teeth again. Adela was uncomfortable, acid building up in her throat from the food she had gulped down only moments ago but, too, from the knowledge that something was not quite right. She couldn't quite tell how old Nine was, but he had the build of an adult. He was taller than Adela and Milo and muscular, though his stubby fingers and childish features betrayed him. Most notably, his teeth had not yet fallen out, so he must have been younger than her. The situation was altogether strange.

"It's probably better if I show you," Nine said, making his way to the door where Adela had heard the commotion before. One by one, he unlatched the locks, starting at the bottom and making his way up. When he was finished, Adela realized there wasn't a doorknob.

How would they get through?

Her question was immediately answered, as Nine rapped a series of melodic knocks on the door.

"Huh?" a small, squeaking voice said from beyond.

Milo grabbed Adela's arm in surprise, and the two stood side by side, peering past Nine's shoulder.

"*Inter spem et metum,*" Nine answered, repeating the phrase that had opened the first door.

Within seconds, a click sounded out and the door creaked open, slow as honey crawling down the sides of a jar. Nine turned to face Adela and stretched his arm out, motioning for them to take the first steps across the threshold. Slowly, they stepped forward, hand in hand.

A grand, cavernous space stretched out as far as Adela's eyes could see: deep earthy colors permeated with crimson, ambers, and golds. The lighting system here was like the one in the enclave they now stepped out of, only on a grander scale altogether. Candles rose from the ground, situated atop metal candelabras. They poked out of metal grommets in chandeliers that hung from the vast ceiling, which appeared to be nearly twice as tall as the previous room, though this was an illusion brought on by the fact that the entire room seemed to be set into the ground by nearly eight feet. Adela marveled at this aspect of the room where they stood, flabbergasted and wondering how the peculiar feature came to be.

Nine interrupted, anticipating the question bouncing about in Adela's head. "It took us months to carve out the bits of stone, which we then used to create our homes. Of course, we also had some special help," he chuckled.

The rambling space featured a small circular pit in the center, with stone benches that fit the curves of the area built into the ground. To prevent the discomfort that Adela assumed would be prevalent with stone, knit pillows and chunky blankets were thrown around the space to protect bony knees and sore backs.

The colors were grand: deep vermillion, shifting maroon, and bright coral, all featured together in loose knits. At the center of the space was another stone pit, covered over by a sheath of semi-circular metal to prevent anyone from accidentally falling in, unwittingly sinking to the depths of the earth. To the left of the pit was a small garden, tended to by a slight woman with frizzy copper hair. She wore overalls, slightly dirty, with a frayed t-shirt on top. The garden she tended to was smaller than Adela's mother's and certainly her grandmother's, but it was mighty.

Tomato vines spiraled up a makeshift ladder that led to a small balcony. Alongside the tomato plants were even more tomato plants, albeit younger, and beside those seedlings were the leaves of a potato plant, insulated from the world by wire mesh that directed it, telling it in which direction to grow. This small garden was a marvel, and Adela wondered how the plants were able to get sunlight in a place so far underground.

As if reading her mind, Nine answered, "At night, the place lights up with these phosphorescent fungi. It looks like mold, really, but we like to pretend it's something different for our own sanity. It's like magic. But the real special part is what's right *behind* the garden. Come, follow me!"

He set off running in the direction of the garden, with Adela scurrying behind him and Milo behind her. Finally, they caught up with Nine, just as he had begun to strike up a conversation with the gardener. The gardener wiped her brow of sweat, brushing dirt along her forehead in the process, and turned to smile at Adela with a gloved hand as an offering.

There they were again. The baby teeth. The sight of them sent shivers up her spine, but Adela did not want to be rude, so she clenched her own teeth and smiled.

"Hi," the girl said, her voice soft and melodic. "My name is Bud."

"Bud? Like the bud of a plant?

She laughed. "Yes, just like that."

"This is Del," Nine said, trying to move the conversation along. "Bud, can I take our guests back there?" He motioned with his head to an area just behind the garden, a large boulder blocking any potential view that Adela could spoil. "I want to show them around. They might be staying a while," he said and smiled at Adela.

"I'm not—" Adela started to reply before Bud cut in.

"Sure thing! It was great to meet you, Del, but I better get back to these guys," she said, laughing and kneeling back down to dig in the dirt.

"Nice to meet you too," Adela replied, as Nine grabbed her arm and pulled her along. Milo scurried behind, trying desperately to keep up.

"Check this out," Nine said, climbing over a large boulder and hoisting Adela up to join him.

Her wrist still hurt from the fall, and her ribs from days prior, when she had slammed into Milo. Adela winced at the pain, biting her lip in response. But the pain would be worth it, for an otherworldly, luminescent lake stretched out in front of her.

"Isn't it amazing? A bona-fide underground lake. I've never seen anything like it in my life! Have you?"

"I have," Adela admitted, remembering the murky, underground lake in the Curling Cave. "But this is far more beautiful. What's in it?" She crouched low to the ground, willing herself to not touch the water, for she didn't yet know what was inside.

"Nobody knows. It's the same stuff that glows on the wall. Either way, Bud uses it to water the plants. We use it to shower. And we use it as our drinking water, too."

"You use it for your drinking water? Isn't that dangerous?"

"How so?"

"Well, you don't know what's in it, for starters."

"But it's water," Nine replied, cocking his head to the side in amusement. Adela was reminded once more that he, and Bud, seemed to be much younger than they appeared. Nine's tour had spurred more questions than it had answered.

"You still didn't answer—"

The tinny tones of a bell sounded from the direction of Bud's makeshift garden.

"Come on, there's still so much for you to see!" Nine exclaimed, clamoring once more over the damp stones and the large boulder blocking the entrance to the watery depths behind them. Adela rolled her eyes but followed behind, checking to make sure Milo was still with her. She needed to learn more about this place. About its people.

As they exited the small rocky section, Adela found that more people had gathered in the center of the room. Nine was headed in that direction and peered over at her, smiling.

She slowly walked behind, taking the opportunity to explore her setting without excited interruption.

Beyond Bud's garden was a stone building, overgrown by ivy and weeds. Every few feet were thick columns, the result of stone bricks stacked one atop the other. Improvised chalkboard and cloth signs were suspended between every two columns of the building, a marketplace of sorts. One sign read *Tinker's Things*, with a hand-drawn depiction of a wrench alongside the shop's name. On the surface of the table were the very stone bricks that the shop was made of, bits of cloth, ceramic garden pots, rusted metal pans and other bits of mangled cutlery, as well as cobbled-together candelabras. Adela picked up a smaller sign, propped up on the table, and read it aloud.

"Welcome to Tinker's Things!

I sell all sorts o' things for your household projects.

Need pots for cookin'? I got 'em!

Need candles for seein'? I got 'em!

Need bread for eatin'?

Sorry, you'll need to go next door for that.

Ask about my bartering system."

Adela covered her mouth with her hand, stifling a laugh. She continued to move along the line of storefronts, which were by now abandoned, their owners rushing to the center of the room where Nine stood watch. Next door to Tinker's Things was a bakery, the smell of fresh bread wafting through the air. Its sign read *Cook's Concoctions* and she closed her eyes, taking in the scents and sounds, the commotion around her. Someone bumped into her on their way to the center of the room and apologized, but Adela continued to stand in place, her senses overloaded, hairs on her arms standing vertically as her frozen hair pushed against her cheek.

"Adela?" Milo's soft voice called out. "I think we should lea—"

A shrill whistle sounded and everything fell quiet. Even Milo and Adela quieted down, their attention stolen by the noise, which had come from Nine. He motioned for them, and they cautiously walked over to the pit, all eyes on the strangers.

"Folks, I have two special guests here. This is Del and Milo."

Cheers erupted, with whooping calls of "welcome" and "glad you're here!" Beaming faces looked back at Adela, and for a moment, she considered taking Nine up on his offer to stay here.

"They'll be staying with us for a while," Nine continued.

But her mother needed her. "Actually—" Adela tried to interrupt, only to be steamrolled by Nine, who clearly had set an agenda for the impromptu meeting. He would not be interrupted.

"First agenda item for the day, we need to come up with nicknames for Adela and Milo. Talk with them, see what they like and report back at tonight's meeting with some suggestions. I personally like Del, but this is a democracy, so we'll vote on it tonight. Second item on our agenda, somebody left the fountain door open again last night. This needs to be nipped in the bud," he said and glanced over at Bud. "Sorry, no pun intended. We can't risk anyone finding out about this place. You all know this."

The group collectively nodded, each making eye contact with one another in a futile effort to visually identify the culprit.

"And finally," Nine concluded, "we need four volunteers for tonight's expedition to Old Kitfalls. It will be more dangerous than usual due to the weather conditions and rampant troll activity, but we need more supplies. If you're interested, come see me. Anyone have anything else they wish to say?"

"I do." Adela bravely stood up, and everyone turned to look at her, mouths agape with tiny teeth.

"Del?"

"I'm looking for someone, and hope you all—anyone—here can help. He may go by George. Or maybe he used to go by George. I need to find him."

Silence filled the space like air filling a balloon, when a voice called out from the corner of the room. It echoed.

"Yes?"

A shadowy figure stood under an archway, arms crossed and leaning against the stone bricks.

Adela could not make out the figure's face, and she squinted and brought her hand to her forehead, attempting to focus her vision. "Are you George?"

"Who's asking?" He strode over, slowly revealing his features.

Unlike the others in the community, George appeared to be a real adult. His teeth had yellowed with age, and one chipped tooth had begun to blacken, its nerves likely dead from whatever violent calamity had befallen his mouth. One of his eyes was a piercing gray and the other hidden by a cloth patch, held in place by an elastic that stretched over his brassy, blond hair. He strode over to Adela and spoke, the sting of his breath slapping her in the face.

"I asked a question. If you're looking for me, I think you'd best answer," he said, though his presence was calm.

"I'm sorry. I didn't think I would actually find you. Can we talk in private?"

He gritted his teeth and directed his attention to Nine. "Has this meeting concluded?"

"Y-Yes, George. Meeting concluded."

In unison, the group of adult-children chanted, "*Inter spem et metum*," that phrase Adela had heard so many times by now, and scurried off in varying directions, none lingering behind to talk to Nine about his earlier proposition.

Nine sighed and turned to George. "Looks like it's just me and you tonight."

"I'll go," Adela volunteered. "Milo, too. We'll both go."

Milo pulled at Adela's sleeves, his breath hot on the nape of her neck. "Adela, are you sure about this? We don't know anything about where we're going. We don't even know these people."

But Adela ignored his pleas and sauntered closer to the two figures standing by the fire pit. Their faces were illuminated by the fire's glow, and the warmth seemed to soften their features somewhat, as if the embers melted away the stress and anxiety of the day.

"It's a dangerous journey," George began. "You may not come back alive."

"That's a risk I'll take right now," Adela said. She gulped, wondering if she was signing her own—and Milo's—death certificate. "But I need to talk to you."

George huffed again, turning on his heel to avoid Adela's requests. "We leave in twenty minutes," he called into the air, walking away from the group.

Nine groaned. "What did you do?" He threw his hands up in the air and filled his cheeks with air, slowly releasing it with a hiss. "Now I need to get you ready and I don't have the time." He thought for a moment, his eyes settling on the marketplace Adela had briefly toured earlier. "I know! Hurry and keep up."

He leapt up on the benches and raced over to one of the shops that Adela had not yet seen, Adela and Milo following quickly behind like chicks following a mama hen.

Manning the table were two young girls, likely twins. The first had braids and glasses, her bare feet propped up on the table while she read a book that was falling apart at the seams. The other girl was crouched low to the ground, rummaging around in a small storage area under the table. Nine gently knocked on the table and the second girl peered up over the edge of the table and smiled. She stood up and straightened herself out, dusting off her pants. "What can I do for you, Nine?"

"Hey, Rough. Hey, Tumble." The girl reading the book grunted a response, but Nine continued, "Listen, we have a small problem. Del and Milo are going to join us on the expedition tonight, but they have no gear. Care to help them out a little bit?"

"I mean, sure, I can set them up with a barter line," Rough began.

"No, no," Nine interrupted, "we don't have time to set up a barter line. They're heading out in less than fifteen minutes. Just let me cover the cost of supplies."

"Are you sure, Nine?"

"Yes, yes, I'm sure. They'll need a holster, some slingshots and stones, and goggles too. Throw in some gloves while you're at it. They'll need those. And a canister for water. Actually, if you don't mind too much, I'll take those canisters off your hands and be right back."

Nine rushed on, canisters cradled in his arms, and Adela stayed behind, staring at Rough's face while she compiled the remaining materials. She towered over Adela and had a smattering of freckles over her nose, reddish-brown in color. Her hair was loosely braided and knotted at the end in lieu of a hair tie. Her fingers moved deftly as she popped down to find the requested items and then back up to test out their individual endurance.

Finally, she said, "Why are you staring at me?"

"Oh, I'm sorry, it's just—I've never met people like you all."

"Us *all*? What is that supposed to mean?"

"Well, you know."

"No, I don't," Rough scoffed, face turning a ruby red. "Do you mean how we look?"

"Yes. I mean, no. I mean—"

But before she could further dance around the topic, Nine returned, a wide grin on his face. In his hands he held small brown cubes and both canisters, overfilled with water from the nearby lake. "These will get us through the night!" he exclaimed.

"What are those?" Adela asked, reaching out to pick one of the cubes up.

"Try it!"

"Try it?"

"Yes, pop it in your mouth."

Adela hesitated, but her curiosity got the best of her. She placed the cube on her tongue and was immediately hit with a strong flavor: a blend of the salty sting of fresh cheese, the warm doughiness of potatoes, and the fragrant bitterness of green onions.

"Is that?"

"Yes! Cheese dumplings! Isn't it delicious?"

"My grandfather made these all the time. He would travel to Brynd Fields just to get this cheese. It looked much different than this, though, that's for sure."

Nine let out a small laugh and offered one of the cubes to Milo, who waved his hand in refusal. Nine shrugged, taking one of the cubes and placing it behind his teeth as he spoke.

"Isn't it amazing?" Nine said, sucking on the treat. "Brew over there has been messing about with some of the strange plants and fungi in this area and working with Cook on a few recipes. They're perfect little bites of sustenance, enough to get you through a longer journey like ours. You know," he said, slightly ashamed, "we don't always have the luxury of real food. That's why we go on these supply runs. Thank goodness Bud came by recently too. Otherwise we'd really be lost. Is that all done?" He turned toward Rough, who nodded while she continued to glare at Adela.

"That'll be seventeen Tinkers."

"Oh, ahh... I don't *have* seventeen Tinkers."

"What *do* you have, Nine?"

He dug around his pockets, coming out with small tokens, rounded coins that were fashioned out of pieces of scrap metal. They were about the same size as a human eyeball, and each had a letter stamped onto the surface. He pulled out a handful of ones with C's, a few with B's, and couple with T's on them. Some were stained certain colors.

"I have five Cooks, three Buds, and two Tinkers."

"You're short by seven."

He dug in his pockets a bit more and pulled out four more coins. "And I almost forgot. I have four Embers! Four Embers should equal out to six Tinkers. Shouldn't they?"

Rough paused, pursing her lips. She turned to her sister and kneeled to whisper in her ear, shielding her mouth from Nine, Adela, and Milo with her hand. Nine looked at his wrist, which didn't have a watch on it, and muttered to himself about the time. Finally, Rough came back up.

"Fine. Four Embers to equal six Tinkers. You're still short a Tinker."

"Thank you, Rough. I owe you one!"

He grabbed at the items on the table and threw them into Adela and Milo's arms, pushing them to a section of the area that had a smattering of up-cycled chairs thrown around. "Stay still, I'll get the holster on. You guys should start to put on the goggles and gloves. Those are important."

Adela obliged, while Nine bent down to help Milo fasten the holster to his waist.

Nine soon moved onto Adela, tugging on the buckles the holster was fashioned out of. "There, that'll do it," he announced, clapping his hands together. "It's almost time."

Adela was outfitted but still had questions swirling in her head as she followed Nine and Milo to the door from which they had entered earlier that night. What was this place? Who were these people? What was wrong with them? Where were they going?

"We're going to Old Kitfalls," Nine began. "It's due east of New Kitfalls, which we're underneath right now. We've been forced to take these longer journeys there once a month since we've wiped New Kitfalls clean, especially in this snowstorm. We can't draw too much suspicion to ourselves, you know." Facing Milo and Adela, he walked backward. "I'll give more instruction when we get there. It's a long walk. But I hope we can answer all your questions, Del."

"How did you know I had more questions?"

"I just assumed."

"You keep doing that."

"Doing what?"

"Answering my questions before I have a chance to ask them," Adela admitted. "What are you, a mind reader?"

Nine was still walking backward and smiled, showing his baby teeth to Adela once more. He winked. "Don't blow my cover, Del." Adela was caught off-guard and temporarily stopped in her tracks. Out of the corner of her eye, George leaned against the door that led to the room by to the fountain's corridor. Nine turned around, his back to Adela now, and called out. "Ready, then?"

"Are *they* ready?" George responded, tilting his sharp chin in Adela and Milo's direction.

"Ready as they'll ever be," Nine responded. "Though I need to show them how to use the slingshots."

"They can learn on the way there. We need to head out now. At this pace, we'll get home right at dawn. Hurry."

He nodded toward a small figure that stood a few feet from the door, and Adela realized it must have been the person who had opened the door to them earlier. He had large ears, like those of an oversized rodent, and his shoes squeaked as he strode over to it.

"Lock it behind us," George warned. "And don't open it to anyone who doesn't know the password. You understand, Little Mouse?"

The young boy nodded affirmatively and stuck his little hands into a small nook, just large enough for him to reach through. There must have been a handle all the way up there, for Little Mouse pulled his hand down and at once, the door began to swing open, the mechanism that they concocted in lieu of a standard doorknob working perfectly.

George grunted, and Nine ran through the door, followed by Milo and then Adela. Finally, it closed, and the room was plunged into darkness; Milo must have extinguished the candles from earlier. The front door squeaked open and a whisper called out ahead, "This way, hurry!"

With only Milo, two strangers, and a thirst for answers, Adela walked out into the winding corridor once more.

# FOURTEEN

# OLD KITFALLS

—

Once the water had flowed away, drained by a mysterious force deep within the fountain's mechanics, Nine poked his head out of the opening in the floor.

"The coast is clear. Let's hurry!" he whispered, pointing to a darkened corner of the city.

Adela rushed out behind Milo, who tripped on his way up. She placed her hands on his back and shoved him forward, her eyes bouncing about in her head as she tried to take in all that the above-ground world of New Kitfalls had to offer.

It was pitch black, but the lampposts gave the faintest bit of light. Towering structures rose around her. The windows of what Adela imagined were the city's inhabitants' homes were black, shut out to the world below, and she understood at once that the hour was late, well past when people would be settling into bed. She shivered. The air was much colder than earlier, the frost cooling the air and blanketing the ground with a soft snow. Adela knew they needed to be under the cover of darkness and wished she had brought another layer or two or three with her.

She searched the pitch black for Nine, trying to track his footsteps, when a movement in the sky caught her attention.

Following it, she managed to catch the swift flight of a peregrine falcon, its belly full and eye trained on the four adventurers below. With a threatening swoop, it disappeared into the horizon just ahead.

*Could it be the same one from Nuimtree? Is it following me?*

But Nine had grabbed her by the arm now and pulled her forward. He pushed her against the stone wall of a nearby alleyway and gently clamped his hand to her mouth. Adela bit at it and he gave out a small yelp, releasing her.

"What was that for? That hurt!"

"What was *that* for? If you need me to quiet down, you can ask me."

"Fine. Just ahead is our transport out of here."

"Transport?"

"Yes, transport. Did you think we would walk all the way to Old Kitfalls?" He laughed, and his eyes became small slivers of darkness, his eyelashes fluttering across his plump cheeks. He stopped laughing when George walked past and immediately pulled his hands off Adela's shoulders, allowing her body to relax once more.

From his rucksack, George pulled out bottles and flasks, much like the ones Clara had pulled out of her satchel on the train, and rested them on the thin layer of frost that formed on the ground. These containers were larger than Clara's, as long as Adela's forearm, and as big around as one of her mother's precious chipped teacups. They were meticulously labeled, and George tilted the labels to his face to read them one by one, hidden in the darkness of the alley but receiving light from the overhead lamps.

Adela crept up to him, leaving Nine and Milo alone by the wall, silently observing one another.

"What are you doing?"

George grunted. "Keep it down, girlie. I'm creating our method of transportation."

"What do you mean?" Adela asked, crouching low and adjusting her voice to match.

He let out a gentle laugh, the first Adela had heard from his mouth. "Why don't you reach into my bag and pull out the last flask? I'll show you," he offered.

Adela obliged, reaching into the bag and pulling out a container. The bottle appeared to be empty and was labeled only *Air (Warm)*. Adela wished she could unscrew the top and let its purported warmth settle around her, permeating into her bones as protection against the frigid air.

"Here," she said, offering the bottle to George. But he shook his head, allowing Adela to hold onto it. At his feet lay two other bottles. The first was labeled *Vapor*, which had some of the phosphorescent water from the Forgotten City pooled within; the jar was filled only halfway, and small pencil marks lined the outside of the bottle. The second bottle appeared to be empty, though inside it was slightly gray and opaque. The label on the front of the bottle read *Smoke*.

"Now, on the count of three, I want you to unscrew the bottle you're holding," he cautioned as he fixed his eyes on the bottle of air in Adela's hand. Positioning his hands over the two flasks in front of him, fingers poised to remove the caps that protected them from the outside elements—or vice versa—he posed the question, "Ready?"

Adela nodded.

"One, two... three!"

Adela unscrewed her bottle, matching George's strength and speed in turn. He picked up the bottle, ushering the flask over the other two and standing them side by side. Crouching over the bottles, his knees popping from the motion, George closed his eyes and began to wave his hands over the three containers in a looping motion, like the doodles Adela had recreated time and again in her journals.

Nine watched them with a straight face, arms crossed over his chest. Milo, on the other hand, looked increasingly confused and pulled a face at Adela, raising his forefinger to his temples in an attempt to indicate just how he felt about George and Nine. But, almost as suddenly, his eyes grew as big as milk saucers, and his mouth gaped open.

Turning around, Adela herself gasped at what was happening.

George had fashioned two substantial clouds, low to the ground and shifting about. The clouds grew, becoming darker and more opaque. George continued to move his hands about for a long while, until as suddenly as the clouds appeared, he stopped, dropping his arms to his sides.

Adela stood in place as Nine strode over to the first cloud and quickly scrambled on top—like magic, the cloud held his weight! He called out to Milo and held his hand out as the cloud continued to gradually peel away from the ground below.

Milo ran over and first placed his hand on the cloud before finally offering the same hand to Nine. Hoisted up behind him, he wrapped his pudgy arms around Nine's waist and turned to face Adela, his features still in a state of shock and awe. George had similarly pulled himself up on the second cloud, as Adela processed what had happened.

Like Milo, she placed her hand on the cloud, as if she could pull her hands through and not capture anything, almost as if attempting to grasp at smoke. But, surprisingly, the cloud was firm and appeared to be capable of holding the weight of not just one, but two people: comfortable and airy, but sturdy. She was amazed, and even more amazed that these clouds seemed to have been conjured from nothing. George held his outstretched arm in front of her face.

*Is he a wizard?*

She gave her hand to George and he pulled her up, directing her hands to wrap around his waist just as Milo's had wrapped around Nine's.

"Hold tight," he warned, "we're going to go up now."

Before he could finish his sentence, the twin clouds rose off the ground at a quicker pace until they were well above the buildings and blending into the cloud cover above them. With a low whistle, Nine leaned to the right and the cloud mirrored his movements, turning and leading the way for George and Adela. He sped ahead of them, at times disappearing in front of the wispy clouds.

"Aren't you going to speed up?"

"Let the boy get his kicks. It's one of the few times he gets to travel on the clouds."

"How did you do that? Are you a wizard?"

George laughed, shifting his body slightly to allow Adela the physical space to take in their surroundings. They were soaring over towering stone buildings and Adela now had an encompassing view of the city below, of snowy New Kitfalls. It was a curiously somber city, gloomy and dark, with towering spires rising in the air at varying heights. Smoke plumed out of chimneys. Rain clouds hung overhead—under even their traveling clouds—threatening to release another icy deluge at any moment.

A stark contrast to the fairy book wonder of Nuimtree, it was even starker still when compared to the bucolic beauty of Sunseree: a different world altogether. In the midst of examining the new world, Adela's ears perked up, realizing George had been speaking. She centered herself on the cloud and stared forward, focusing on his words.

"Alchemy is quite interesting, you know. It deals with bending matter and conforming elements of the world to however you see fit. In a way, it is a form of witchcraft. You're dealing with creating something out of nothing. You need to understand the elements you're bringing into a spell, or a concoction, or a potion. But I wouldn't call myself a wizard, no."

"Was that alchemy, what you did back there?"

George nodded, his hair scratching up against Adela's face, and the cloud suddenly bobbed up and down. He laughed sheepishly, his demeanor softening among the pillowy clouds. "Sorry about that. It has a mind of its own at times. But yes, it was. With something special thrown in, I reckon."

Adela sat silently for a while before asking her next question. "Don't you want to know how I knew about you?"

George paused. "I have an idea," he admitted. His back stiffened and straightened slightly as his muscles tensed up underneath Adela's hold.

She continued, knowing this may be one of her only opportunities for a straight answer. "My grandmother left behind a brooch. It had your name on it. Did you gift it to her?"

"Yes. Clarissa," he admitted, without hesitation. "How is she?"

"I'm not sure at the moment. I'm trying to find her."

"She certainly isn't here," he said, letting out a barking laugh that surprised her.

Adela tightened her grip as the wind picked up and the atmosphere grew colder. Her hair was frozen now, small icicles forming that threatened to snap off with the slightest of touches. She could not even fathom how the rest of her body was reacting to the extreme, damp cold.

"I know she's not. She's a witch. Did you know that?"

"That I did."

"Did she teach you what you did back there?"

"In a sense, yes."

"You're not offering up much information."

"Do you think you're asking the right questions?"

Adela wrestled with the barrage of thoughts in her head. Right now, she was unsure what Old Kitfalls would have in store for them and unsure how much she should trust George and Nine. Then there was a different line of questions altogether. What was the Forgotten City, and how did Nine and George find it? How did the children find it, and why were the children the way that they were? She gulped down a breath of air and began.

"What is the Forgotten City?"

George didn't answer for a while, and some part of Adela thought she had offended him. She was embarrassed and decided to turn her attention back to their frigid surroundings when George spoke, low and growling so Adela needed to strain her ears and hug her body close to his in order to hear.

"I used to live underground, in that small alcove where you first enter the complex. Way back when, I was a scientist. I hated living among everyone. They used to stare at me and call me a monster. And I didn't want to deal with that."

"Why did they call you a monster?" Adela asked, confused.

George first pointed to his eyepatch and then pulled his pant leg up to expose his knee, knocking. The sound was hollow. He had a false, wooden leg.

"I'm sorry," she said.

"What are you sorry about? Not any of your fault. That's for sure. Either way, I had no family—parents died when I was a youngin'—and that's why secluding myself from everyone made the most sense."

They had caught up to Nine and Milo, who had turned around on the cloud to wave back at them with unbridled joy, one hand white as it firmly clutched Nine's sweater. Adela smiled and waved back while George maneuvered to follow Nine's path. Straightening their cloud out, he continued.

"I guess that's to say my home was always forgotten. It just grew into a city when Nine came, and the others, too."

Before he could finish his words, Adela had her next question lined up. "What's the deal with the kids there?"

"You mean, why are they there, unsupervised?" George laughed. "Other than myself, of course."

"Well, that but also..." She trailed off, unwilling to complete her thought, but willing George to catch on: the seemingly adult bodies and faces, the high-pitched voices that escaped from behind tiny milk teeth.

"There's something you have to realize about the kids in the Forgotten City. Nine, and Rough and Tumble, and Ember and the others. They've been forgotten by the world around them. Neglected and uncared for, they were called to the underground world because they had no place in the overworld. Nine over there," he lifted a crooked finger to point in Nine's general direction, "is the youngest of nine children. His parents had no business having one child, let alone nine. They were cruel, and they hurt him, and, one by one, his siblings took over the various parental duties that typically burden an adult. And then, one by one, they all moved out of the home, leaving Nine abandoned many times over.

"And that cycle continued, on and on, until he was the only one left at home. His parents didn't care for him. They didn't feed or clothe him. He was growing up entirely too fast, though he was just a little one!" George shook his head, looking down momentarily before releasing a heavy sigh, fraught with emotion and empathy.

"He left home one night, wandering the streets. I had just been returning home, late at night, when I saw him, crying alone by the fountain. That fountain has some kind of drawing power. It acts as a homing beacon for anyone who is downtrodden, who needs a kind word and a helping hand. So that's precisely what I did. I brought him downstairs and gave him a cup of tea. It was five days before he would say anything to me, but eventually he did. His parents never came looking for him, you know."

Adela focused on the back of George's head just in front of her face, urging herself to not cry, for her tears to remain locked behind their emerald prisons. Nine had such a sad story—a story that felt wholly familiar to her own.

"Back to your question. One day, I took a long journey to gather supplies for the underground alchemy lab I had been building. And when I returned a week or two later, the most curious thing had happened. Somehow, Nine had managed to carve out a section of wall. He had tunneled into the stone, forming part of the alcove that you saw earlier today. It was so strange. And oozing from the walls was this blue water. The surprising part was not that it was blue, of course, but that it *glowed*."

Adela nodded, realizing George had been talking about the water in the lake, the strange water that she had been curious about herself, for it seemed to possess magical properties, much like the glossy cave pearls currently tucked into her shoe and rolling about.

"I don't know what it is about that water. But over the next few years, Nine grew... yet he didn't. He grew taller and broader and stronger, but his baby teeth never fell out. His voice never deepened. And his legs and forearms never grew hair. It was like he was older, but a child still. I haven't figured it out, but that water... that water gives you what you need. We all use it for drinking and cooking and cleaning. I use it to create clouds from magic. Bud uses it to nurture her plants. And I think Nine used it and thought about how he wished he could bring his childhood back. And that's what it did for him. And all the other children, too."

"How old is Nine?"

"By now, he must be..." George let out a deep breath, calculating years in his mind, imaginary numbers appearing and disappearing in front of his face. "He must be seventeen years old. He's been with me twelve of those years."

"And the other children?"

"Over the years, they came, drawn to that same fountain, drawn to that magic water. All forgotten, one way or another. Neglected, orphaned, deformed. Some have these abilities that are quite special. With time, I learned that Nine had a fierce physical strength. He was able to carve out blocks of stone using just the pads of his pinky fingers. Slowly but surely, we carved out a space for ourselves. We have a thriving community. And yes, all of us look a little strange," he admitted, turning around to face Adela, "but we're family. And that's what matters." He winked, and Adela gave him a sullen smile.

"So," he finished, turning around, "that's the story of the Forgotten City. Forgotten by society. But not by us. And, hopefully, not by you."

"I don't know how I could forget it now," Adela admitted. "It's all fantastical and strange."

George let out a small laugh that turned into a cough. The cloud swayed side to side before finally settling in place, like a boat floating and righting itself on turbulent waters.

"We're almost there," he announced, peering over the wispy cloud to the ground cover below them.

The environment had changed slightly. Behind them, the spires of New Kitfalls' buildings reached the heavens, stretching toward the moon, but ahead of them, the cloud cover gave way to a vast expanse of mossy greens and honey yellows, seemingly mimicking the glow of the sun that had left them behind. Bunches of green rose to touch the bottoms of the cloud as they descended.

Adela leaned over the clouds and realized that the collections of green were trees, situated on rock instead of the usual tree bark. Wrapped around the base of the trees were strings of lights, casting an otherworldly glow to the treetops, which swayed in the breeze as George's clouds passed over them.

The cloud ducked under a jutting cliff-face, from which a gushing stream of water sprayed out, pooling into a small, semi-frozen lake below. Nocturnal birds swooped down at Adela's head as she and George instinctively ducked, and she again saw the faint markings of a peregrine falcon at her side, seemingly following her.

"There she is," George interrupted.

Adela shook her head, bringing herself back to the present and taking in the beauty of the surrounding country-scape that vaguely reminded her of her home in Sunseree with the addition of rocky trees and sparse wetland blanketing the ground. "It's beautiful. Where are we?"

"This is Old Kitfalls," he answered matter-of-factly, leaning his body to one side to begin the descent down to the swampy floor. Adela was nearly thrown back from the sudden motion, and she scrambled to place both hands firmly around George's waist once more.

"Old Kitfalls? Is it related to New Kitfalls?"

"See all the stone?"

"How could you miss it?"

"Legend is that the City of Kitfalls rose from the earth, centuries ago. It used to be a coral reef, believe it or not, and the shells of dead animals formed the stone you see today. It became compounded and compacted and made the area what it is. But years and years ago, two factions emerged. One wanted to keep the existing ways how they were, and another faction wanted to advance technology. They decided to divorce—amicably, of course—and divided the land. New Kitfalls to the west, and Old Kitfalls to the east. One interconnected to the other."

"That's fascinating. Why are we here?"

"Old Kitfalls has natural resources that are integral to our livelihood. We're in a city with minimal access to what we need to survive. The creatures here trade in far-off goods, magical stuff."

"Creatures?"

But George was bracing for impact, his long legs dangling to the ground in an attempt to stop the cloud's impending crashing momentum.

Within seconds, George had deftly dismounted and reached his hand out to Adela to assist her off the cloud. As her feet touched the ground, somebody slammed into her back, wrapping his arms around her. It was Milo, a near-identical greeting to the one she had afforded him days prior; her ribs remained sore from that encounter, and Adela sucked her teeth as she felt them bruise under her skin once more.

"That was amazing!" Milo shouted. His face was frozen in a goofy grin, eyes wide and breathing heavily as he came down from his adrenaline rush. "I've never ridden on a cloud before!"

Adela gently pushed him away and dusted herself off, beginning with her shirt. She had yet to take a shower and was starting to feel itchy and dirty. She did not want anyone to touch her in this state, least of all Milo.

"Settle down," Nine warned, sauntering over to the two children as he descended from the cloud. With the two boys as company, Adela glanced around for George, realizing he had moved away from the group. He was near their cloud and blowing it back up into the atmosphere.

"Wait, what are you doing?" Adela shouted, running over to him with arms flailing above her head as the cloud began its ascent into the sky. "How are we going to get back?"

George simply rustled the side of his rucksack, the jars clanging together and creating a cacophony of clamors. Breathing a relieved sigh, Adela regained her composure and followed George back to the group in time to overhear the ensuing conversation between Nine and Milo.

"We have a few things we're going to try to get during this expedition. Del and Milo, since you're both new, you'll take turns going with each of us. Del, I'll need you for the second journey. Milo, I'll need you for the first. Let's meet back here once we're both done to swap places. When we're done, we can return back to the Forgotten City."

Without another word, without allowing any opposing sentiments or questions, Nine turned on his heels with Milo racing after him, stumbling on his shoelaces as he did.

Of course, Adela was grateful to be able to spend more time with George. She wanted to learn more about her grandmother, who seemed to have known George intimately. George pulled an item out of his pocket, which Adela assumed was a pocket watch, and nodded to himself as he took mental record of the time.

He grunted and pointed in a direction. "This way. Keep close."

# FIFTEEN

# CURSE

——

Adela followed, staying firmly on George's heels to the point where she stepped on his shoes every few steps. At one point, George turned around and glared at her, his mood clearly shifting to the sterner variant of his personality, and Adela distanced herself ever so slightly to avoid tripping him. Around her, the trees built on rocks emanated a soft glow. Their roots grew toward the murky water that nearly hid them in plain sight, were it not for the fact that Adela was walking alongside the thick roots herself. The surface of the ground was soft, giving way to the body of water from which Old Kitfalls had sprung millennia before. Adela was careful to watch her step at first, growing more confident of her movements with time.

After nearly an hour of walking, she spoke again.

"You still haven't answered one important question. How do you know my grandmother?"

George sighed, forging the path forward and testing the ground for soft spots to avoid. "Clarissa is really your grandmother?"

"Yes."

"Does she know you're here?"

"Maybe part of her does. But no, I don't think so."

George nodded. "She did have that sense about her, always aware of what was happening around her, especially with her own family. She was a master with herbs and plants, creating pastes and healing salves with ease." He stopped, turning to keep eye contact with Adela and balancing on one leg as he rapped on his wooden one with his knuckles. "I met Clarissa when this happened. I lost my leg in an explosion one day, working with chemicals. She was passing through the area, picking up wares on her way to Nuimtree, just there." He pointed, and Adela followed his finger instinctively, certain she would not be able to see Nuimtree from here, though she could picture it perfectly in her mind.

So her grandmother has passed through here before. Perhaps on her way to Nuimtree.

*Was that the time when she had met me?*

George answered her question almost instantaneously. "She later told me she was trying to secure magical ingredients for a summoning spell. You see, she had lost someone back in Nuimtree and had scoured our little corner of the world to find what sundries she needed to procure. But on her way there, she ran into poor me with my leg blown off. And so she stayed behind a week, and that week turned into a month, and all the while she made these pastes and various ointments to keep the pain at bay and help my stub heal."

"Did she have a baby with her?"

"She did. I almost forgot about that, but how could I? That baby had the most peculiar birthmark on her forehead. I sensed she was special, too. I'm sorry to admit, I fell in love with your grandmother, and I think she fell in love with me too, but her life called to her back in Nuimtree or Western Wilerea or wherever she deigned to call home. For a moment in time, I thought we'd be a misfit family of our own, but

Clarissa eventually left. I gave her that brooch before she left, to remember our time together. A sad ending, but an ending nonetheless."

"I'm sorry," Adela offered, becoming uncomfortable as she thought back to her own family, and her grandfather and his gentle blue-gray eyes and kind voice and unconditional love for her and her mother. She side-stepped a particularly slimy piece of ground, the wetness of the earth seeping into her shoe; she hoped the cave pearls would be safe.

"Stop saying that," George whispered, lowering himself in the tall grass around them.

Adela followed suit, taking in the world: the grass was nearly Adela's height, providing the optimal amount of cover. It was thick and bright green, mimicking the color of the treetops, though the world around them remained pitch dark. Adela held her hand in front of her, only able to make out its outline due to the lightning bugs that whizzed by, providing the minimal amount of light with which to see. The air was warmer than in New Kitfalls, and Adela appreciated the relief from the biting cold.

"Move." George's order broke through the silence.

Adela focused her attention on what was in front of them. Ahead was a grand tree, its base made of stone, but at the top of the tree, hidden among the treetops, was a suspended home. Made of a deep brown wood, it was cobbled together in sections: the main room was the largest, with a beautiful white door made of material that did not appear to be wood, while the windows opened to the air around them, blocked only by a pair of sheer curtains, swaying in the soft breeze.

Out of the treetops, a plume of black smoke released into the air, and Adela traced its origin to a stack of circular wooden rooms to the left of the main room. There were no rooms here, and Adela imagined it was a kitchen, closed off to the world with rows of cabinets lining the curved walls. From a deck suspended across two tree branches, a ladder led down to the swaying grass below.

George was beginning to climb the ladder.

Adela raced after him, trying to keep up, her braided hair furiously whipping her in the face.

"George," she hissed, "where are we going?"

He offered only a grunt in reply and kept climbing, stopping only when he had reached the platform. This time, he did not offer a hand to Adela, as he had done with the cloud. Instead, he strode to the door and knocked twice. Adela hoisted herself onto the weathered platform, one leg at a time, and stood tall just in time for the door to open.

An elderly woman opened the door. Her nose was crooked, with a flesh-colored wart on the side, and one of her teeth protruded slightly outside her mouth, taking residence outside, perched on her lip. She held a cane made of what looked like bones in one hand, and she grasped the top, a rounded flourish that appeared to be a small rodent skull. She was short, shorter than Adela even, and had a permanent hunch.

"Jezibaba," George greeted the strange woman, curtsying out of respect.

"About time. I've been expecting you for weeks," she snapped, her voice hoarse and wavering as she turned back into her home. George scurried after her, kindly leaving the door open and swaying on its hinges, prompting Adela to come inside. Jezibaba's scratchy voice caused Adela's ears to ring, not the ringing like when Clara laughed in Nuimtree, alerting Adela to a special connection. No, this was a different type altogether.

Threatening. Dangerous.

While George and the woman continued their conversation, Adela crept inside the hut slowly, taking in the hodgepodge of items scattered throughout the home. It was cluttered, jars of animal parts and books covered with layers of dust stacked one atop the other. To the left was the circular structure, which Adela realized housed a large stove that took up the length of the room. Behind wrought-iron doors, a fire burned brightly and fiercely, on the verge of being out of control.

"Who is this?" Jezibaba asked, swarming toward Adela, her face only a finger's length from Adela's own. With her thumb and forefinger, she reached out and pinched Adela's cheek, holding onto it a second too long. A flint of gray disappeared behind her, showing itself to Adela only from the corner of her eye. "What a sweet little girl," she cooed menacingly, her eyes glinting in the warm fire's glow.

"Hello," Adela answered, her voice wavering.

Jezibaba smiled slightly, a small growl emitting from her lips. "Looks familiar. Doesn't she, Kocur?"

George ignored this exchange and Jezibaba's calls into the ether; he seemed nervous, as if he had been caught doing something he was not supposed to. "We don't have much time. It'll be dawn soon, and we need to get back before everyone wakes." He looked around anxiously. "Can you help me?"

Jezibaba leaned on her cane of bones, leering at Adela before turning around swiftly and striding toward George. "Yes, yes. What is it?" The house creaked and seemed to sway in the soft wind, held in place only by the trunks of the trees and their roots embedded in the watery sediment.

Adela stood with her back toward the giant stove, peering through the entryway as Jezibaba dug around in her jars with George nervously peering over her shoulder.

"Who *are* you?" a wily voice asked, just behind her back.

Adela gasped, jumping in the air. Her eyes focused on a blob of gray, tips of his fur glinting with a silvery sheen. Vibrant green eyes shining, he emerged from the inky darkness. A Cat, perched high atop a shelf stacked precariously with pots and pans. The shelf hovered over the warm, iron stove, threatening to come crashing down with the slightest nudge.

"Did you just say something?"

"I didn't *say* something," the Cat replied, its pink tongue lolling about in its mouth. "I *asked* who you were. And as a follow-up, what are you doing here?"

Adela blinked once, then twice, and by the third time, the Cat had gotten up from its hiding place and leapt onto the dusty wooden floor, making its way toward Adela. She tried to back away, but the Cat was quicker and weaved in between her legs to trip her. Attempting to escape the Cat's dizzying route, Adela lost her balance and fell on her backside, using her wrist to brace for impact. She flinched, having applied pressure on her wrist again. It was becoming beat up as the night went on, just as her ribs had been newly disturbed.

Turning, Adela looked around for George and Jezibaba, but they had secluded themselves to a corner of the other room, whispering in hushed voices and occasionally opening a jar, which they held up to their noses to take in.

The sharpness of the Cat's claws dug into Adela's hand, and she quickly moved it. The mysterious Cat had dug into her skin in an effort to catch her attention. Adela's throat became dry, and she was finding it difficult to breathe, sitting on this dusty, weathered floor.

"Are you going to answer my question? Or are you mute?"

Adela gulped, blinking. "I'm not mute."

"Well?"

"I'm here with George."

"Naturally. Why?"

"I don't know. I volunteered to come here."

"Why?" The Cat circled her once more, forcing Adela to whip her head to keep up.

"To get answers to my questions."

"Answers? To what?"

"I'm trying to learn about my family."

The Cat stopped dead in its tracks, and his hair stood up on its end. "Your family?" he repeated, slowly as if trying out the phrase on his barbed tongue. He looked to Adela, and his slit-shaped eyes began to expand, seeking out every inch of light from the darkness that had spilled out into the home.

"Yes," Adela replied.

"I've heard of you, you know," the Cat admitted, circling again.

"Of me? How?"

"I'm perceptive. That, and Jezibaba mentioned that you looked familiar. Now I know why."

So this must be who Jezibaba was talking to; his name was Kocur, a curious name.

"Why?"

The Cat erupted in a deep purr, like the deep whir of a machine springing to life, clearly amused with the information he was hiding. With an agile swiftness, he leapt back on top of the stove, padding along the surface while keeping his emerald eyes on her at all times.

"Your mother. The poor woman. Cursed."

"Cursed? How?"

"Cursed with abilities. Cursed in love."

"I don't quite understand," Adela admitted. "You're not making much sense. Then again, you're only a cat."

"Hold your tongue," Kocur warned. "I know more than you ever will. I creep in the shadows. I travel through the night, under cover of the pitch black. I've been to the edges of Western Wilerea, and I've communed with fortune tellers in Nuimtree. I know more about you than you know yourself."

Adela was silent, allowing the Cat to continue its tirade. From the other room, the hushed voices grew louder and agitated. She ignored them, drawn to every hissing word out of the Cat's jaws.

"Tell me more," Adela implored, positioning her body forward and leaning into the Cat's hypnotizing voice.

"Before the Last Sun, long before I settled in with Jezibaba, I met a Witch in the Isle of Vila. For a moment, I considered being her companion. But truly, she was far too cruel for even my liking," he said, licking his paw gingerly. "She had grown angry and callous, seeking revenge on a little girl—like you—who had wronged her. You see, while the little girl thought she had evaded her over the years, the Witch was scheming and devising plans to capture her soul once and for all. She had taken the first step to do so, but it wasn't enough. She needed something more."

The Cat began grooming itself, smoothing down its gray coat with the mauve pads of its paw. From behind Adela, the sounds of jars being filled permeated the room. George let out an interrupting cough.

"Go on," Adela said to encourage the Cat, wanting it to finish its story before they had to leave. She had an old-world sense that Kocur's story was important, that the Cat was not lying, and that this may shine light on what was happening to her mother.

"You see, it just so happened that she set a trap. And, oh, what a marvelous trap it was! She had found the man this woman loved and lured him into her home. After a few days of torturing him and destroying his spirit, I watched as she began replacing his soul with bits and pieces of her own. He would be lost to the world forever. It's a dark magic, you know, none that I had seen before. Naturally, I was intrigued. Slowly, this man began to lose his humanity. But she left a bit of him inside, of course. So as not to arouse suspicion. That's important when practicing magic, you see."

Adela nodded, enraptured.

"She had released part of her dark soul into this innocent human, poor thing. And of course, in turn, she became weaker. And so she needed to seek out power in all its forms. The young girl, by now, was a woman, with a young girl of her own. The young girl who had wronged her, she had a twin brother, one that the Witch plotted to capture in an effort to tap any magical youth from him. But, still, the Witch ached for feminine power, would have done anything to get her hands on it. And she set the plan in motion to do just that. She released the innocent man back into the world and influenced his every behavior from that moment on. This Witch spurred the Last Sun. This Witch has wreaked the havoc you're escaping from today."

Kocur stopped, watching Adela intently.

"What does this have to do with me?" Adela asked, aware that the commotion behind her was quieting.

The Cat smiled and leapt back to the floor, landing elegantly on all fours. He strode over to Adela and brushed his fluffy tail against her leg. "Don't you see, little girl? You've wondered for ages what happened to your family, why Conrad has been unimaginably cruel to you."

Adela's ears perked up at the mention of Conrad.

"How do you know—"

"I watched his soul be overtaken that night, replaced piece by piece by the soul of something much darker. Something intent on destruction."

Adela jolted up, yanked upright by the firm grip of George's hand on her arm. "We're leaving," he barked, a new satchel of goods under his armpit. "We need to meet Milo and Nine. Now."

Adela could only be dragged away as Jezibaba and Kocur watched her leave through the front door. She climbed down the ladder, trying to process the information she had learned on her expedition with George. But her ability to process was cut short as, from within the grass, she heard the huffing and puffing of someone running frantically toward them.

Before she had a chance to understand what was happening, Nine had caught up to them and began speaking in hushed voices with George, voices rising on the still air. They both looked back at Adela and then sprinted forward, back to their original meeting site.

Something was wrong. Adela broke out into a run, letting the wind blow through her braid, still caked with dirt, until she caught up to them. Doubled over, she limped to where the two were standing. They were looking down and, as she joined them, she realized what had gone wrong.

Atop the dense grass that covered the ground lay a small figure, eyes open and mouth frozen in a gaping scream. Thick, pale hands were folded over the figure's chest, where a pool of bright red blood had stained the clothing above. Unmoving, the figure looked like something out of a storybook.

But this wasn't a storybook. For before her eyes, before her and George and Nine, lay a body.

Milo was dead.

# PART FOUR

## SIXTEEN

# MILO

———

The air was still. And cold. Despite this, Adela gasped for breath, a distinct constriction overtaking her, clogging her airways as if the cool air had just filled with impenetrable smoke, snaking its wispy fingers around her throat and curling them closed, restricting her access to the fresh air around her.

"What happened?" she asked, finally choking the words out, directing her question toward Nine in particular.

"I-I don't know," he admitted, hand running through his long, black hair. His eyes were wide, pupils dilated until they nearly filled the entire expanse of his irises. "We were just... I was just..." Nine couldn't—or wouldn't—answer the question.

Milo's face was frozen in place, stuck in a permanence of shock and horror. He was paler than even before, his hands curled up over his chest, fingers seemingly mangled but intact, all ten of them attached to his requisite limbs. Eyes wide and unblinking, he appeared to stare up into the heavens as if petitioning for life anew, his mouth fixed in a perfect circle. Adela admired the still body, unmoving in its grotesqueness. George walked toward Milo and gently placed his rough hand on his face, nudging his eyes closed.

Adela felt only shock. Her mind cycled through a range of emotions and questions, like one of Sunseree's world-renowned acrobats perfecting a routine.

*Is Milo truly dead? Of course not! He's only sleeping. But then, why isn't he blinking? Or breathing?*

*So he is dead. How? How could Nine let this happen?*

*I should have been there! If only I could grab hold of something, anything, to travel back to that moment.*

*He was my only friend. And he has a family.*

*They'll need to plan a funeral now. I'll need to get the body back to Sunseree.*

"Where did you go?" George asked, directing his question to Nine and simultaneously snapping Adela out of her dazed trance.

"We went to the swamp. He wanted to see the trolls."

"The swamp? The trolls?" George repeated, his body stiffening. "Who gave you permission to go there? You were meant to meet the merchants at the bridge."

"Yes, but..."

"Your carelessness and thoughtlessness cost a young boy his life," George said, his voice rising as he literally rose to face Nine, his body creaking with age. His face took the form of a scowl now, grimacing at Nine with an intense anger Adela had only witnessed a few times in her short life. It was frightening and she knew, at once, that Nine must be terrified of George.

But instead of lashing out, George sighed, rapping his hand against his alchemic rucksack. He did not raise his voice, nor strike Nine, nor scream and throw things about; he allowed himself the momentary pleasure of a handful of breaths, in and out, before at last focusing his attention on Adela, scared and still in the middle of the marshland.

"You," he said, as if only now acknowledging her presence.

"Yes?" Adela asked. She remained in shock, staring down at Milo's body with little emotion behind her eyes.

"Assure me again that you're Clara's granddaughter."

A pause while Adela processed the question.

"Yes."

Another pause. George continued to bore his eyes into Adela's face, as if discovering it for the first time. Finally, he said, "We need to return to the Forgotten City. And quickly."

"But what about..." Adela's sentence trailed off, and the three brought their eyes back to Milo's unmoving body, lying in the middle of the mossy grass, as if discarded and forgotten, the earth slowly beginning the process of returning him back to it as beetles and toad bugs crawled about the surface of his skin, spindly legs leaving small imprints to mark their journey. The call of frantic cicadas sounded in the air as a response to the warm temperatures, the droning sound increasingly agitated and equally agitating. George put his hand on Nine's shoulder, a motion aimed to temper the anger from moments ago.

"Nine, you'll need to bring him back. Can you handle it?"

Nine nodded, and Adela only now noticed the tears that had built up in his eyes. He, too, was distraught by the events that had unfolded, impacted by whatever had happened in the swamp. He had almost certainly witnessed Milo's death itself. While seconds prior, Adela had harbored ill will toward Nine and the place where they now stood, she knew now that this had truly been a mistake, that Milo's demise had been unintentional.

But, nevertheless, he was dead.

Their return back to the Forgotten City was uneventful. George artfully dodged between towering trees and over climbing skyscrapers that clawed their way into the atmosphere itself, using shrill whistles to communicate with Nine, who had stretched Milo's body out on his own cloud and was taking special care to balance their mode of transportation as best he saw fit. He maneuvered around opaque clouds that threatened to bounce them backward in their journey while Adela internally processed all that had befallen the group, refusing to take in the scenic beauty on the way back. It would feel like a luxury, morally indulgent in light of the grim circumstances.

Under cover of darkness, they landed in New Kitfalls, nearby the alleyway that was in turn nearby the fountain, prepared to be swallowed into the depths of the earth once more. Whereas four had left hours ago, only three—and a body—returned.

Nine had propped Milo's body carefully over his shoulder, taking great care not to rustle or rouse the body much, though Milo would surely not feel any accidental smacks or shoves that would strike his arms or legs.

As Nine and Milo started their descent underground, Adela prepared herself to enter behind, chest heaving with worry, knowing she would need to release her token soon and deliver a corpse to Milo's parents. She imagined a casket blown entirely of glass, all of Milo's favorite colors swirling about. Favorite colors that she had never asked for, now unable to picture the scene in her mind. Before she descended into the fountain, a hand caught her clothes, gentle but firm.

"Listen to me, because I won't repeat it again."

Adela slowly nodded at George, the mechanical sounds of the fountain settling in place and assuring her that Nine and Milo's body were safely underground, that they had not been suddenly seized by the inhabitants of the city who were now waking, gas lampposts signaling the morning hours that the sun would not. Only she and George remained above ground.

"Take this," George said, carefully prying her fingers open with his own and folding an object into the palm of her hand. It was a wooden whistle, intricately carved and depicting elegant waves of water swirling about. Or was it sand dunes? Its color was light and singular, like the golden hue of the honeycomb that Miss Sona collected back in Sunseree.

"What am I meant to do with this?"

"Away from here, far from where you came, there is a water oasis. Foretold in the journals of alchemists who lived and died before me, this oasis holds two springs, forever kept apart, that ultimately converge as one. These are the Waters of Life and Death. Find them and you hold the ability to grant life. The ability to grant life," he repeated, "and bring anyone back from the dead." He said this last part slowly, allowing the words to seep into Adela's ears.

"Do you mean..."

"I do."

"But why are you giving me this whistle? What does it have to do with anything?" Her stomach churned. Though she feigned confusion, Adela knew what the whistle stood for and what she could do with it.

"This whistle was carved in a town not too far from the springs. Find the town, and you find the water. Find the water, and..." He nodded in the direction of the fountain, leaving his words unsaid but teeming with meaning.

"I have no idea where this place—this oasis—even is, or what's there."

George appeared to flinch slightly, though he did not immediately respond.

Adela's hair fell about her face, purposefully shielding George from her eyes at that moment, while imaginary gears began to devise a plan, frantically in motion as her feet stood locked in place. She allowed the question to be unanswered, posing a new one: "What do I do with this whistle?"

George laughed softly, so as not to attract attention. "Do you think I don't know who you are?"

She paused, wrapping her fingers tightly around the whistle, her knuckles turning white. "What? How?"

"I know everything that happens in this city, both above and below ground," he said, crouching low to keep hidden, as New Kitfalls continued to wake, lights humming on in the houses that surrounded them. "I remember the conversations I had with your grandmother long ago. It's easy to put one and one, or three and three, together. You're her magic girl."

"I don't think I'm quite so magical after all," Adela sobbed, looking down to avoid eye contact. "I couldn't save Milo."

"Hush, girlie," George said, his small eyes darting about. "We don't have much time at all. You know what to do with the whistle. You *know*. Now, if you'll excuse me, I need to go back into hiding. I can't risk being found out, today of all days."

"Wait." Adela tried to grab a hold of his clothing as a last attempt for more answers, but he pushed past her and ran down the stairs of the fountain, disappearing—like the soft mist that had formed his clouds—below ground to the bustling underground city where Milo's body now lay. Adela was frozen in place, passing the whistle from hand to hand as she balanced the various bags on her shoulders and emitting a small laugh as she again remembered how her grandmother had looked when entering the Curling Cave, bags strewn about her body.

Yet worry creased her forehead and overtook her spirit. She had never transported in the middle of traveling before. What would happen to her? Would there be two copies of her original body now? One in the forest and one here? Where would she return when all this was over? And how would the tokens work?

Her head hurt. Her innate ability to worry had reared its ugly head; she was nervous and knew that the people of New Kitfalls would soon be leaving their homes. If she didn't move, she would be caught, a strange girl, cold and dirty, without a home. Surely, they would not allow her to simply exist as she was, free to move about without parents to watch over her. And so, without another thought, she followed the path that Nine and George had taken moments before, moving deftly into the mouth of the fountain, like the quiet mice that inhabited it, and secured it behind her.

Below ground, she could no longer see her hand in front of her face, for the space was dark and yearning for the flickering flames of candles or lamps to pierce its shadows. But for her purposes, this would be the ideal hiding place: one in which her second original body—was it even an original body anymore?—would surely be safe, tucked in the depths that no reasonable person would dare enter. Her head possessed a certain lightness, and she stumbled down the stone steps, careful not to go tumbling down. Careful not to break all the remaining bones in her body. Adela curled her gaze around the corner of the staircase she'd climbed countless times over the last few hours; behind the stone steps was a tight opening, just wide enough for her to squeeze into, at other times surely a home to the crawling creatures below ground. The space was damp but currently devoid of any critters that could nibble on her reclining body. It appeared to do just fine.

She sat on the ground, her lower body quickly becoming soaked from the fountain water that had pooled below. Despite the less-than-pleasant circumstances, Adela knew it would be safe—assuming, of course, that a version of her body would stay here, in the Forgotten City's long hallway. She shook her head, daring herself to not think of that any further; it was decidedly out of her control and not worth the space of another thought filling her brain.

With the drips of the fountain as her lullaby, the cave pearls rolling about in her sock, and the whistle in her hands, she took a deep, musky breath and closed her eyes.

# SEVENTEEN

# AL AINAB

———

The smell of salt hit her first. Her mother kept a rock of salt in the kitchen, using it to season the meals they enjoyed together. It was considered as precious as gold in her village, the mineral upon which life itself stood perched. But this smell was different, as if entrenched into the atmosphere and the air Adela now breathed, circling her head like a flock of falcons circling their prey. The air was sticky and warm, unlike many of the environments with which she was now familiar, and Adela peeled her eyelids open to observe the world she had entered.

It was a quaint city, not nearly at the scale of New Kitfalls, condensed and compact. The ground was made of packed material, something soft and beige and pale, and coarse gravel, opposing textures mixed together to create a surface that was stable, under which she presumed animals could amble and people could walk without fear of falling to the center of the world itself.

Adela knelt down to pick up what she presumed was sand, letting it run through her fingers. She had only ever heard of the material before, Conrad returning from a faraway city, spinning tales of pale houses that sprang from the ground, equally solid but fragile. He spoke of streets lined with the hot material that shone when the sun's rays touched it just so. At night, it would cool to the touch yet retain its initial warmth, as if holding onto the memories of the earlier day.

This sand was cold, though, and Adela deduced that she was still in the time of the Last Sun. It was evening here, the sky a deep, midnight blue—though Adela was unsure precisely what time it was—and from among its vastness shone a smattering of white lights, stars illuminating the sky and the city beneath it.

The air filled with the smells of homemade cooking, fragrant spices converging to fill Adela's nostrils with the anticipation of a home-cooked meal. The smells reminded her of her grandmother's house, the stove always burning as it magicked a thick, savory stew from its iron depths.

She dared to step forward, the soft sand giving way under her tired feet. Adela marveled at how the material formed around her shoes, molding itself to their varied curves and ridges. She clutched the whistle between her fingers.

"Who are you?" a whisper carried itself across the air.

Adela spun around, nearly dropping the whistle and kicking up granules of sand. Yet, she could not find the person who had uttered the question. She appeared to be completely alone, standing in the middle of the pathway, a lone traveler standing on the side of the road, determining where to venture next. Looking down and up, Adela checked sandstone balconies for people lurking in the shadows, sending her gaze down compact alleyways where white cats leapt from windowsill to windowsill in search of scraps.

Nothing. She must be imagining things.

"Who are you?" the voice repeated, its whispers creeping closer like ivy.

Adela was quicker this time, her body on alert, able to track down the voice with relative ease. It came from the direction of a lamppost in the center of the street, though nobody was to be found. Shivering and mustering up all her strength, Adela shuffled over, expecting to find someone veiled within the darkness.

Nothing.

"You're looking right at me," the voice said softly, as if riding on the air itself.

Adela strained her eyes, only now making out a faint outline in front of the light. Barely opaque, and in the shape of a young girl perhaps even younger than she was herself. But it wasn't a living girl, for her shape was not quite solid and the coloring of her skin was a dull gray rather than the fleshy tones that covered the surface of skin. She had charcoal-colored eyes that shone when lit from behind, and her nose was straight and solid, slightly upturned at the tip, like the curious angle of a ridge on the South Mountains, where Adela would sled in the winter and catch the air gleefully. The edges of the girl's mouth curled upward, and her lower lip was dwarfed by the size of her upper lip. Her lips were gray. A loose, flowing dress was slightly worn at the edges of the head opening and both sleeves, in bright colors reminiscent of food: peaches and oranges and eggplants. Her feet were bare and her hair, tightly curled and perfectly thick; its color, too, was gray.

"Who are you?" Adela murmured, moving closer to the light.

"Fine then, I'll answer first. But you'll have to answer me, too, you know. My name is Zaila."

"Zaila," Adela tried on her tongue. She liked how it sounded. "My name is Adela."

"Adela." The sound repeated, and Zaila's gray eyes twinkled as she phased through the lamppost and out the back, circling toward Adela. Rather than walking, she appeared to drift through the air, findings pockets within which she could take up space temporarily, staying only a moment before venturing on to the next.

"What is the nature of your visit here, Adela?"

"How do you know I'm only visiting?"

"I've been here long enough. Only centuries by now. I can tell who belongs and who's new. And you," she threatened, jabbing her smoky finger at Adela's chest, "don't belong."

"I guess I don't," Adela stammered. Though Zaila seemed to be made of the consistency of smoke, her finger felt firm and real on her breastbone. It was unnerving, and Adela wondered what type of creature she had encountered. "I've been sent here by someone." She twirled the whistle in her hands, only having a destination in mind and no other means to decide her next steps. Or where to go.

"You've been sent here? To Al Ainab, of all places?" Zaila snorted. "And for what reason might that be?"

"My friend... he died."

Zaila froze, and her demeanor changed entirely. Her body tensed as she moved away from Adela. "You should be burying him then, not making small talk with me in a deserted street."

Adela flinched, balking at the statement. Zaila was blunt. It stung in the moment, like the sting of a garden spider that had implanted itself on Adela's pointer finger two summers ago, refusing to let go until swatted at with a wooden spoon. But Adela could tell a mystical quality was at play here; perhaps she could use the situation to her advantage.

With Zaila's help, she could learn why George had sent her here in the first place.

"Well, the thing is," Adela continued, "I would like him to not be dead anymore."

"Is that so?" Zaila snapped in her direction, crossing her wispy arms over her grayed torso, her foot bouncing in place, restless and constantly moving with a fury.

"Zaila, have you heard of the Waters of Life and Death?"

The shadow girl stopped, her shape swaying in the wind like smoke being pushed through the top of a chimney. "The Waters of Life and Death?"

"Yes," Adela said.

"I have *not*," Zaila firmly answered, moving away from Adela and down the alleyway, leaving Adela in her wake. Adela collected her things and ran forward, trying desperately to keep up with Zaila's quickened pace.

"Are you certain you haven't?" Adela asked again, exhaling as she struggled for breath. Her ribs were still sore from her journey, and her wrist stung as she placed the satchel gingerly across her shoulder. "I've heard of the rivers, found in an oasis not too far from here."

Zaila refused to answer, instead attempting to lose Adela, phasing unceremoniously through walls and around corners. But Adela had by now trained her eyes to make out the shape of Zaila's translucent body as it mixed with the fog of the early evening. As she ran, she corrected the placement of the items that were perched on her shoulder. A stray piece of string hung off a bag, and she paused for only a moment, unraveling it and breaking it off until it was an appropriate length to tie around her neck. Fingers moving quickly, she attached the whistle to the string, knotting it a few times so as to fasten it in place and against her skin. Collecting herself, she searched the horizon for Zaila once more, finding her in the corners of the cityscape.

She turned another corner, finally passing through the sandstone wall of a tan building, bearing cutout windows and a small gray door that was itself weathered with age and the barrage of sand against its wood. Around the wall was a similar series of doors and windows, all different colors and sizes, all lit from within. As if on cue, the windows hummed on, emitting a soft orange glow that stayed steady, a gentle candle in the still wind. Scents of lemon and fig, smells that Adela recognized from her mother's small garden, escaped from the window and into the air.

"Are you in there? Zaila?" Adela asked, keeping her voice low and hushed.

A moment passed. Then another. And then finally, the door creaked open, as if gently pushed from within. Zaila stood in its frame, eyes turned to the floor and tiny hands clenched at her sides.

"Do you know how many people have attempted to steal the Waters' magical properties? Hundreds!" Zaila's eyes met Adela's and glimmered in the starlight as she rushed to answer her own question. "And none have succeeded." She raised her gray eyebrows, mouth upturned to form a concerned and serious scowl.

"What do you mean?" Adela asked, shaking her head. When she did, her whistle dislodged from under her shirt, and Zaila glanced down, taking it in. "I don't understand. Why would he send me here if it was impossible?"

"What is *that*?" Zaila's eyes were trained on the whistle but, once more, she allowed no space in the conversation for Adela to get a word in. "Never mind that. I don't know who sent you or why, but I do know this. While the path may be short, it will be difficult to come out unscathed, to come out alive even."

Her words hung, suspended in the air, mirroring the clouds in the air above.

"That said, you do have me on your side. Something nobody else ever had."

"What's that supposed to mean?"

"Can't you tell?" Zaila flung her arms out at her sides, twirling around quickly for Adela a few items, the hem of her dress lifting up and manufacturing a soft wind.

"What am I supposed to be looking at?" Adela asked, confused.

"I'm a Djinn!"

"A Djinn?" Adela echoed back. She blinked once, then twice, then three times and furrowed her brow. "What's a Djinn exactly?"

"You've never heard of us before?" Zaila let out an amused cackle, nearly doubling over in place. "Where are you from, exactly?"

"I'm from Sunseree. I'm not sure how far that is from here."

"You don't know how far it is? How did you get here? Were you dropped off by a firebird?"

"A firebird?"

Zaila sighed, sitting down on the mix of sand and gravel underneath her feet and rubbing her translucent fingers against her temples. "I can tell this conversation is going nowhere fast. You don't know the first thing about this part of the world. Do you? And yet you expect to traverse it, to take what you need and leave?"

"No. I'm having a tough time understanding why I'm here, in fact. And who you are. And where to go next."

"I'll tell you all about me then."

Adela paused, staring Zaila down. Tired and exasperated, lungs still burning from attempting to keep up with Zaila only moments ago, she refused to be pulled about once again, privy only to Zaila's meandering words. There was too much at stake here. It was time for her to stand her ground, as terrified as she was.

"No," she spat out.

Within seconds, Zaila had whipped around and flown straight at Adela's face, letting the air billow and build around her as she created a volatile pocket, akin to the air that formed ahead of a thunderstorm. Her face morphed, cracked and gritty. It appeared like stone that had tumbled down a mountainside too many times or ice that had dropped and shattered into a million little pieces.

Adela gulped.

"What did you say?" Zaila asked, her voice taking on a new form: scratchy and strained, deep and imposing.

"I'm sorry, but no."

"No?" Zaila's shadowy face was mere inches from her own, and Adela could see the outline of her features even more, augmented and pulled into a distinct scowl. In this state, she was terrifying, and Adela knew that her face would invade her future dreams, stealing away her sleep little by little. She had half a mind to drop the whistle now, to forget about this entire journey.

To forget about saving Milo.

To forget about finding her grandmother.

To forget about saving her mother.

But instead, she mustered up her remaining courage, the courage she had found more and more of as the days passed, and stood up for herself. "Zaila, I need to save my friend. And if you want to help me, if you want to take me to the

Waters of Life and Death, you can tell me all about yourself on the way there."

Zaila backed off, her features settling into that of the little girl Adela met when she first entered the city limits.

Adela held her gaze, refusing to blink in fear of shedding tears that would roll down her cheeks and surely dampen her shirt. She had not yet fully processed what she was about to do, nor were her mind and body primed to do so.

It took everything in her power not to cry; Adela had often felt powerless, as if the world was against her. But this was different. People were depending on her. She bit her tongue, tasting blood on her lips, her breathing erratic as she willed Zaila to speak again.

"Very well," Zaila said, heading off in the direction of a vast desert dune in the distance, one that seemed to loom over the small city below. She drifted backward as she maintained eye contact with Adela, charcoal eyes to viridescent ones. "Follow me."

# EIGHTEEN

# OASIS

———

Adela let out the deep sigh she had been keeping hostage. She checked that the whistle was still against her skin, setting out to follow Zaila. At night, the city was quiet, with not much to look at. Houses carved of stone dotted out of the landscape of rock, small caves lit from within, carrying only fellow humans in their spaces. Cats slinked about in the night, yowling only when they encountered one another and stopping briefly to take in the sight of Zaila and Adela—the Djinn and the traveling girl.

Ahead of Adela was only sand. Here and there, leafy palm trees dotted the landscape, joined by the humble olive tree, its silvery-green leaves providing opportune areas for their white, feathery flowers and underripe green olives to grow. Verdant greens were unlike the beige world around them. Wells stood in the center of sideways streets, creating makeshift courtyards alongside shopfronts and chairs and tables that had been set up outside, a gathering-place of sorts. It was at one of these wells that Adela and Zaila now stopped, thirst threatening their expedition. Next to the refuge stood an animal, long neck and slim legs with strange undulating humps that sagged on its back. Its face, long and drooping, was covered with plush fur around its small ears.

"What is that?"

"That's a camel."

"What does it do?"

"It's one of the most amazing creatures in all the universe."

"Really?"

"Yes. I know of a camel that got lost and wandered the desert for over a year before returning to its owners. They're like wayfinders of the animal world, able to withstand anything that comes their way."

The camel approached the girls and stopped a foot's length from Adela; from this angle, she could see its thick eyelashes, curling toward the midnight sky above. The smell from its mouth was unbearable, its crooked and yellowed teeth chewing on bit of straw with its tough lips.

Zaila brought up a bucket of water with her hands, somehow firm enough to pull up the frayed rope from which the container was loosely suspended. Adela was too tired to question these physics, the same physics she had experienced when Zaila had touched her earlier in the evening. Instead, she dunked her head into the bucket, allowing the cool water to rush over her face. Her braided hair flowed in place, the dirt from earlier in the day loosening, and she took a few deep gulps of the muddied water, savoring the feeling in her mouth for just a moment. As she opened her eyes, a face filled the space at the bottom of the bucket. Adela stumbled backward, landing on her backside and knocking the bucket over as a manic laugh filled her ears.

"Did that scare you?" Zaila wheezed, circling around Adela.

"Y-y-yes," Adela sputtered, blowing her nose to rid it of the water she had accidentally inhaled.

"That's one of my best tricks. It's a crowd favorite."

"It's definitely not mine. You shouldn't do that to people," Adela said, composing herself and wringing the water out of her braid.

"Says who?" Zaila slowed to a halt in front of Adela, hands on her hips in an act of defiance.

But Adela did not want to further engage the actions of her Djinn acquaintance. "We should continue on our way," Adela said, beckoning to the deep night sky. They had walked for a number of hours, adrenaline coursing through Adela's body and keeping her from feeling undue pain. "I don't know what time it is, but I imagine people will be waking up shortly."

"Soon enough," Zaila agreed. "But you promised me you'd let me tell you about myself. And where we're going. You wouldn't break your promise so easily now. Would you?"

"Well, we don't have much time for you to tell me. Get on with it, then."

A creeping Cheshire grin took over Zaila's face. "Very well, the basics first. Do you know what this place is?"

"You said it earlier."

"Al Ainab."

"Right."

"This is the city the Djinns created," Zaila said, pausing as if awaiting a certain response from Adela. When none came, she continued, flabbergasted. "Nothing? That means nothing to you?"

"I'll be honest, we don't have Djinn where I'm from, so I don't know what that means, really."

"How totally ignorant of you," Zaila scoffed, whipping the air around Adela as she continued edging closer to the outskirts of the city. She continued to lead Adela. "The Djinn are the oldest magical creatures in all the universe. Forged from fire and made of air, we were here long before man and we will be here long after."

Adela shivered, the chilled night air settling in her bones and whipping wind freezing her wet hair in place.

*Or is the shiver an involuntary reaction, a response to the story Zaila is telling?*

"Like you, we live out our days and care for families and stumble through life, like feeble men or women unable to grasp their true purpose. Like you, we come in many races: Marid, powerful and strong, roaming the edges of cities, protecting the townfolk from invading forces; and Ghouls, dreadful entities that can shape-shift and turn into a camel or a cat."

Adela laughed, quickly covering her mouth in an attempt to stop the sound from escaping, but it was too late. She had caught Zaila's attention.

Zaila smiled before carefully releasing her next words. "It seems humorous, yes, but think about it. If somebody upsets them, all they have to do is turn into a snake and give them a gentle little bite. Problem solved. And that's not all, of course. They prey on travelers and children, roaming graveyards and the dark corners of the world."

Adela gulped. "What kind of Djinn are you?"

"I'm a Jann, in fact"

"A what?"

"A Jann. I sit in the shaded areas between the night and day, revealing myself to whoever I find worthy. I can control the air around you, the waves of the sea, the very earth on which you walk. At this moment, I could rip the ground out from under you and send you plummeting into the shifting sand."

Adela stopped in place, her heart pounding.

Zaila stopped as well, turning to look at her and smirking. "I won't do that to you."

Barely assured, Adela continued forward. The mental and physical stress of the day overtook her with haste, and her legs collapsed out from under her. Zaila swept in, moving swiftly on the air. Her presence kept Adela temporarily suspended, arms flopping in front of her body as if resting on an invisible pillowcase.

"Careful now, we're just about there."

And they were.

A few steps forward and Adela and Zaila had made it out the other side of the dunes. Beyond was a small oasis: two rivers had carved out a place in between the red sand and stone of the desolate wasteland. The area was flat, sand dunes creating artificial waves on the surface of the land, as if mimicking the waves of an ocean.

Just like the whistle.

In the center of the land was a large and luscious palm tree, its long and plentiful fronds overlapping one another and providing shade to any travelers who may happen to come across it. The rivers in question curved around the tree, never joining but traveling side by side. Each was its own brilliant shade of blue. One was a bright cyan flecked with white spots that glimmered in the moonlight. The other was a deep blue, like that of the deepest points of the lake by Adela's home in Sunseree. Around the river lay scattered a bed of rocks, golden and deep charcoal, jutting out of the sand just so.

"Are those the Waters?"

"The Waters of Life and Death themselves."

"What do they do exactly?"

"They do exactly what they say in the name. They provide life, and they also take it away."

"You said people have died trying to find this place."

"That's right. It's typically more hidden than what you see before you now. I helped reveal it to you."

"Why?"

Zaila did not answer, only allowing her eyes to drift toward the whistle that swayed from Adela's neck.

Adela forced her attention back to the oasis, hands yearning to collect the water to bring Milo back to life.

And then once she did that, she could find her grandmother. And help her mother. She reached into the satchel she had been carrying, moving items around until she found what she was looking for—the container Nine had given her back in the Forgotten City. Removing it from her belongings, she unscrewed the cap and emptied its phosphorescent contents onto the cool sand at her feet. She was ready.

Adela raced toward the rivers, not knowing which was which, ignoring both Zaila's yells from behind her and the pain in her legs while keeping her steely gaze fixated only on the lush palm. If she could only reach it...

But when Adela was mere steps away from the rivers, she was propelled high into the air, tumbling through the atmosphere and barely missing the city limits. Landing hard, she was dazed for a moment; all breath had been knocked out of her and she could barely inhale without feeling a sharp pain at her side. Her ribs were now surely broken.

Zaila must have intervened, preventing her from reaching the river. She thrashed her head about, face flushed with anger as her breathing returned, becoming heavier with every passing second. Adela had thought Zaila was on her side. That she was willing to help her.

*How could I be foolish enough to trust her?*

That was when she saw it.

A scaly monster, nearly twenty times as long as Adela stood tall.

Emerging from the sand, it gleamed like the brightest gold in the world, the bony ridges along its spine resembling the carcass of a bird, colored in yellow and black. On its neck were loose flaps of skin that resembled a beard, and its tail was as thick as the palm tree's trunk ahead of her, coiled around it with a fierce possession. The Dragon had been burrowed in the sand all along, disguising itself within the muted colors and shades surrounding it, the perfect camouflage for the desert oasis. With a small, fire-filled roar in Adela's direction, it settled back into the depths of the earth, disrupting the soft sand as it did.

A sudden gust of wind whipped Adela's hair in her face.

"I didn't tell you about the Dragon."

"No," Adela said as Zaila appeared behind her, "you did not."

# NINETEEN

# DRAGON

———

The gauze bandage was cool to the touch, and Zaila's fingers moved deftly. When they touched Adela's skin, there was a slight burning sensation that quickly cooled when exposed to air. It was a strange feeling, unlike any Adela had felt before, but it was welcome among the blistering pain that enveloped her sides.

"That Dragon did some damage," Zaila said, breaking the silence.

They had taken up residence in an abandoned cave, a few hundred steps from the oasis itself. Zaila had carried Adela here and placed her on the stone floor with care, the movement itself making Adela's chest burn as if set on fire. It was difficult to breathe, and Adela winced as invisible hands pressed on the gash in her side. The significant blow she had suffered hours ago had not been Zaila after all. It had been the Dragon, on alert and ready to defend the water source Adela had sought for the better part of an evening.

"You should have warned me." Adela forced the words out behind clenched teeth.

"You ran off before I could."

"You didn't think to tell me that a Dragon was guarding the very thing I sought?"

"You should have been more cautious."

"Cautious? You don't understand what's at stake."

"I do." Zaila sighed, dropping her hands to her sides. "I've heard tales of travelers who seek the Waters of Life and Death. Who have, over the centuries, sought it for both nefarious reasons and noble ones. I'm choosing to help you. Count yourself among the lucky ones. Most who venture this far die before ever reaching the oasis. I'm the one who chose to make it visible to you."

Adela fell silent, allowing Zaila's small hands to continue their act of securing the bandage around her waist.

"How do we defeat it?" Adela asked.

"Defeat it?"

"How else can I get to the oasis in one piece?"

Adela saw the outline of Zaila's body, getting up and moving to recline against the coarse wall. The small cave, despite being currently unoccupied, showed signs of life, a rest stop for poor and weary travelers to seek shelter before they moved along.

"I don't know how to defeat it."

"What do you mean?"

"I've never gotten this far, and I've never heard of anyone else defeating it."

"I don't understand. We got this far. How do we not have a plan?"

"We? Up until this point, you've treated me with animosity, distrustful of my intentions."

"You offered to help me!" Adela shouted, the sound reverberating off the cave. She flinched as the action of straining her vocal chords made her chest spasm in response.

The whistle around Adela's neck caught Zaila's gaze once more and, watching her intently, Adela picked it off her chest, holding it between her fingers.

"You keep looking at this."

"Do I?"

"You know you do. Why?"

"That whistle," Zaila mused, leaving her perch against the wall and inching forward, "it's curious. Where did you get it?"

"It was gifted to me."

"By who?"

"Someone I trusted."

"*Very* curious." Zaila reached forward, her wispy fingertips mere inches from the whistle, before recoiling. Meeting Adela's gaze, she smiled. "Do you know what they say about whistles? Whistling in general?"

"No. Tell me."

"Whistles are special. The holder of a whistle holds court over the Djinn. And your whistle, well, it's even more special. It was carved here, ages ago, depicting the oasis itself. Whoever carved it would have known the Djinn intimately. How did you get it again?"

"It was given to me."

"But how did that person get it?"

"I don't know."

The statement hung in the air, heavy and brimming with tension.

"Right," Zaila said, breaking the silence. "We need a plan to get you close to the Dragon."

"Not just close enough. I need to defeat him."

"Right."

Zaila pulled at her hair, mindlessly brushing her grayscale lips with its dense strands. It seemed this was a unique tic or habit, much like Adela had the habit of biting at her lips and insides of her cheeks. The young girls sat in silence, as the paler midnight blues of dusk turned into deeper midnight blues of the late evening, the sky permanently a varying shade of navy and black. Adela imagined that each time it shifted to a slightly lighter color, the townsfolk would venture outside, hopeful that day—finally, that day—the Last Sun would end, and the sun's beams would kiss their faces once more.

In two months' time, it had yet to happen.

"Well," Zaila interrupted, "there's a way to defeat it, of course."

"How?"

"The first step is to have someone who can control the weather. Someone who can cause the skies to rumble, the atmosphere to grow thick and heavy and wet, the clouds to rain down on the smoldering desert land below, securing its heat in place." She paused for a beat, smirking at Adela. "Check."

"How does that help?"

"He's a Dragon of the sand. Right? By nature, water will hurt it. Or disarm it. Theoretically."

"Right."

"The second step would be to get close enough to incapacitate it. Making it rain is easy enough, but it can easily escape by burrowing into the sand. To steal away its attention, we need to create a diversion."

"A diversion?"

"And we need to use you as bait."

"Are you crazy?"

"Perhaps. But look at it this way. If you die, I can just bring you back to life. I think."

"Why am I the bait?"

"There's only two of us."

Adela's fingers grazed her neck and the whistle that draped across her collarbone. While Zaila spoke, she was devising a plan of her own, bolstered by the knowledge that Zaila had volunteered just before.

"I think I have a better idea."

Before Zaila could react, Adela put the whistle to her lips and sounded it. Nothing came out. All Adela could hear was air passing through the small windpipe, resulting in a short, wet sound not unlike a child blowing spit bubbles between their lips.

But there appeared to be a reaction from the beings it was intended for, for Zaila's body became stiff immediately, as if held together with wires that ran up to the sky. Her eyes grew a dark gray, and Adela imagined a storm brewing within them, getting more intense with the passing moments.

A low groan sounded from two humanoid figures at the mouth of the cave. Adela could only see the feet of the first and the outline of the second, the shape blocked out by the light of the moon behind them. As she let the whistle fall against her neck once more, Zaila pushed her into the rock of the cave wall and approached the strangers.

"Asim. Qadira. What brings you here?"

"Same as you. We heard the whistle. It summoned us."

The voice met Adela's ears, gravelly and low, like the growl of a feral tomcat. Its originator spoke in short phrases, pinched and forced, expelled from the depths of their belly.

"Did you get here before us, Zaila? My, how you always are ahead of the pack."

A feminine voice this time, soft and lilting but malicious in its tone. Silence followed, which was in turn followed by an exasperated sigh.

"Are you going to stand aside?"

A sound caught in the depths of Adela's throat as Zaila made her way to the back of the cave, the smaller of the two shapes following behind. Adela could now make out the figure in the moonlight. Her hair was short, reaching just above her ears, and white as freshly powdered snow. Between her eyes lay two blue pools—her eyes—that were freckled with pale, ghoulish flecks. The woman was older than Adela and Zaila, perhaps older even than Adela's own mother. Face sallow and lips thin, her cheekbones came to a point alongside a nose that zigzagged across her face. Unlike Zaila, she walked on two feet and seemed corporeal in nature, as if Adela could reach out and touch her.

Rocks and dust fell from the ceiling when the second figure entered the cave. Or, not so much entered as elbowed his upper torso into the small gap. He had a long beard, unruly and black, wiry hairs going every which way. Whatever hair was on his face made up for the lack of hair on his head; the surface of his head was bumpy and his skin tanned, a warm shade of beige. Adela could not make out his eyes from her position in the cave.

Perhaps the most distinguishing feature of all, he was muscular and huge. The Marid.

Which meant the woman in front of her was the hungry Ghoul.

"Who is this?"

"This is Adela. She—"

"I see," the woman interrupted. Naturally, her eyes found the whistle, the one Adela carried around her neck. The one that now seemed inexplicably warm to the touch, burning Adela's skin underneath. "You called for us?"

Adela mustered up the courage to speak. "I need the help of the Djinn."

"What do you know about the Djinn?" the woman asked, stepping forward.

"I know only that I need to defeat the Dragon. And I would like your help with my plan."

Zaila threw a cursory glance toward Adela. "What plan?" she muttered under her breath, hoping the words would be unheard by the other occupants of the cave. But they were not. The Ghoul had heard her.

"Yes, what plan is that?"

"I need a diversion."

"Simple then. You can be bait."

"That won't work."

"Really?"

"Qadira, hear her out. Please," Zaila pleaded, gray eyes shifting from Adela to Qadira.

The woman nodded, motioning to Adela to continue with the flick of her wrist, her eyes remaining trained on the carved whistle. With a deep breath, Adela outlined her plan.

It would be relatively simple, as far as plans concerning dragons go. As Zaila promised, a deluge of rain would befall the oasis at once, a storm conjured out of nowhere.

Then, the Marid—whose name was Asim—would convene in the center of the oasis by brute force alone. With his commanding size, he would serve as a noble distraction for the Dragon while everyone assumed position. He was, after all, the protector of the people.

Qadira, of course, was the leader of the Ghouls, beings who could shift into other creatures. She would work closely with Adela, provoking the Dragon in the sky while the young girl made her way to the waters.

It was simple.

"Why should we help?" The rumbling voice sounded from the mouth of the cave, and the women turned to face Asim.

Qadira cackled, a tinny, snorting laugh that seemed as if it should not be coming out of her mouth. Rolling her eyes, she turned toward Adela, her arms crossed against her spindly frame. "He's right, of course. Why would we help you? Of all people?"

"Because I have this whistle," Adela argued, holding it in front of her face, as if it were a talisman.

"That whistle is nothing. It merely calls us. You have no power over us otherwise," Qadira countered.

Adela's heart was racing. In order to save Milo, it was imperative that she had the trio of Djinn at her side. Sure, she had never liked Milo much, never confided in him, or felt particularly close to him. Rather, she had merely tolerated him. But, like her, he had been an outsider. Other children did not want to play with him, and he would walk home from school with his head hung low. Their friendship had been one of convenience, wanting to escape their respective impending solitudes.

But Adela had a moral responsibility to save him. She knelt on the ground, removing her shoe, and then her sock, and then slowly pulled out one of the small, circular beads she had kept on her body throughout this journey.

One of the cave pearls Alby had gifted her gleamed in the moon-kissed recesses of the cave and, for a moment, everyone's eyes fell on Adela's hand, where the pearl had settled in the crooks of her palm. It wasn't brilliant, nor was it faceted, like a gemstone. Instead, its smooth surface was perfect, and the circular shape held a unique beauty. In order to save her friend, her family, she was willing to part ways with one.

"What is that?" Zaila exhaled, enthralled by the pearl.

"It's a cave pearl."

But that answer came, not from Adela, but from Qadira, inching closer to the young girl.

"How do you—"

"They're quite mundane, as natural formations tend to be, but this one is special. Isn't it?" Qadira asked.

This question was directed at Adela, who nodded in reply. "Yes. Gifted to me."

"Under what circumstances?"

"Troubling ones."

Qadira tilted her head to the side, as if nonplussed yet understanding all the same. "And if we help you?"

"I'll give you one. These cave pearls allow me to bend space and time. Perhaps, if in your hands, it can help you do the same."

"Child, I have lived thousands of years. What use does that have for me?"

"And in all those thousands of years, you can't pinpoint a single moment in time you'd like to return to?"

Asim's deep, lumbering breaths rolled through the cave, joining the wind that whistled around its curves. Moments passed that felt like hours, and Adela worried but refused to convey it. She could not show weakness any longer.

"Very well, let's put your plan in place."

A grunt from the cave's mouth indicated that Asim, too, was on board.

"Now?"

"We need to do it today. While it's dark out and the clouds are preventing the stars from shining into the desert," Zaila said, looking backward toward the entrance, where the oasis stood only hundreds of feet away. "We need to go now."

Qadira followed. And then Adela after her, cold sweat forming on her brow. She slinked away into the night, her quest as a north star, the air cooler this time of night. While the feeling on her skin was refreshing, it only proved to send a shiver down her spine. Her body tensed in anticipation of the upcoming battle.

"Everyone knows their role?" Zaila asked, leading the group of misfits to the edge of a stone wall on the outskirts of the oasis. "When I start the dust storm, you'll need to take cover. In a storm of that nature, it's easy to lose your bearings. With the Dragon out of the hole, I'll whip up the thunder. With luck, you'll sneak in and grab what you need and return to where you came."

"Wait," Adela said, reaching into her sock once more. "The pearl. You should have it. As an insurance of sorts." She placed it firmly in Zaila's hands, manually closing her fingers around the sphere.

With that, Zaila phased through the wall and inched toward to the oasis in an attempt to lure the Dragon out if its hiding spot. The storm crackled at first. The whistling of the air whipped around Adela's body and the wall she crouched behind. Small, granular particles hit her in the face as sand rose off the ground, floating on thin air.

Closing her eyes, she crouched down low and used her hand to steady and guide her along the wall. Heading for the section where she had landed awkwardly hours ago, she attempted to get back in the open area.

Asim, too, lumbered forward, his heavy steps muffled on the surface of the sand. Only now could Adela get a good look at him. He was nearly four times as tall as Adela and exponentially larger, too. But if one would assume that meant he was clumsy, they would be wrong. His stride was confident and sure. As his steps were considerably longer than Adela's, he approached the center of the oasis in no time, ready to meet the Dragon as it emerged from its hiding place.

Adela stumbled forward, pain searing at her sides as the storm picked up speed and ferocity. She felt the ground under her feet give way as the large, scaly figure emerged from the sand.

His long tail whipped back and forth in excitement and a hypnotizing frenzy. In the reflection of the glimmering waters, the sand Dragon seemed to dwell on his own reflection a moment too long, as if mesmerized by the shine of his scales under the moonlight. A split second later, his attention turned back to the granules. Adela moved closer, testing the boundaries of his line of sight.

But the Dragon had seen Asim in his periphery, and so he tried out his powers for a moment, taking off for a brief flight. His roar was deafening, and it took everything in Adela's power not to scream at that very moment. She wondered how the people in the neighboring areas could not hear it. Were they immune to it? Was the roar reserved only for those in the vicinity of the oasis? Or did they simply ignore it?

A final roar was punctuated by a puff of fire. While the Dragon flew above her head, Adela could feel heat suspended in the air.

Asim continued to move about the area, a perfect distraction as the Dragon trained his eye on the single figure, ignoring the worsening forecast and the converging troop of Adela and Qadira moving toward its hiding spot. With the weather devolving, it was time for the next phase.

"Ready?" Adela heard Zaila's whisper in her ear, seemingly out of nowhere.

"Ready," Qadira's voice reverberated in her right ear.

"Now!" Adela screamed. It took every muscle in Adela's body to propel herself forward. She faced the Dragon's back, only a few hundred steps from the Waters themselves. Under the cover of darkness and behind the solid wall, she had been safe. But now, she was the perfect prey—out in the open and running toward danger. Her feet sank into the soft sand that, as it had for Asim, provided temporary cover, her footsteps silent.

Roars sounded around her; the Dragon had grown tired of its distraction. Asim was retreating now, readying the battlefield for Qadira.

And there she was, soaring through the sky on feathered plumes of magenta and gold. Her wingspan reached nearly ten feet across as she aimed at the Dragon's head. The Firebird herself.

When Zaila had spoken of the legendary firebird, Adela knew it would be one of the few creatures that could venture a run at the powerful, mythical Dragon. Qadira had been happy to oblige. She had never shape-shifted into a firebird before, and she yearned for the opportunity to spread her arms and glide on the air.

But the Dragon's attention was piqued; the swirling atmosphere was on their side. As the Dragon beat its papery wings, it turned its body to track the Firebird, which had dipped low, as if to entice its opponent. The storm had kicked in by now. A resounding boom echoed in the sky, and dark storm clouds rolled through the oasis. With a puff of smoke and a glance toward the sky, the Dragon swayed in place, abandoning Qadira's Firebird altogether.

With a final pass, Qadira retreated, off to the outskirts to meet with Asim and Zaila, as the Dragon attempted to burrow back into the ground and escape the raindrops now falling.

It was Adela's turn. The plan's success depended on her.

As she approached the Dragon, she unbuckled her ruck-sack, rummaging around with one hand to grab what she had only thought of using mere moments before. Clara's hair comb. Pulling it out, she clutched her fingers around it tightly, terrified she would lose it. She was only fifty steps away from the Dragon and victory was in reach. For she had a plan now.

And then he saw her.

Once again, Adela flew into the air and landed on her back, the wind knocked out of her and the gash at her side opening once more. Rain continued to pick up, thunderous bolts of lightning peppering the inky sky. She struggled to get back in position, rolling onto her stomach and peeling an eye open. As she had expected, the Dragon was enticed by the glinting bolts in the sky. As suddenly as his attention fell on the bolts, he turned his gaze to Adela with a hiss, stomping over to her, ready to finish her off.

His tail curled closer, preceding him slightly, the same tail that had lifted her off the ground twice now. The Dragon cornered Adela, edging nearer while her injured body struggled to crawl over the smooth sand.

She reached, slowly, for the Waters of Life and Death, as his heavy footsteps and huffing breath drew closer, deafening among the patter of the rain on the dunes. Rain fell heavily, pulled back to the ground with a magnetic force. Adela could no longer tell where Zaila or Qadira or Asim were situated, and she didn't know if they would be able to intervene if anything befell her.

She was on her own.

Finally, she pulled herself up to the small rock outcropping that lined the edge of the oasis. Using her elbows to prop herself up, she opened both eyes. She was situated above the twin rivers, in which she saw the Dragon reflected. Her small figure was dwarfed by his mammoth one, and his foot pressed down on her lower body, claws beginning to push into her thin and battered skin. Her body was bruised and broken, blood puckering out of the cuts in her arms and hands, fingers throbbing from holding the comb tightly. His tail swatted her arm as he pressed down, sending an excruciating, sharp pain up her spine.

Adela acted quickly. Before he could crush her body under his foot, she stabbed the tip of his tail with Clara's hair comb, driving it through the fleshy bits. With all the might she could muster, and the images of Milo and her mother racing in her head, she drove the object deeper still, into one of the rocks framing the oasis. She removed her hands only to pound down on the pin with both fists, grunting each time she took a breath or moved her upper body, bloodied and sore.

Her plan appeared to work. She had noticed earlier how infatuated the Dragon had been with his reflection, with the glints that bounced off his scales and the light that pierced the night sky in the form of lightning bolts. She remembered a story her mother told her, long ago, of a Dragon enamored with shiny objects, until he encountered a silver dagger that proved to be his weakness, his greatest love and desire his downfall. Adela laughed, wheezing in pain, as she recalled how Clara's hair comb had saved her on multiple occasions now.

The Dragon flailed and roared, immobilized in place by the silver weapon; his body was weakened, even more so when incapacitated by the watery deluge that poured from the skies. Unable to retreat into his dry haven below the sand, he thrashed about while Adela deftly rolled out of harm's way and pulled herself closer to the Waters.

Adela knew the pin would not hold the Dragon very long. She needed to get back to Milo.

"Which river?" she whispered, willing Zaila to speak to her once more.

"The darker blue."

So the deep blues sloshing gently in place would bring life to Milo's cold body. Her container in hand, she scooped up the water quickly, careful to avoid her fingers for fear of adverse effects, keeping a vigilant eye on the Dragon who had now resorted to biting at the comb with his sharp fangs.

"I need to leave," she announced, realizing she was in grave danger if she stuck around longer. "Thank you all for your help," Adela gasped, knowing the Djinn would somehow hear her.

"Where are you going?" the gravelly voice asked.

"What will you do next?" the lilting voice added.

Zaila's soft voice broke through the noise. "How will I find you if I need you?"

"I need to go back to where I belong. I need to finish this."

At that moment, the Dragon escaped his confines. Acting quickly, Adela tore off the makeshift necklace that secured the whistle at her nape and let it fall into the depths of the Waters, from which she had collected what she needed. Chest heaving, trembling and battered, she once again stood behind the stone staircase in the corridor outside the Forgotten City.

# TWENTY

# ISLE OF VILA

---

The sound of dripping water echoed through the hallway. In one hand, Adela grasped the container, fearful the water would spill, that she would drop it at any moment, or that it would just as suddenly vanish from between her clenched fingers. She had returned to her original body. Not the one in the forest, but the second one that lay on the cool stone in the underground corridor that led to the Forgotten City.

This time was different than all the others prior. She struggled to stand and nausea slammed into her with the full weight of a freight train. Her eyes took longer to adjust to her surroundings, watering slightly as she pried them open. Transporting had, of course, been a physically taxing action. The presence of one less pearl in her possession would have surely impacted her further, making the effects of traveling even more potent than before.

And that was without the battering her body had undergone in Al Ainab.

Moments passed before Adela could hoist herself up on her elbows, and she blinked a few times to allow her eyes to finish adjusting. She moved slowly and laboriously, her feet shuffling against the floor as she struggled to keep her eyes open, the pain that reverberated through her body the only impulse keeping her awake at that very moment. Lifting her face up, she was enveloped by the smell of spices wafting through the air, and she knew she was closing in on the main door. Only a few steps forward. And then a few more. And then a few more, repeated an infinite amount of times until finally, she felt the wood beneath her fingertips and began beating with her fists, simultaneously crying out, a cathartic release after the events of the past few days. As she beat at the door, she devised her next steps.

With the Water of Life, she could save Milo.

And with the knowledge Adela gained in Old Kitfalls, she would set out for answers.

And she would finally find the Isle of Vila.

When the door swung open, she collapsed, sinking to the floor like a bundle of dirtied clothes. On her way down, a pair of hands caught her by the armpits and pulled her across the threshold. Everything went dark.

When Adela awoke, she was in a cold, damp, and dark room she did not recognize, lit only with a handful of candles, each tucked in the corners of the room. As she blinked, her eyes adjusted to the candlelight. The walls here were stone, gray in color and smooth in texture, as if carved out of a mountain cliff and sanded down by someone running their hands over the walls each day for centuries. The tick of a clock in the corner echoed off the walls. In that corner, a figure hunched over a workbench, another candle by his elbow as the primary source of light; this was a small living area, with only bare furnishings filling the cavernous space. Adela had been reclining on a small bed. To her side, a humanoid figure was placed on a chair and draped in a tablecloth. Milo's body. Which meant that the person at the bench was—

"George?"

The chair creaked as it turned, George angling his tired and weathered face toward Adela's.

"You're finally up."

"Yes."

"You came back."

"I did."

"And I see that you were successful in your quest," he said, gesturing to a small iron end table on the opposite side of her resting place. On it lay the canister gifted to her by Nine, who had bartered for it with Rough, wet and shiny on the outside, carefully guarding the life-giving contents within.

Adela nodded, quickly planning her next question and refusing to give George an opportunity to make any additional gratuitous comments. "Did you know?"

"Know what?"

"That a Dragon was there? Guarding the Waters?"

George sighed before answering, shifting his position so Adela could see only his side profile. An impatience had set in his voice when he spoke, and his demeanor signified that he cared little for this line of questioning.

"Yes, I did."

"And you sent me there? Without warning?"

"I had a hunch you could do it. I had a hunch you—"

"A hunch?" Adela interrupted. She moved abruptly and flinched from the pain, nearly forgetting why she had been resting, the circumstances under which she awoke in this room in the first place. Slowing her movements, she continued, "I could have been killed based on your hunch. I barely made it out alive."

"But you did."

"That Dragon could have killed me."

"But it didn't," he said, waving her away with his hand as he turned his chair back to focus on the item he had been tinkering with when Adela woke. He pocketed it and walked to Adela, a scowl imprinted on his face.

"Monsters," he said, "are only monstrous when you give them the power to be so. Monsters are everywhere in this world. I can be a monster. You can be a monster." His eyes shone in the dim light, the flicker of the candlelight reflecting in his pupils as they dilated to the shifting light levels.

"I—I don't understand."

"We create monsters in our lives. Our response to them determines how our stories unfold. You can choose to cower in fear and ignorance of them, or you can choose to confront them head on, gathering the intuition and courage to defeat them."

"But I didn't do any of that. That Dragon is still there, guarding the oasis."

"In that moment, you surely confronted your fear of dying. Your plan was rooted in courage and physical strength and mental stamina without the smallest dependence on your powers. Isn't that special?"

"How do you even know all that?"

George smiled, his lips curling over his teeth in a wide grin. "An alchemist doesn't reveal his secrets," he said before making his way to the table beside Adela. "Well, you brought it back. The Water of Life itself." He picked up the bag, considering it for a moment before placing it down and walking away, his back to Adela.

"I did. What happens next?"

"What happens next is that you leave. You forget about this place."

"What?"

"You need to leave. Take the kid with you and forget about the Forgotten City. Never return."

"Why not?"

"We're just a small, jagged stepping stone on your journey. If Clara was right, you're meant for bigger things. Here."

He dug into his pockets, pulling out a small book, slightly larger than the palm of his hand. It was bound in leather, and the binding was hand-stitched. On the front was a small letter embossed into the cover—a faint, curled C.

"What is this?" Adela asked, reaching out and letting her fingers touch the soft fabric, which darkened slightly from the oil on her fingers. She savored its feeling on her skin.

"It's your grandmother's. You should have it. In return, I ask only for one thing," George added, his voice a gruff whisper.

"What's that?"

"The brooch."

Adela shook her head, meeting George's pleading eyes. "I need it to return home."

"But you don't, not really. Once you release it, you'll be back in Sunseree. And this book will lead you to Clara."

"What about Milo?"

"She'll know how to help. Trust me."

"But why the brooch?"

Silence filled the air, and George let out a small laugh, one that felt entirely out of character yet altogether filled with a certain sadness and longing. "Tell me again where you found it."

"It was in an ivory box filled with my grandmother's belongings. She gave it to my mother, to give to me."

"Which means it's been forgotten, passed on without a second thought."

"I don't believe that's true."

George paused once more, smiling down at Adela. "If it weren't true, Clara would have kept it herself."

Adela picked the brooch from her shirt and held it in her hands, running its grooves through her blistered fingers, savoring the cool metal and the worn engraving that had led her here. George was right. She didn't need the brooch to return back home. Or wherever she ventured next. And her grandmother had truly left it behind, a memory of a life foregone.

"Deal."

"Deal," George repeated. He walked over to Milo, lifting his limp body into his arms and standing in front of Adela. "You'll need to take him with you."

Adela nodded as Milo's weight pushed down on her upper body. For a brief moment, she caved under the weight, her knees buckling from under her before she caught her bearings. A searing, white pain spread from her neck to the backs of her knees, and she held her breath for a handful of clock ticks before she stopped seeing the popping lights behind her eyelids. Finally secure, Adela inhaled as George passed her the canister.

"You'll need this, of course."

"Thank you."

Adela contemplated prying Milo's mouth open at that very moment, fighting against the rigor mortis that had surely set in by now.

But George had read her mind, or anticipated what she was thinking. "The Waters of Life and Death, they're powerful."

"I know."

"It would be best to consult with a witch to help bring Milo back to life."

"I know."

And she had a witch in mind, too. The witch who could help her save her mother. The witch she had been looking forward to seeing since she had set out on this journey.

Her grandmother.

She grabbed the canister and pushed it down into her satchel of items, small knick-knacks and treasures from both home and the journeys along the way collecting there. An item lay at the bottom, one which Adela had yet to reveal to anyone—a jar with dried petals. They were once a deep orange, or so Adela imagined, but had turned a hazy, brackish brown with age. They appeared to be nothing special, unassuming really, but Adela knew what power they held.

"And this, too," George interrupted, holding the bound book out in front of him. George, understandably, believed Adela would go to see her grandmother now, and would use the journal to find her.

She would not.

Nor would she break this spell and return back to her body just yet.

Grabbing the book, she turned her back to George as she dropped it into her satchel, joining the cohort of items. She shielded her actions from the room's other inhabitant and, with her pointer and thumb, plucked the dried flower from its hiding place. Holding the brooch over George's outstretched palm with her other hand, she closed her eyes and released it, keeping this final journey a secret.

Adela was not ready to travel again. Her injuries proved to be wholly disorienting. Her brain could best be described as foggy and a severe spell of nausea whacked her in the face just as she had been whacked about before this all started.

When she opened her eyes, she recognized the setting immediately.

The sound reached her first: the gentle murmur of water joining the deluge of rain that fell from the heavens, drenching Adela and the limp body on her shoulder at once. Adela blinked. In each direction, dense trees rose from the ground on thin roots that converged to form a substantive trunk branching in multiple directions. Atop this trunk were spiraled leaves of a green color. Adela leaned in to touch them and scrunched her nose at their pungent smell.

The noises continued: the belly groan of frogs that hid themselves in the roots of the trees around her; the high-pitched chirp of bugs that lived in the ground, finding a home between the overworld and underworld; the flitting wings of butterflies and firebugs and other winged creatures that danced around her face, occasionally forcing a landing that would be quickly disrupted by the swat of Adela's hand across her nose. And then the chirps rang out.

Hidden in the vast trunks of the tree were a collection of nearly fifty birds, all gazing intently at the young girl who appeared out of nowhere. They were large in size and quite long. Altogether, they were nearly as long as Adela was tall, their colorful tail feathers following behind their backsides majestically. Each was a lime-green color, a red band just above their foreheads. Though their tails were pale blue and red, their backs featured a streak of cobalt, as if someone had begun to paint the morning sky when breathing life into them.

Strong, black beaks squawked and gnashed in her direction. One among them spoke, its voice harsh. "Where did you come from?"

"I'm here for the Witch," Adela said, her voice strong and confident. It was time to finish her story.

The birds looked at one another for a brief moment, as if silently communing.

The Bird spoke again. "We know of no Witch."

"But you must. She's here. Isn't she? This must be the Isle of Vila."

They exchanged glances once more, and Adela sensed a darkness in the air. Fear, perhaps. Or death. From above, wings fluttered once more, rising above the treetops. Adela sought out the flash of green in the night sky, but she saw only pitch black. It was not one of these birds, then, that had flown away.

"We cannot help you," the voice sounded, ringing through the air.

"But you must."

"We must not do anything," the Bird answered before letting out a call not unlike the prolonged screech of the chickens that called Sunseree their home. Like thunder in the night sky, the birds rose abruptly, leaving the branches where they had been perched in favor of another imposing tree to call home.

"I can help you," a gentle voice said, whispering into Adela's ear.

Adela nearly fell backward, dropping Milo in the process, as she scanned the air for the source of the sound.

"Where are you?"

Without answering, a small woman flew right at Adela's face, hovering between her eyes. She was tiny, about the size of a hummingbird, with a thin waist. Her hair was a golden color and tied up with a small ribbon, falling around her face delicately. While Adela could not make out her features at this size, she could make out that the woman had two translucent wings, shifting between a deep purple and a vibrant yellow, continuously moving and keeping the woman in place.

"What are you?"

"I'm a Fairy, of course! Or you can call me Vila."

"You *are* real!"

"Why would there be an Isle of Vila without any Vila, silly?" The Fairy let out a tinny laugh that sounded metallic in Adela's ears. "Now then, what is that on your shoulder?"

It was as if being reminded of the weight that she was carrying was just enough to make her feel the pain of doing so, and Adela's knees buckled under her before she regained her strength. "I'm here to find a Witch."

"I know. I don't understand why. But if you really wish to find her, follow me."

The Fairy motioned behind Adela. Turning, she saw only the dense forest that surrounded them at all sides.

"I don't understand. Where are we going?"

"Just beyond the rubber trees."

Without hesitation, Adela pushed the lush foliage out of her path, her hand coming back wet with rainwater; she was drenched, of course, and Milo's body was growing heavier as his clothes dampened. As much as the tree cover had protected her from the worst, Adela was hopeful for a moment of pause from the deafening rain around them.

She turned to speak to the Fairy but found that she was now in another clearing, not unlike the first, surrounded by dense forest. Disoriented, she closed her eyes, tears of anger threatening to spill out. With her eyes clamped shut, she heard the water. It was low and trickling at first, but as she pushed forward, hands in front of her body, the sound picked up until it was an intense rushing. Her hands came back dotted with blood, scraped slightly from the branches and twigs and creatures that undoubtedly lived in the foliage. But when she opened her eyes, Adela laid eyes on the stone house.

"There you are!"

The Fairy hopped off the broad leaf where she had been standing, the leaf bouncing from the motion. While Adela could not make out her specific features, she could see that her eyes shone with anticipation.

"Is this it?"

"It sure is."

"What do I do?"

"I don't know. Whatever it is that you set out to do. I'm only here to help you along."

It was just as her mother had described it in her story.

Lightning bugs rushed up to fly into her face and the sound of gentle water from the nearby river filled the air. The stone house was in front of her: dead ahead, lights off and still. Adela was uneasy, her body on the verge of collapse. But she knew this was her only opportunity to get answers.

About the story Kocur had told her.

About Conrad and his cruelty.

Groaning, her body on the verge of collapse, Adela approached the hut, the Fairy not far behind; it was quiet, and Adela did not see any movement inside the house. She waited in the silence, circling the stone house and wary of any movement within. None came.

Instead, after a few moments of bated breath, a hand fell on her shoulder.

The woman, the one with the thick black hair, stood with an apron tied around her waist. She smiled at Adela, eyeing her, as a look of utter bemusement grew on her face. "Now then, you look vaguely familiar."

## TWENTY-ONE

# DEFEAT

———

Adela froze, considering dropping the dried petals clutched in her palm right then and there, wondering if she should just return home, go back to Sunseree to pack up her life and leave forever. She struggled to get the next words out, and she imagined that one of the frogs from earlier had leapt inside and taken refuge within her throat. But she was bolstered by a newfound bravery.

"Of course, I do. I was just here last week."

"Last week? I don't remember you," the Witch said, tilting her head to one side and squinting her eyes, as if the slightly blurred image of Adela would spur her memory.

Adela continued, the story her mother told ringing in her ears, details sticking out with pure necessity. "I promised I'd teach you how to paint."

"That was decades ago."

"It wasn't."

"It was."

"Prove it."

"I can't, not like this. But if you let me inside, I may be able to do so."

The Witch eyed Adela, briefly glancing at the body draped across her shoulders. If she noticed the Fairy, she did not let on. Crossing her arms on her chest, she smiled. "Very well, it'd be rude of me to leave you out here in the rain."

Adela had barely noticed. The rain had been cooling, cleansing the stench and grime of her journeys and carrying them away far, far from here. But she needed to put down Milo, for her body was starting to shake and convulse, broken ribs and sprained wrists just a few of the countless injuries that screamed with pain now.

And so she followed the Witch inside. As she entered the hut, Adela found—again—that the room mirrored that from her mother's story perfectly. She placed Milo's body on a small chair tucked into the corner of the room, pushing her chest out in a small, yawning stretch as she did.

"Do I still look the same to you?" The woman stood in the middle of the room, hands on her hips while she observed Adela. Evidently, the Witch did not trust that Adela was the girl from decades prior, which of course, she hadn't been.

But Adela had an advantage here. In the story, the woman appeared based on the likeness devised by whomever had encountered her; for the Golden Girl, the Witch appeared to have raven hair and pale skin, lips as red as blood.

"Dark black hair, down to your waist." Adela said, parroting the words her mother had used in the story.

"Very well," the woman said, her eyebrow arching in surprise. "And my name?"

"You don't have one to me. But you do. All things do."

"Clever girl."

"Will you finally tell me your name?"

"Why would I do a thing like that?"

"We're friends now. Aren't we? And if you do, I can teach you how to paint like I do."

"I know how to paint. I've done it before." The Witch laughed, mocking Adela.

"Yes, but you haven't mastered it like I have."

The woman's eyes shone, beady and dark. She strode over to a bench, replete with containers and herbs thrown haphazardly across the surface. A gilded cage hung from the ceiling and, as Adela leaned forward, she saw the Falcon.

"You!"

"I see you two have met before," the Witch said, releasing the Falcon and letting him dig his long talons into the side of her pale arm. "You know, he told me all about you. About your encounter in the woods. About the woman you were with. About the twins. Dreadfully sorry about that, of course. No need to lie any longer."

The Falcon chattered, as if he was laughing at Adela's expense.

The Fairy had snuck behind Adela's hair, resting on her shoulder. She was silent, the sounds of her small wings only a minuscule noise in the quiet darkness; to anyone but Adela, it was as if she didn't exist.

Adela stared forward, allowing silence to fill the room before she spoke.

"It doesn't matter. That was only days ago."

"Was it? To him—to me—it has been decades. Decades of plotting. Planning. Waiting for you to show up at my doorstep."

All air had dissipated from the room. Adela found it hard to breathe, and she struggled to maintain her composure. She had now existed in multiple time periods. The concept of time was dizzying and maddening. She grew increasingly aware of just how much she had confided in the Falcon those nights.

"You've been following me."

"Of course. I was sent to follow you," the Falcon replied, his eyes boring into Adela's soul.

More silence.

"What were you plotting?"

Overjoyed, the Witch clapped her hands together, as if Adela's question was a present she yearned to open. Her mouth curled into a vicious smile, canines subtly jutting out from behind her lips. "Oh, I can show you! Wait right here." She walked down into an opening in the floor, a small trapdoor leading to the damp and dark basement below the house.

"This doesn't feel right," the Fairy whispered, tickling Adela's ear with her breath. "We should go."

But Adela's head was spinning. She was on the precipice of answers, and she needed to learn more, to see this through. Clutching her head, she lowered herself onto the floor slowly as the Falcon watched.

"I still don't understand," she said, hoping the Falcon would divulge more details. "What does this all have to do with me?"

"Stupid girl," he said, spreading out his wings and making his body larger in an attempt to appear threatening. "Don't you see? This has nothing to do with you. And everything to do with the Golden Girl. Your mother."

"My mother?"

"Isn't it sad? Your mother is the main character of your own story. How that must hurt."

But it didn't. Adela pressed on, grasping for more answers that appeared to be within reach.

"What about my mother?"

"News spread far and wide that Nuimtree was a kingdom in upheaval, cursed by a dastardly witch. And then, just the same, news spread about the children. A Golden Girl and a Boy, and the celestial powers bestowed upon them, the abilities to bring balance to the day and night. And perhaps, powers far greater than that."

Adela nodded, remembering the story Clara told her in the caves, long ago.

"Then word from Western Wilerea came. A healing witch, a student of practical magic, had been summoned to the kingdom. Ha! Of course, my master sent me to learn more, to understand the motives of the King and Queen. To learn about the babies. And that's where I met you." The falcon let out another squawk, a chatter of sorts among the quiet.

Downstairs, sounds of a struggle and items being thrown about climbed up the stairs, though nobody emerged from the darkness.

"How foolish you were to tell me all about your life back home! How foolish you were to lead me to Clara and the castle itself. It's quite surprising what you can accomplish when you are invisible in the night sky. I listened that night, and I learned how you and Clara would plan to steal away the young girl in the morning. I listened as you spoke with the old woman by the fire. And then, I reported back to my master. And she devised her plan."

"And what plan was that?"

"To conquer the daylight."

Sounds of footsteps clamored up the stairs as Adela's breath caught in her throat. The Falcon's attention fell to the Witch's movements.

In this moment, the Fairy found her opportunity to speak. "Miss, we need to get out of here now."

"I—"

"No, don't talk. You'll give us away. Just listen. I know this Witch. She stole away the sunlight, bringing about the Last Sun. I don't know how, but I know it with all certainty. Up to no good, conjuring something or another. I remember that day, the day we saw the light beams begin to dissipate, as if being sucked in by a black hole. All of us creatures were disoriented, confused. Rising above the tree canopy, we watched as the sun disappeared into a small house—this house—day by day, until one day it was all gone. We don't know how she did it. But if all of that is true, we need to le—"

"I have someone I'd like you to meet. It's a family reunion, you could say." The Witch emerged from the shadows, another figure alongside her: a man, strongly resembling her mother.

His eyes appeared to be kind, if not sad. His clothes were beautifully embroidered, yet tattered, as if he had been wearing them for months. Around his hands and feet were shackles, bound by an iron chain the Witch held in her claws.

Surely, this was her mother's twin.

While the rainforest's creatures may not have understood why the sun disappeared, Adela had begun to piece the events together. The Witch had disrupted the balance of night and day, the very thing that had been prophesied when the twins were conceived. With the knowledge that the Falcon had shared with her those decades ago, the Witch had set her sights on her mother and uncle, villainy coursing through her veins.

But Adela still did not understand where she fit into the plan.

"You look confused," the raven-haired woman said, laughing and inching toward Adela.

In response, Adela moved ever closer to Milo's body and the small bench of herbs and knick-knacks strewn about. "I am. I still don't understand your plan."

"Really? That dense, are we? It's quite simple. Your grandmother, Clara, had set the plan in motion with the Queen, of course. Separating the twins was incredibly helpful for me. With it, the balance of night and day were primed for disruption."

The man looked down, his chest heaving as he gently sighed. Adela sensed he knew this story, knew the outcome. Still, she allowed the Witch to speak, needing to learn more.

"The tricky part was getting my hands on both the Golden Girl and this one," she said, jerking a thumb over at the figure attached and bound to her with the chain. "How easy! The little girl practically fell into my lap. And that's when I learned she had more powers, greater ones than I had even dreamt of—of course, she was deeply suspicious of me, though I couldn't understand why. I knew she would never come back, so I sent something dark back home with her: fear and loneliness and all their counterparts that would eat away at her until just the shell of a young girl remained.

"Around that time, my dear Falcon returned with news of a young girl who could transport herself by touch. 'What a curious thing!' I thought, reminded of the young girl I had met only weeks prior. And the more he spoke, the more it clicked for me. You were related. She would be your mother. And I now had intimate knowledge of your home life.

"Working within time is tricky. But by that point, I had the next three steps of my plan in place. The first, to find Conrad, your stepfather, and lure him to my home during one of his long journeys selling ice to the furthest corners of the world. And then, to curse him. The second step was to use Conrad's darkness to harm your mother, knowing that weakening her would disrupt the balance further. Step three was to find your mother's twin, capturing him to lure out the King and Queen. And I'd exchange their children for the kingdom."

The Witch paused, as if anticipating applause or a smattering of accolades. But Adela, during this speech, had inched ever closer to the workbench and Milo's body, at once taking in the information and devising a plan to get out of this situation. She had become a master at devising plans.

"What a clever plan," she lied, grabbing hold of Milo's hand.

The woman smiled, eyes growing larger as her neck craned forward. "Isn't it?"

Adela nodded, opening her satchel and reaching in to grab the journal with her other hand, readying herself to drop the petals on the floor, to meet with her grandmother, to use her powers to bring harmony back: to her world, to her family. She closed her eyes and...

"I wouldn't do that if I were you."

Adela opened her eyes, the Witch glaring back, having snuck up on her and mere inches from her face. "What do you mean?"

"Do you really think I'd let any magical being use their powers in my house? No, of course, I wouldn't." The woman's eyes dilated, and her mouth screwed itself up into a devious smile.

Adela's heart fell. "I promise I'll be back," she lied. "I just need to find help for him. He's dead."

"Absolutely not, I fell for that trick with your mother, and I'm not doing it again. You're mine."

But before the Witch could finish her sentence, a bright light filled the hut, forcing her to shield her eyes from the sudden disruption. The light emanated from Adela's shoulder—bright and harsh—and the soft voice spoke.

"Run. Run for the door. Run into the rainforest. Run. And don't look back. Now!"

So she did. Without another thought, Adela picked up Milo, her body finding its strength, and raced toward the door, slamming into it with her arm, another casualty of this treacherous journey. Behind her, the beating wings of the Falcon and the screams of the Witch carried into the night air, closing in on her. The Fairy had stayed behind, using the light that seemed to pulse from her body as a deterrent of sorts, a method to keep Adela shielded and protected. But Adela was quick, nonetheless. She slid into the forest cover, skidding her knees on the mossy ground before slowing to a stop. Milo's body bounced against the ground slightly, but she would not feign interest at this time. Her primary goal was to get out of here alive.

Defeated, with shrieks and screams surrounding her, and in the safety of the dense and lush greenery, she dug into the satchel once more. Adela turned as the Fairy fluttered toward her and landed on her shoulder. Grabbing hold of the journal—finally—Adela released the petals.

Her grandmother's home.

Western Wilerea.

She made it.

She had only visited this place years ago, as a small child, before she and her mother decided to settle in Sunseree for the remainder of their years. This was back when her grandfather was alive. After the move to Sunseree, her grandparents would visit every few months, taking the long journey to visit their family. Neither she nor her mother had visited Western Wilerea since, but Adela sensed in her heart that this was it.

Herbs sprung out of the wet dirt beneath, and the house was slightly misshapen, welcoming, warm, and comforting, entirely unlike the one she had just escaped from moments prior. A puff of smoke emitted from a chimney, the house slightly elevated, surveying the grounds beneath it with care. Her grandmother's garden rivaled her mother's, replete with herbs and the leafy bits of carrots poking through the ground alongside bundles of what looked like thyme and sage

Adela nearly collapsed in an effort to reach the front door, her body and the door alike gnarled and battered by the elements. Adjusting Milo with one hand, and clutching for dear life to the journal that George gave her with another, she knocked.

A clanging inside the house stopped at once. For a moment, Adela wondered if she had appeared at the wrong house, her face clouding with worry as her brow scrunched upward. Then, like magic itself, the door swung open and in that opening stood her grandmother.

A wave of surprise swam over her face as she took in the small girl in front of her; and that surprise quickly turned into bewilderment and then a knowing smile that signaled to Adela all that she needed to know.

"You remember?"

"Of course, I do. Come inside then, you'll freeze to death out there! What are you doing here?"

Her grandmother ushered her into the main room, warmed by the stove. Homemade paintings dotted the walls, not unlike the ones seen in the Forgotten City. The walls were circular and featured splashes of color and texture. On one wall, an amber sweater was nearing completion, while a patchwork quilt of cyan and marigold squares lay finished atop a rocking chair. This house was unlike any Adela had encountered, and it immediately brought comfort to the anxiety swirling within. She felt at home.

"Where'd you go just now?"

"Sorry, I was just taking everything in."

"That's alright," her grandmother chuckled. She stopped, only now eyeing both lumpy shapes atop Adela's shoulder. "What are you..."

Her voice trailed off, as Adela shuffled over to the small daybed at the corner of the room, depositing Milo's corpse carefully on the cushioned surface.

The Fairy flew off her shoulder and into the center of the room as, turning around, Adela found her grandmother's face, eyes big and mouth agape in shock.

"That's Milo," Adela said. "He's... dead. And that's a Fairy. And, in fact, I have a lot to tell you."

"Dead? What do you... oh, heavens." Her grandmother's hand covered her face, and she lowered herself into an armchair that was conveniently situated by the front door. As she sank into the soft cushions, her eyes roamed Adela's face, searching and ever questioning.

"Milo had an accident. But I found something that can bring him back to life. George said you could help."

"George? How'd you find *him*?"

"I found your box of things. Mama gave it to me before..."

"Before what?"

The air was heavy, stale with words left unsaid. Adela shook her head, willing herself to forget about the events of the past hour, hoping that if she only forgot about them, they would cease to be real.

"I have the sense you're not telling me everything."

"You're right." Adela paused, lowering her gaze. Remembering the herbs she'd collected, the ones Conrad brewed for her mother under the Witch's direction, she emerged from her satchel with the glass jar.

"Is that..." Her grandmother stifled a laugh that had started in her belly and worked its way up and out of her mouth.

"It's one of yours. I kept it after we were separated."

"When was that?"

"A few days ago."

"Feels like forever ago."

"I know. I thought I'd never see you again."

"But you would. You just didn't know it yet."

Adela nodded. "Grandmother, Mama is sick. And Conrad too, in a way. Here," she said, placing the jar of herbs into her lap. "Can you tell me what this is?"

Her grandmother eyed her suspiciously and then opened the small jar and stuck her nose into the opening, taking a deep whiff before making a face and screwing the lid shut. "Let me see what we have here."

She got up from her seat, her round body creaking with age. Only then did Adela realize that her grandmother had aged, quite a bit, since she saw her last. Not even since the journey on the train, or to Nuimtree, or into the caves. But since the last time her grandmother visited Sunseree and held her in her lap and read her a bedtime story, tucking damp hair behind her ear. Despite her abilities to circumvent time itself, Adela could never loosen time's ugly grasp on her loved ones.

She followed her grandmother outside, and the Fairy too, to the very garden where her grandmother had taught Adela's mother about various healing plants, their properties and benefits. It was an expansive space at the side of the home, a small wooden sign with a sprawled *Clarissa's Greens* the only marker to alert you that this was someone's private garden. The plants themselves were haphazardly dug into the earth, with cauliflower jutting against pink roses that grew alongside a cherry tree.

Adela didn't notice when her grandmother knelt beside the flowers and began whispering. It was only when she heard the whispers responding back that her attention was drawn to the stifling air. Walking over, she watched as her grandmother conversed with a spider, yellow patterns dotting its dark body, legs spindly and long as it climbed atop her grandmother's hand.

"Hmm," he said, "I haven't seen this in some time."

"Precisely why I came to you. You've traversed this garden backward and forward more times than even I have. Surely, in your journeys across these grounds, you could remember."

The spider tilted its bulbous head toward the jar. *"Atropa belladonna."*

"Really?"

"Oh, yes. Terribly poisonous. Paralysis, blurred vision, confusion. Where did you get this?"

"I didn't. My granddaughter did."

The spider at once noticed Adela, its multiple eyes blinking in disbelief. "What is a young girl like you doing with belladonna?"

"It's not mine. But I found it. My mother, she's sick. And this was used to poison her."

"Dreadful news."

"Right, well, we best go back inside. We have quite a lot to discuss. You," her grandmother said, diverting attention to the Fairy.

"Yes, ma'am?"

"You'd be useful here. Would you like to stick around?"

"Here?"

"Yes, here. I can teach you about the botanicals of the world. You can reside in my garden. Providing protection."

The Fairy appeared to think for a moment before breaking into a tiny grin. "There's nothing left for me on the Isle of Vila. I'll stay here, with you."

Her grandmother nodded, smiling. Then, with a sudden and darkening change in mood, she grabbed Adela by the arm and dragged her back into the house, closing the door shut behind them. "Where did you get this?" she asked, slamming the door shut and suspending the jar in the air, her face stern and serious.

"From home."

"Home?"

"Yes. I stole it."

"Stole how?"

"From Conrad."

"What does he have to do with all this?"

"I told you, he's hurting Mama."

Her grandmother stared ahead, as if boring holes into Adela's skull. Finally, she nodded. "We'll have to do something about that then."

She strode over to Milo's body. "What do you have to help him again?"

Adela reached into her satchel, one that had become increasingly empty over the last few days and hours and moments. Her journey had led to some casualties, naturally: the original train ticket, the one that had started this journey. Clara's comb, which held the Dragon in place at Al Ainab's oasis. The Djinn whistle, discarded unceremoniously into the depths of the river after her battle with the Dragon. The brooch that led her to George, led to Milo's death, left behind. And the browned petals that lay fallen on the ground on the Isle of Vila.

The only remaining token was Clara's journal, the one she held tucked under her arm, fearful of letting go. And the ivory box, tucked into the recess of the bag, clanging against empty jars.

"Here," she said, pulling out the canister that held the Water of Life.

"And what might this be?"

"It's the Water of Life."

Clara paused, hand outstretched and brushing against the warm leather of the canister. "That's impossible. How did you get this?"

The question broke a dam of emotions. Running toward her grandmother, Adela wrapped one arm around her legs and cried and cried, for a good long while, explaining to her the events of the last few days.

How her mother was in danger, slowly being poisoned by the evil Conrad. How Conrad had become evil, cursed by the Witch's darkness. How the Witch had devised a plan so evil, capturing her mother's twin. How the imbalance had caused the Last Sun, plunging the world into darkness. How she met George, and how Milo had died, and how she had defeated the sand Dragon to capture the Water of Life. And most importantly, how she had come here—now—cradled in her grandmother's arms. The story took only minutes to tell, and Adela found it horribly amusing how the events of the last few days had left such an indelible mark on her experiences, yet felt so small.

"You defeated the Dragon?"

"Yes."

"That was very brave of you."

"I had help."

"I'm sure you did, along the way. It doesn't change the fact that you devised your plan. That you saw it to completion."

"It's nothing special."

"The girl I knew in the Whitt Woods would have never done what you did. She was too afraid. You've grown so much."

Her grandmother smiled, grabbing Adela's chin gently and rubbing it between her thumb and forefinger. She sighed. "I knew when I realized who you were, way back then, that you'd find yourself on many an adventure in your own time. Little did I know all that you'd accomplish. Now then, let's start by bringing Milo back."

Tucking the book into the band of her skirt, Adela moved forward while her grandmother unscrewed the cap of the canister. Leaning over Milo's body, she pulled at his mouth with her fingers, trying to pry his teeth open. His face was pale now, eyes sinking deep into his bones. Adela turned her head while her grandmother carefully poured the water down his throat.

The change was instantaneous. Within a few heartbeats, the ruddy pink had returned to Milo's cheeks, and his skin filled with water, plumping his cheeks and skin in turn. His mouth settled back into place, teeth grinding against one another while Adela's grandmother fell back, retreating to her chair in the corner of the room as she screwed the container closed.

Adela herself stayed in place, kneeling on the floor as she crouched over his body.

Milo's eyes opened. "Adela?" he asked, his voice hoarse and soft and weak.

"It's me."

"How? Where are we?"

"We're in Western Wilerea. At my grandmother's. She saved you."

"No," her grandmother interrupted. "*You* saved him."

Milo spoke again, his voice strengthening. "How did you do that?"

"It's a long story, complete with a Dragon and Djinn."

"And your mother?"

Adela's smiled faded. They had saved Milo but her mother's life was still in peril.

And her mother's twin.

And the world, truly.

"She's still home. I haven't figured out a way to help her just yet," she admitted.

From behind them, a chair creaked as Adela's grandmother settled into soft cushions that blanketed her chair. "Come, I have a story for you both."

# PART FIVE

# TWENTY-TWO

# WITCH

—

*By now, you both know the story. When I was a young woman, I was sent for by the King and Queen of Nuimtree. They did not tell me why they sent for me, only that they needed my magical expertise. And I returned over and over. And on one journey there, I met a young girl. Utterly precocious and full of herself, but young and scared and terrified. She trusted me, though she should have been more careful. You see, she divulged secrets to the wrong creatures. And they, in turn, used them against her.*

*When we arrived at the kingdom that time, I was asked to care for a baby girl. I was terrified. But I heard rumblings of a dark Witch on the Isle of Vila who was watching the kingdom. And I felt it was safest to take her, to use my powers to hide her from the magical world, like pulling a veil over everyone's eyes.*

*And so I did. I stole her back to Western Wilerea and raised her like any young girl. When the people of the island asked about her golden sun, I responded, "It's simply a birthmark, see!" and left it at that, hoping nobody would find out. But I didn't know, at the time, that there was more to this young girl.*

*On the island, there was a forest. It was small, as forests go, but housed a handful of animals that called it home. Among those was a sly red Fox. At the time, I raised little chicks and hens, and he would hang about the house, but curiously, he* would never attack them. Rather, he watched me. Or, more accurately, he watched my daughter.

And one day, she slipped away into the forest and didn't come back. I was terrified. I thought the dark Witch had stolen her, found her at her most vulnerable and killed her. We sent out a search party, poring over the woods to no avail. When we returned home, there she was, sitting in front of the door, rolling cave pearls around in the palm of her hand. She was giddy! She had met a Fox, and he had given her these pearls.

Cave pearls, you see, seem rather mundane. But they can hold mystical qualities. Together, they hold immense power. But once you begin to remove them from their grouping, their power begins to dissipate, slowly seeping away until there's nothing left.

And so then I realized the Fox had granted her abilities. Had realized how lonely she felt, how much of an outsider she was, with her golden sun marking her. He wanted to give her the gift of escape.

My daughter loved to draw and paint. One day, she came bounding up to me, hair flying about and her grin stretching from ear to ear.

"Mama," she said, "I painted a door."

"A door, my little sun?"

"Yes," she answered. "And I went through it."

I could hardly believe it. I thought these must be the ramblings of an imaginative mind. But it was real. I never followed her through a door, but I would watch as she painted a scene, beautifully vibrant, and then created her door. And then her doorknob to enter. And then she disappeared, returning mere moments or hours later.

And I let her do so, never once admitting that I knew. I allowed her this small pleasure, for I had taken so much from her: her real family, her brother, a life in Nuimtree. Many times I found her, panting and bruised, clearly escaping some kind of monster. And I learned, from those around me, that the doors she drew were a purgatory of sorts. Only those of decent heart could pass through it. The rest, even if magicked, would be stuck forever.

Before I go on, you have to remember that the Isle of Vila and Western Wilerea are both home to covens of witches. But we lead very different lives. On the Isle of Vila, witches are sparse, scattered across the rainforest, keeping to themselves. They each find it difficult to share a combined power, so they plot and plan ways to steal power for themselves. Here, on our little island, we use our powers for good. For healing. For saving. Our gardens overflow with flowers and herbs that we then trade with one another. Our singular goal is the betterment of the world. Safety. The Isle of Vila is magical, filled with all kinds of creatures. And unspeakable horrors as well.

One day, I fell ill. I suspected it was the work of the dark Witch on the Isle of Vila. Lying in bed, I heard my husband tell my daughter about the magical golden flower. If I had more strength that night, I would have called out "No!" and prevented her from ever leaving. But I knew she would. And I knew she had found that Witch.

The very next day, her golden sun disappeared, and I feared that something had come through her door with her. She changed overnight: fearful, apprehensive, sad. I wanted to help her, but I couldn't. So I did the only thing I saw fit to do. I placed the cave pearls beneath my heel and ground them into the ground, leaving only a sliver of a piece behind.

She would paint after that day, trying to escape the loneliness that enveloped her like a dark cloud. But she struggled to go through a door ever again. She was never able to create *her doors, for her powers had waned. For years, it was quiet. I continued to send my familiars to scout the goings on but came up short.*

*No new intel. We let our guard down.*

*And then she gave birth to a little girl. And I worried again. Worried about the Fox that continued to hang around our home, this time watching not my daughter but my grand-daughter. I encouraged my daughter to move, to find a new home. And it meant saying goodbye to our regular visits. But I knew it was the safest path. Or so I thought.*

*As you know now, there's still one part of the story left. To save my daughter and to defeat that evil Witch once and for all. And I could do that myself, lead the charge. But I'm too old and frail by now. And it's fitting that you have your moment of redemption, little one. And so I'll tell you something that will grant you power over the Witch on the Isle of Vila.*

*Her name.*

*Her name is Eva.*

## TWENTY-THREE

# THE END

———

Adela froze, captivated by the story her grandmother had told her. The pieces were beginning to fit together, like a jigsaw puzzle whose parts had been strewn about the universe, waiting to be collected and placed back together. And now, it was time to bring them together in the place where it had all started—her home.

Understanding the next steps, she sniffled and wiped her nose on the back of her hand. Before all this, she would be defiant, refusing to take the next step, uncertain and conjuring up scenarios of the sundry ways in which this situation could go downhill. But now, she had been victorious before. She knew, with the right plan in place, defeating Eva was possible.

Saving her uncle was possible.

Saving her mother was possible.

Returning the sun to the world was possible.

She clutched the leather book under her arm, aware that letting it go would mean leaving this place forever. And so, placing Milo's hand on her shoulder, she let go, letting it fall to the ground with a thud. Transporting was difficult by now, and the experience threatened to rip her body in half. Her realization had been confirmed by her grandmother's story. The cave pearls' esoteric qualities had allowed her to transport and now threatened to steal her abilities from her. When she had met Alby, there were three pearls, perfectly gleaming and replete with power. Now, only one lay tucked into her shoe.

As suddenly as the book thudded to the floor, so she and Milo rose from their original bodies, hidden in the forest. It was dark, of course, but the soft lights of a cottage in the distance pulled her forward, as if magnets finding each other and pulling one another close.

She knew what she needed to do; adrenaline coursing through her bruised body, Adela headed straight for the front door and knocked.

When Conrad met her, his face first reflected a jolt of surprise, softening to a neutral gaze before forming a sinister smile. "You're back. How stupid. Right into my little trap."

"I know what happened to you," Adela blurted out, her heart racing, knowing that Milo would be watching her from the safety of the thinned trees of the forest as they had agreed. "And so I'm here to speak to the cursed part of your soul."

"Oh?"

"You must be wondering why I'm here. Where I've been."

"I know where you've been."

"You do?"

"Being cursed is like a two-way communication. I speak to the Witch. The Witch speaks to me."

"I see. And if I wish to speak to the Witch?"

"There's nothing you could say that would be of interest to her."

"She needs my mother, of course. To finalize her plans."

"Yes, but—"

"How do you expect to deliver my mother to her? Across the vast lands that span between Sunseree and the Isle of Vila? And then to Nuimtree again as ransom?"

Conrad appeared to consider the line of questioning, his eyes growing dark and mouth moving slightly, conversing with voices within his mind. Moments later, he replied, "You have a point."

"Of course, I do."

"No need to pat yourself on the back," he snarled. "Is there something you propose?"

"There is. Does the Witch know how I disappeared from her clutches?"

Another pause while Conrad conversed with his mind. "She does not."

"I created a door," Adela lied.

"A door?"

"Yes. Similar to the one my mother created herself, decades ago. Similar to the one you tried to draw under her bed."

"You're able to use the door?"

"Yes."

"You're able to use the door?" The question was repeated, but the voice was different, soft and feminine. It was the Witch, speaking through Conrad in an attempt to reach Adela once more.

"Yes. And I can let you through."

"Why would you do that?"

"I've already lost. I lost my friend. I lost my mother. There's nothing left. I only ask for one gift in return for helping you."

"Which is?"

"You let me go. You never bother me again. You allow me to use my powers to travel far from here, far from you and

Conrad and all the evil in the world. You let me live out my days in the darkness."

"How pitiful, how depressing. But yes, yes, I agree to the terms. Now, let me through."

"One other condition. You let my uncle come through with you."

"Well, naturally, I would. Do you think I'd be stupid enough to leave him here alone? He'll be in front of me the entire time."

"Very well." Adela pushed past Conrad, her feet walking the halls of her home once more. She hoped she had stalled just enough for Milo to have snuck into the bedroom. For Milo to have helped her mother to the floor, to force her thin fingers to draw the final doorknob on the door under the bed. She hoped the remaining fragment of her mother's own cave pearl, picked from the recesses of the ivory box where her grandmother had hidden it, had been enough to create the hatch.

Pushing the door to the bedroom open, she found the curtains billowing in the wind and smiled. Her mother was propped up in bed, eyes slightly opened and pale lips cracked and dry. But Conrad's footsteps sounded behind her and so, without saying a word, Adela lowered herself on all fours and crawled under the bed where the door took up space.

Slightly ajar.

The last bit of magic in the pearl had worked.

"There. The doorknob. That's what was missing here." Adela feigned opening the door in an attempt to sell her story. She hoped with all her might that this final plan would work, that she could lure the Witch through the opening. "Conrad, please. Can you help me move the bed? Nobody will be able to climb out in that small crawlspace."

With a grunt, he obliged, pushing the wooden bed to the side, against the window that was letting the wintry breeze indoors. The door was exposed, ajar and waiting for the inhabitants of the other side to crawl through.

The feminine voice pushed out from Conrad's body once more. "Is that what fixed it? Is it safe to come through now?"

"It appears to be so," Conrad grunted.

"Where are you right now?" Adela asked the Witch, discontent bubbling in her stomach. She pushed through the fear, emboldened by the courage that had found its way into her soul over the last days. "Are you at the door my mother painted, years ago?"

"That is the only door I've found on the island."

"And you believe it will bring you here?"

"It must, for that is where your mother lies."

"Right. Very well, it's safe to come through."

"It'll be a tight squeeze, but I think we can make it. You, ahead of me," she said, clearly speaking to Adela's uncle. "I don't want you escaping." The clanging of chains sounded until finally, the door in the Isle of Vila was opened and Adela, on her hands and knees, could see to the end of the corridor, where the soft eyes of her mother's twin met her own. Adela nodded, giving a small, comforting smile, and motioned for the man to come toward her.

The Witch followed closely behind, with Conrad breathing down Adela's neck.

From the bed, her mother gave out a low groan.

After what seemed like hours and days and weeks had passed, the man reached the end of the corridor, stretching his hand out to Adela. With all the strength in her broken body, she pulled, hoisting him onto the creaking wood floorboards of her home in Sunseree. Her uncle was safe.

It was time to learn whether her grandmother's story was true.

"Eva," she said, "come through."

The Witch was caught off guard, surprised by the mention of her name, one which she had never given to Adela before. The shock sent her back and, with a swift motion, Adela leaned backward, sliding along the floor until she was firmly situated behind Conrad. Aiming at the center of his back, she used her feet to give him a robust push, sending him into the door to convene with Eva, the Witch.

"You little brat!"

But her grandmother had been right. Nobody came crawling out of the door. As Adela pulled herself forward, peeking her head over the edge of the door, she saw Eva and Conrad, faces fuming and filled with darkness, stuck in purgatory for all time. Hearts doomed to the darkness of the door forever.

Defeated not by her magic, but by Adela's cleverness.

The story had come to a close.

Letting out a deep sigh of relief, Adela closed the door. It creaked into place. And at that moment, the weight of the last few days, the pain in her battered and bloody body, overtook her and she collapsed, sinking to the floor.

When she woke, she rose from her bed, piled high with numerous blankets and pillows, the sun beaming through the paned windows of her room.

The sun.

Filled with adrenaline, she leapt out of bed, the floorboards under her feet creaking and giving way. A sharp pain shot through her leg and up her side, and she took an intake of breath and flinched; her body was broken, of course, beaten from her journeys.

Limping to the window, she took in the marvelous sight. Townspeople, standing in the middle of the field, conversing and laughing with one another. The yellowed fields were drenched with sun, returning to their vibrant greens, as if overnight. A single honeybee buzzed by her window, and a grin formed on Adela's weathered face. Miss Sona would be pleased to have her bees back. She could already taste the honey on her lips, and Adela's stomach growled fiercely in anticipation.

The door swung open.

"Hungry, are you?"

"Grandmother!"

"You're awake. About time!"

"How long have you been here?"

"A while."

"How long was I sleeping?"

"A while, too. As soon as you left, I knew I had to make my way back here as quickly as possible. I called on the Fairy to get in touch with an old friend and called in a favor. You didn't tell me how magical riding on clouds would be," she said, winking. "When I got here, there were the requisite reunions. Your uncle, of course, didn't remember me, but I remembered him. We caught up while I nursed your mother back to health, detoxing her of the belladonna. You were already in bed, resting, so I healed your cuts and wounds and set some bones back in place. It'll be a long time to heal. But you'll get there."

"And my mother?"

"Doing better. Thanks to you."

"I was the reason all this happened."

"How so?"

"My foolishness. In the Whitt Woods that day. I was too trusting."

"Not at all. You were a young girl, figuring out the world around you. You needed someone—anyone, anything—to talk to about the way in which you experienced life. You could never have known that would come back to haunt you." She moved to sit on Adela's bed, patting at her side for Adela to join her.

"I will say, the young girl I met that day was a scared girl. I worried, after meeting you and after realizing who you were, that being blessed with the abilities you had would cause you to be complacent. To become reliant on your magic. To never grow or push outside your comfortability. I feared that little girl, like my daughter before her, would use her abilities as a crutch. I lay in wait for years, anticipating the moment I would need to carry out the same injustice as I did years prior. That I'd need to rid you of the pearls, equally a blessing and a curse.

"But never did I think the girl I met on that train would go on to change the course of the world. Never did I think that scared girl would grow into a young woman, courageous and curious, dauntless and determined. Never did I think my granddaughter, blessed with magic, would end up finding magic within her. I'm more proud than you know."

As her grandmother spoke, a frail figure climbed up the stairs and entered the room, striding toward Adela.

Her mother.

"I'm glad you're back," she said, beaming. "No more journeys for a while for you. Not without me."

"Deal," Adela said, smiling as her mother kissed her forehead. "I'd rather stay with you any day."

And from the window, a red Fox watched the small family huddled over Adela's bed before scurrying away.

# EPILOGUE

———

The sun rose early that morning, and Adela bounded down the stairs to the kitchen, where her grandmother, mother, and uncle were enjoying breakfast together.

"Good morning." She smiled, cozying up next to them on the small bench. Today, her grandmother had made scrambled eggs with cheese and green peppers, just the way Adela liked it. Waiting for her was a hot cup of tea with honey, of which they had in abundance now that the honeybees had returned to Miss Sona's beehives.

"I can't wait for today," Adela said, her hands grasping at the mug. Her palms still held the scars of some of the deeper cuts she had collected during her journeys, and she loved how the healed-over skin had its own unique appearance. It made her feel almost magical, the imperfections that made up the girl she was today: full of hope and courage and, most important of all, love for her family.

Her mother let out a small laugh. "Me too. Our first adventure since the Return."

The Return marked the sun's appearance in the sky again. It had mysteriously coincided with the night that Adela defeated the Witch and reunited her mother and uncle. The moon and sun, in perfect harmony. They would go on to meet with the King and Queen of Nuimtree, the Prince eventually moving back to the kingdom, destined to preside over its inhabitants one day. Her mother, of course, decided to stay in Sunseree.

"Can we go now?" Adela asked.

"You didn't finish your breakfast."

Adela eagerly scarfed down a few spoonfuls of breakfast, ravenous but wanting dearly to get on the road. "Now?" she mumbled, food spraying the plate in front of her.

"Clean that up, and then we can go."

Adela leapt to her feet and cleared the table and dishes in no time, maneuvering around her grandmother and uncle to do so. When her mother got out of her chair, Adela raced to the front door and began pulling her shoes on.

"Bye, Grandmother. Bye, Uncle!" she called over her shoulder.

As her mother, too, pulled her own shoes on, Adela grabbed the small suitcase that was stationed at the front door, excitement bubbling up in her belly.

"Ready?" her mother asked.

"Ready."

The two stepped outside the door, hand in hand, side by side.

They were off to explore the world together. Ready to experience the magic just outside their front door.

# THE END